The Ven Hypothesis

Kepos Chronicles Book 2

Erica Rue

ISBN: 1-945994-34-7

ISBN-13: 978-1-945994-34-0

This is a work of fiction. Any similarity to real persons or events is coincidental and not intended by the author.

Editing by Jessica Hatch of Hatch Editorial Services

Cover Design by Sanja Gombar
fantasybookcoverdesign.com

Published by Tannhauser Press
tannhauserpress.com

Visit ericarue.com for more information.

For my parents, Jane and Ralph.

For my best friend, Maggie.

The Ven Hypothesis

Extinction is the rule. Survival is the exception.

- Carl Sagan

1. OBERON

Run. Fight. Hide. Those were the only options. Professor Elian Oberon was panting even though every breath fed him more oxygen than he was used to. That was just one more unfamiliar thing about this place. He slowed his sprint to a jog, then paused, just for a moment, to regroup. The humming of the insects all around him made him itch, and the birds, waking in the faint light of dawn, startled him with every squawk. He had no idea where he was going. He didn't even know what planet he was on. All he knew was that he couldn't afford to stop for long. He could hear them, following behind. Low growls, the crunching of twigs, the stamp of feet. They did not try to hide their approach. The message was clear. *We are coming. Run.*

Just a few days ago, after the attack on his ship, the *Calypso*, he had been surprised to wake up on a Venatorian ship. They were not known for taking prisoners alive. In fact, he was fairly certain that one of the Vens had stayed his execution, standing between him and the club poised over him when he came to. At the time, he thought they were going to dissect him, or maybe sell him to another Ven clan, but his savior turned and carved a mark, a crude spiral, into his arm with a claw. It was making some sort of claim over him. Perhaps his rescuer was higher up in the hierarchy. But why not just kill him?

When they had landed on this planet, four Vens had taken him from their ship and brought him to the woods. They had removed his bonds, and each painted herself—he could make out the scalloped edges along their plating that marked them as females—with a white symbol. The spiral, bisected triangle, spiked circle, and three nested rectangles painted on their faces must mean something. Rank, possibly, but when they carved the symbols into his arms, too, he had his doubts. He had three new cuts to match his spiral. They were familiar. They had been the same symbols that were painted on the blue Vens of the boarding party. If the blue Vens had truly been juveniles, could these Vens be their mothers?

He really hadn't studied much Venatorian culture, and for the first time in his life, he was regretting it. Four giant, viridian Vens, like gorillas with an armadillo's plates, and long, deadly claws, stood before him. Sharp-toothed snarls and hard eyes with strange rectangular pupils urged him back a step. Then another, until he was fleeing. He knew what they wanted from him, even if he didn't understand why. They wanted him to to run. Soon after, they began their pursuit.

Oberon picked up his pace. His head throbbed where he had been hit a few days ago, but his wound had scabbed over. His entire body ached. He couldn't run all day, and he wasn't sure if he could hide. All he knew was that four large Venatorians were chasing him, and he had to keep moving.

He was still proceeding rather slowly, but the Vens never seemed to catch up. They lagged behind, just enough to menace, to threaten, to keep him moving forward, but they never got close enough to be seen.

They were trying to scare him.

It was working. He tripped, losing his train of thought and his footing, and fell. Immediately the growls grew closer, the stomping louder. They were herding him, that was clear, but to where? The only reason he was still alive was because they were planning to kill him in some spectacular manner.

The manumed on Oberon's wrist beeped, its first sign of life since he had been released on this planet. While in captivity on their ship, he had been able to look up a few things about the Vens, but it never worked for more than a minute or two before going back on the fritz. He looked down at the device, and his heart sank. The *Calypso* had picked up his manumed's signal and connected him to its network. He was back in range of his students, Dione, Zane, and Lithia. Bel's manumed did not register. Maybe hers was broken, like his. They must be on this planet or in orbit if he could transmit. He tried to call them, but at that moment his manumed blinked back off.

"Damn," he said out loud, and picked up his pace. As he ran, he considered the *Calypso*'s signal. They must have come here in the ship, but there was no way to know if they had been captured. And where was here? They were supposed to jump to clean space, then find a colony with a near real-time comms array. They couldn't have possibly done that in such a short time, even if they had realized they could use the emergency beacon's charging matrix. The only planet in range was Bithon, and he didn't think that planet had any jungles like this. Unless he had been unconscious longer than he thought.

None of that mattered right now, though, so he pushed it from his mind. If his students were here, he had to find them. He had to make sure they were okay. He had to lose the Vens.

He began testing the boundaries of his course. He moved on a diagonal to his right, but soon growls came from that direction. He pressed on until he finally saw the Ven with the bisected triangle running almost parallel to him. Almost. He saw that it would soon intercept him and block his path. They did not want him to go that way.

Oberon put on a burst of speed, hoping to beat the Ven and pass the interception point before the Ven could reach him. For a moment, Oberon thought he had succeeded. Then he felt it grab his arm and wrench him backwards, hurling him onto the ground. The pain in his back reached a crescendo in his bad shoulder, but his assailant had backed off. With a loud groan, he popped the joint back in. Immediately he felt relief, though the ache was still there. This was not the first time he had dislocated that shoulder. The Ven stomped and feinted in his direction. He knew what it meant. *Get moving.*

They were definitely keeping him alive for some reason, and he needed to find a way to escape before they changed their minds. He maintained a slight diagonal toward the right, but kept the Ven out of sight. After another ten minutes, he could barely jog. He thought he heard running water, but it was probably his imagination. He was so, so thirsty. Maybe they weren't herding him to a place, maybe they were running him into exhaustion. If that was the case, he didn't have much time. Oberon fell again, and scrambled back to his feet. Not much time at all.

Just when he had nearly given up hope, he figured out why they had been herding him away from the right side. With no warning, the jungle dropped away, and a steep ravine took its place. The water he had heard rushed below, loud and fast.

This was it. His final chance. If he didn't escape now, he would be too drained to even try again. He jogged to the edge of his permitted runway, stumbling. This time, it was for effect. The Ven with the triangle appeared, leaving a small gap between itself and the edge. That was all he needed. Once he closed that gap, gravity would do the rest.

Oberon winced, knowing that if his escape worked, it would hurt like hell. He ignored the growls coming from the Ven and trudged ahead. He pretended he was veering back onto the approved path, but instead, accelerated, aiming to beat the Ven to the interception point, just like before. The Ven anticipated him, putting on speed. He was banking on the Ven believing he was stupid and tired, desperate enough to try the same thing. At the last minute, Oberon shifted his weight, ducked, and managed to pass behind the Ven. A few more strides, and he tucked himself into a protective ball and proceeded to roll down the treacherous ravine.

Oberon used his hands and arms to protect his face and head, and the short, wiry grasses left dozens of small, painful cuts on his exposed skin. He didn't know if the Ven was in pursuit, but a horrible screech filled the air.

When at last his momentum slowed, he unrolled himself. The world was spinning, and he thought he might vomit. He looked up to the top of the ravine and saw two Vens picking their way down after him, and they were surprisingly agile for their size. The other two stayed at the top and proceeded to hurry along the edge. There was no way to outrun them. Climbing up the opposite side of the ravine was out of the question. There was only one option.

At that moment, his manumed beeped back to life. Oberon didn't waste any time. He sent a call to all three of his students' working manumeds.

"It's Oberon. I'm on a planet. There are four Vens hunting me. Some sort of ritual, I think. I'm about to jump in a river and try to escape. My manumed's not working right, but I'll get in touch when I can."

After a moment, he heard Dione's voice. "Professor, you're alive! We're all here. We can help you. I'll send—"

His manumed cut off before she could finish. That was probably for the best. The Vens were getting close. He knew nothing about this river. How deep was it? Where did it lead. All he knew was that it was fast, and the Vens, while they could swim, preferred to wait out their prey if it made it to water. He couldn't stay in the water forever, and he knew that they would be tracking him from above and behind. As he ducked his head below the surface and let the current take him, a grim realization presented itself. He had just made this fun for them.

2. DIONE

"Professor?" Dione said, holding Lithia's manumed. "We sent you a map. Did you get it?" Her own manumed, along with her machete, was still in the smuggler's den. Brian had advised her to leave it there only yesterday.

So much had happened in the few days since she, Lithia, Bel, and Zane had escaped the Vens in the *Calypso*, only to find themselves stranded on Kepos.

Dione looked around the living room of the apartment they had claimed in the Mountain Base. Breakfast interrupted, all four StellAcademy students were on the edges of their seats. Even Brian, the Ficaran who had helped them, looked concerned. Her heart was pounding.

"Connection's gone," Zane said. "If his manumed starts working again, it might go through."

"He's still alive," Bel said. Dark circles ringed her eyes, even though the anti-parasitics had cured Bel of her Ven-induced infection. A few days ago, Dione and Lithia had gone down to the planet with the simple goal of finding these meds, but had gotten caught up in the feud between the Aratians and Ficarans. The latter had broken off from the Aratians because the Aratians arranged all marriages through the Matching ceremony. The hostility between the two groups had only grown due to a Ficaran food shortage and an Aratian trade embargo.

Of all the strange things that had happened on this planet, hearing from the professor was the most unexpected. "We have to go find him," Dione said. "He'll know what to do." She couldn't believe it. Professor Oberon had survived. The last time she had seen him, he was lying in a pool of his own blood on the Ven Maurader class vessel that had attacked them. And she had left him behind, thinking he was dead. Guilt bubbled uncomfortably in her gut. "Zane, where is he?"

Zane was already on it, his half-eaten meal bar cast aside. "It looks like he's in the forest near the Ven ships."

"Then we have to go find him," Dione said. Zane nodded in agreement.

"What about my people?" Brian asked. "I thought you were going to help us fight off the Vens."

She expected to see anger in his eyes, so the betrayal there caught her off-guard.

"Brian, I… the professor…" She hardly knew where to begin. "It's my fault he's in this mess. I thought he was dead. I owe him my life."

Brian nodded. She had told him about the professor before. He seemed to understand, and she thought she saw his frown relax, just a bit.

"I'll go with you, Brian," Bel said. She looked at the Ficaran as she stood and braced herself on the back of the couch. "We owe it to Kepos to help."

Dione was surprised. Bel hadn't been caught up in the conflict between the Ficarans and Aratians like she and Lithia had. In fact,

Bel had just met Brian. Dione wondered if it had to do with Bel's vendetta against the Vens, the aliens that had killed her family.

"No, Bel" Lithia said, before even Zane could object. "You're staying here. We need someone to coordinate everything, and you'll be no good out there while you're still recovering. Keep researching the Vens. I'll go. I'll drop Dione and Zane off in the forest, then take Brian to the settlement."

Bel opened her mouth to argue, as she often did with her StellAcademy classmate, but even that effort seemed to exhaust her. "You're right. I can barely keep my eyes open right now. I'd be a liability. But you can't just drop them off in the woods. The Vens will see the shuttle and send another hunting party, and there are already four Vens after Oberon," she said. "You can't fly in to the professor."

"Then how do we get there?" Dione asked. "He doesn't have much time."

"Maybe you can find a machi somewhere?" Lithia said.

Dione preempted Bel's question by explaining. "It's like a tapir mixed with a horse. You ride it."

"A machi won't have the endurance to get you there in time," Brian interrupted. "Take Canto."

"Are you sure?" Dione asked.

"Yes, he likes you," Brian said.

"Thank you." Dione almost hugged him, but despite this generous offer, he seemed cold.

"If I'm going to be stuck here," Bel said, "at least let me tell you what I know about the Vens."

Brian sat back down, gaze fixed on her.

"From what I've learned, attacks inside the Bubble are rare. Even on the Dappled Rim, a planet-dense region at the edge of the Bubble, most of the places they hit are unprotected. People just choose to take the risks because the mining is good, and, well, regulations outside the Bubble are a lot looser."

"Like what?" Dione asked.

"Slave labor, basically."

Dione tried to mask her surprise. Bel had already called her out once for being sheltered. No, *naive*. "So why'd they attack our ship?"

"I don't know. There must be some reason, but the alarming thing is there have been more attacks inside the Bubble this year alone than in the last decade. It's still not a lot, but the trend is what's troubling."

"How does that help us?" Brian said. Dione thought there was a challenge in his voice.

"Any change in behavior might tell us something useful."

"I appreciate that, but what can you tell me that will actually help us fight them?" Brian said.

"They have redundant organs," Dione said, "so they can take more bullets than you or me. The hood plate that protects their brain is extremely thick, and their brains are segmented in such a way that there are redundancies for motor control and autonomous functions."

"Translation, Dione?" Lithia said.

"If you manage to break through the plating and shoot them in the head, there is a good chance that another part of the brain will kick in and take over things like breathing. They'll still be able to move and attack you."

"And they heal quickly," Bel added.

"Yes. It's kind of like rapid growth. They can heal parts of their bodies, but this takes a lot of energy. We don't actually have a lot of info on their process of rapid healing, but they don't do it every time they get injured. Bel, do you know anything else?" Dione asked.

"There's a theory that they do it to repair damaged blood and fluid vessels so they don't bleed out," Bel said.

Dione hadn't read that, but it sounded plausible. She would defer to Bel, the expert.

"Okay, but what's the best way to kill one?" Brian asked. "Sounds like bullets aren't much good."

"Neither is my stun rifle," Lithia said.

Bel nodded. "Energy weapons aren't especially effective. If you use enough bullets, you can take one down, but you can never be certain. Sometimes, you think they're dead," she paused for just a moment, "but they're not. They're just in a low metabolic state, healing."

"They can't be invincible," Brian said.

"They're not," Bel replied. She rubbed her temples, and Dione wondered if she had a headache. "The best way to kill them is to take them down, and sever their neural connections. Completely. If these are cut, they're dead, but you have to sever every single link." She turned to Dione. "That's what happened on the *Calypso*, you didn't cut through everything."

Dione felt the guilt and shame well up inside of her as she recalled her hesitation in cutting the Ven's neural connections. She thought she had killed it, but it had come back to life and nearly killed Bel. Dione was a firm believer in learning from mistakes. Her failures in the lab usually conveyed the most valuable information, but this was a situation where her mistake had left Bel at the mercy of a Ven. She realized she was staring at the spiral cut still healing on her friend's cheek and looked away. Dione would not hesitate again. The Vens might be sentient creatures, but they were horrible and vicious. *Why are they such violent hunters?* Dione would probably never find out.

"How do you sever their neural connections?" Brian's question pulled her out of her thoughts.

"Slide a blade under their hood and cut. It's not easy, but it does the trick," Bel said.

"I can show you," Dione said. "There's a dead Ven in the cargo bay of the *Calypso,* in a refrigerated container." She shuddered at the thought of coming face to face with it again, even if it was dead.

"Good. We should leave as soon as possible. Neither of us can afford to delay for long."

"Brian," Lithia began, "I have to ask, since I'm coming with you. Aren't you worried that Victoria will do something to you if you go back? She thinks you're a traitor."

"If I left them to the Vens, I would be. I don't think they'll kill me," Brian said.

Lithia raised her eyebrows. "You don't *think*?"

"Everyone respects Victoria, but they don't all like her. She's not the one who slips them a few extra rations when their kid is sick. I'll be able to convince a few to listen. Remember, they saw the ships last night, too. We'll be ready to fight."

"Think about it. Your settlement is open and vulnerable. It's in the middle of a field. The Aratians have significant natural defenses that protect them, but your people just have a wall," Lithia said. Dione saw where she was going with this.

"We have the guns," Brian replied. "You said enough bullets would kill them. We'll just have to make sure it's enough."

"My settlement had guns, too," Bel said softly. "The Vens still overwhelmed us."

"Why not evacuate?" Dione asked. "Activate the Flyers and bring everyone here. Sam, can you accommodate six hundred people?" She knew the AI would be listening. Samantha, a research scientist known to the colonists as the Architect, had uploaded her consciousness to the Mountain Base's mainframe to protect all the people of Kepos from outsiders.

"Yes, but not as a long-term solution. Space would be tight."

"Then what's the point?" Brian asked.

Dione hesitated. "With the Vens here, there has to be a way for your people and the Aratians to work together and defeat them. Maybe you could shelter at their colony and work together."

Brian laughed bitterly. "They wouldn't trade us food as we starved. You think they'll help us against the Vens?"

"But the Vens are a threat to them, too. It only makes sense," Zane said.

Brian seemed to consider it for a moment. "I don't know what Victoria will decide to do. All I can do is go back to my settlement and warn my people. They need to know what they are facing."

Before anyone could respond, Sam interrupted. "There's another matter to consider. Because the dampening field is down, the Venatorian distress beacon is still transmitting. It needs to be disabled before more Vens pick up its signal."

Dione had forgotten about the beacon. A Ven scout ship that had crashed here decades ago was transmitting a distress signal, calling any other Vens in the area to the hunt. Sam had managed to block the signal with a dampening field. When she and Lithia crashed on the planet a few days ago, that same field had also blocked their manumed communications. Zane, who had stayed on the space station to take care of Bel, neutralized the field so that he could communicate with them on the planet. They had all been unaware of Sam and the Ven distress signal at the time.

"I could try," Zane said. "Is it close to Oberon?"

"It's within two days' journey of your professor's last transmitted location," Sam said.

Dione turned to Zane. "We could disable the beacon after we find the professor."

"I've sent the location to your manumeds," Sam said.

At that moment, a little girl no more than ten years old joined them in the common area. Dione gave her a distracted grin. Evy was a stowaway who had left her parents at the Vale Temple to come adventuring with the StellAcademy students. The fact that her parents were Aratian nobility didn't matter to her. She just wanted to collect bugs and hang out with her new friend, Lithia.

"There's one more thing," Zane said, "that I think you all should know. I took a look at the matrix last night, and after the modifications we made, I'm fairly certain that we'll never be able to reintegrate it into the *Calypso*."

The room was still for several moments as the news sank in.

"So we're stuck here," Dione said.

"Yes," he replied. "The professor might know some tricks—it's his ship after all—but I don't think it's possible."

Dione looked immediately to Lithia, who clenched her fists, but said nothing. Evy went up to her and gave her a hug. She only came up to Lithia's waist, and Lithia patted the girl on her back.

"I heard you talking about the Vens," the girl said.

"It's okay, Evy, we'll beat them."

"I know."

"Can you wait a little while to go home? This really is the safest place for you right now."

Dione could see the tears welling up in Evy's eyes, but she nodded. "Remember how I was telling you about my friend who liked bugs, too? Well, that's Bel. You can stay here with her, and once she's rested a little more, she'll show you her bug collection."

"I hope you like dragonflies," Bel said.

Evy smiled, but it was a sad smile. Dione wondered about the girl's cousin, Cora, the Aratian Regnator's daughter. Cora was Lithia's cousin, too, through their shared grandmother, Miranda Min—an unexpected revelation that Dione was still getting used to. Despite Cora's attempt to steal the anti-parasitics Bel had so desperately needed, Dione hoped she was okay.

"Let's not waste any more time. Show me the Ven, then you can go disable the signal. I need to get back to the Field Temple." Brian went back to the kitchen to grab some more food.

"He's grumpy this morning," Lithia muttered to Dione.

"His settlement is about to get destroyed by a bunch of aliens. Can you blame him?" Dione whispered back.

Lithia shook her head all the same. "I'll get the shuttle ready," she said.

Dione stood to take Brian to the Ven and show him how she had finally killed it.

"Come on, Brian. This way." she headed for the apartment door.

Now it was time to face the dead Ven. She felt sick just thinking about it.

3. DIONE

Dione opened the refrigerated container and gagged. Vens stank whether they were dead or alive, no matter the preservative measures taken. Brian stared at the corpse for a few moments, then covered his face so he could get in close to where it lay facedown in the container.

"I thought Vens were green," he said.

"They are, but the ones that boarded our ship were blue. We think it's a juvenile. See how its shoulders are tinted green?"

Brian nodded.

"Here," Dione said, pointing to the small gap between the hood and the first pectoral plate. "That's where I was able to get through."

"Is that the only weak point?" he asked.

"Some plates are fused, and some aren't. I don't know if it's consistent throughout the species or varies by individual which are and which aren't, but I'd try this plate gap first."

"So how do you get it down?"

"Aim for the feet?" Dione said, uncertain. "We had some stun gas that helped us knock them out. I failed to kill this last one, and it attacked Bel. Even injured, it was hard to take down. It was already limping when I had to face it, and I was able to use that to get it on the ground. Zane also came in, so it was distracted. There's no way I could have taken on this Ven alone and survived if it hadn't been badly injured."

"So find a way to wound them, knock them down, then strike," he said.

"That's the best advice I have right now. And work in teams. The Vens rarely work alone."

That was an aspect of their behavior that some observers had speculated about. There weren't many survivors of Ven raids. Most of them were out of their minds with fear, or didn't see much because they were hiding. A few survivors said they worked together, and the professor said that four were hunting him, the same number as had tried to board their ship.

There were a lot of unknowns, or as Bel believed, findings undisclosed to the public. Well, if there was a gap in public knowledge, Dione would record as many of her observations about the Vens as she could. When she made it back, she would share these revelations with anyone who wanted them. She could discover something that might save lives, and that meant she would have to survive this invasion.

Zane joined them. She saw him shudder as he looked at the Ven.

"Don't let them bite you either," he said to Brian.

"Why? Poison?" Brian said.

"Not exactly. They dose you with adrenaline and some other stuff and make you crazy. You're more aggressive and stronger, but you lose track of who you are. It's like a frenzy, and you'll attack anyone," Zane said.

"Why would they do that?"

"We're not sure, but we think it's either to increase the challenge or to set their opponent to make mistakes," Dione said.

"Can we turn it over? I want to look at the front, too."

"Yeah," Zane said. "Bel actually sent me here to see if we could bring it back to one of the base's labs."

"Why? I don't think we'll ever get the smell out of the *Calypso*, and now she wants to stink up the base?" Dione said.

"She wants to dissect it," Zane said.

Dione nodded in approval. There were records of dissections, but maybe Bel would discover something new. After all, this Ven was almost entirely blue, and that was undocumented. Maybe she could confirm their juvenile theory.

"All right," Dione said. They easily wheeled the storage container into one of the labs in the base, and Brian figured out how to link it up to the base's power supply. The last thing anyone wanted was for the decomposing Ven to warm up too much.

Brian headed for the stairs, but stopped abruptly and turned. "I almost forgot, I need to teach you Canto's commands. If you're going to save your professor and disable the beacon, I'll need to give you info about the locations Canto knows, too."

"Yeah, Zane, can we borrow your manumed for a few minutes? We can pick up mine on the way, but for now, we need a map," Dione said.

"Sure," Zane said, handing it over. "I'll go tell Bel where the Ven is." He headed off to the apartment where Bel had gone for a nap.

"When Lithia and I get to the Field Temple, I'll send Canto to the smuggler's den where you left your manumed and machete. Though I see you grabbed a replacement." Brian motioned to the machete she had strapped over her shoulder.

She had never felt the need to carry a weapon before, but this planet, the Vens, and that strange angler worm that had nearly killed Lithia? It all had her on edge. She still didn't trust her aim, so she'd probably see if Zane wanted the pistol that was also there.

"So, you've already learned some machi commands. Maximute commands are similar, but you have to be much more precise."

"Why is that?"

"I don't know, but that's the way it works."

He taught her the mounting sequence, as well as how to speed up, slow down, and turn. Even though the tunes were simple, his voice made them come alive when he sang.

The rendez-vous commands were much more difficult.

"First, you prime him with the home command," Brian said. He sang a seven note arpeggio. That will send him back to the settlement. If you want a rendez-vous point, each one has a different note following it, and you hold it for a whole note. I've taught him five different locations near the settlement, including the smuggler's den where we stayed."

The one where you kissed me.

Dione needed to shake that memory. There were more important things to focus on. Besides, Brian had been distant all morning. Before, he had been welcoming and inquisitive, but now he seemed closed off, especially from her.

She wondered if he blamed her for the Vens, and for her hesitation before agreeing to hand over the charging matrix. She couldn't blame him on either front.

Dione practiced the tones and took some notes. She even recorded Brian's beautiful tenor singing a few of the harder sequences, but mostly she tried to map them onto children songs from home to help her remember, turning all of the words into the command she was trying to sing. The slow-down command was exactly like the first line of a simple children's song.

Brian laughed as she sang, "Slow down slow, slow down slow," to the command's tune, and for a moment, she saw the light in his eyes that had been there before the Vens arrived.

She kept practicing with Brian until Sam interrupted them. Sam seemed to do that a lot. It was unnerving, knowing that their conversations weren't really private, even if they were alone.

"Brian, it may interest you to know that the communication devices that Jameson hid away are here. Long-distance communication may prove useful in the coming days."

Brian's eyes it up. "Where?"

"As long as you leave half for the Aratians," Sam said. "Everyone will need the ability to communicate. The Vens are a threat to everyone."

"I guess you're right," Brian said. "Though if you're hoping that Michael and Victoria will work together, I wouldn't hold your breath."

"People may surprise you," Dione said. "I just hope it's not too late at that point."

Her fate hinged on their cooperation, too, and she hated how helpless she felt under the mercy of polarized leaders. If they refused to cooperate at least on some level, they would all die. Dione felt cold, but Brian didn't seem fazed.

Soon, he was filling a bag with communicators. They were nothing like manumeds. They weren't sophisticated, but they did look sturdy, like they could stand some abuse in the field. These must have belonged to the terraformers. Personal comms like manumeds really weren't designed for extensive field work, though Dione's was an athletic model designed for durability. It had been a present from her uncle, to replace the one she had destroyed digging through mud on a trip just a year ago.

Sam gave Brian some instructions, since his experience with communicators was limited to manumeds.

"Each one has an ID number, but you can program names to each one," the AI said. "They're all networked, so once someone programs their name in, that name will show up instead of the number."

"Okay, can I reach Dione or Zane with these?"

"Yes, but you'll have to add them separately," Sam replied.

"Here," Dione said. She took a communicator, programmed it with Brian's name, then added all of their manumed designations. She laughed, realizing she had just given Brian her number.

"You can send voice and text messages, as well as share data. I've created a hub here where information can be stored and accessed, like a map of the area," Sam said.

Brian seemed to like the potential of the communicators.

Zane's manumed buzzed in Dione's hand. It was Lithia. "Zane, I'm ready. Get Dione and Brian, and let's go."

"It's me," Dione replied. "We'll get Zane."

"All right. Light a fire, though. I just saw the images Sam got from the space station and things don't look good."

Fifteen minutes later, they were in the air.

4. LITHIA

Lithia was nervous. She had already dropped Dione and Zane off at the edge of the woods. It wouldn't take long for them to reach the smugglers' den according to Brian. As much as she worried about them, she feared more for her own safety.

Sam's latest images showed the Ven landing site. It was far off across the plain, but the bird's-eye view made it seem so close. There were hundreds of them; doing what, she didn't know, but it couldn't be good. Preparations of some kind?

"Brian, the hangar's not open. Where do you want me to land?"

Brian didn't even glance at the external camera feeds before answering. "The town square."

"What?"

"The town square. In front of the Temple."

"Why not that nice, grassy area over there by the wall?"

"I want everyone to see us and hear what we have to say."

Lithia ground her teeth. "What if Victoria shoots us first?"

"She won't," Brian said.

"And you know this how exactly?"

"Because we've got something she wants."

"Which is?"

"The key to the Flyers."

"She might kill me out of spite. She won't need both of us."

"I just need enough time to convince her that we're here to help. You can bet she saw those ships last night and knows that something bad is going to happen."

Lithia was still uncertain, but she figured he was right about at least one thing. She would land somewhere with witnesses.

It was midday when they landed, and after only a few minutes the square was packed with people, many holding plates of food. *We must have interrupted their lunch*, she thought as she parked the craft.

Brian opened the back of the shuttle and stepped outside, hands raised in surrender. "I'm not here to fight. I'm here to warn you all about the ships that flew overhead last night."

Lithia followed his lead, saying nothing. She scanned the crowd for Victoria, but she wasn't there.

"The ships that landed last night are full of the demons from the old stories," he continued. "They're actually aliens called Vens. The Icon destroyed one of the ships, but not the others. They are probably already on their way here now. I've come to unlock the Flyers so we can go to the Mountain Temple. We'll be much safer there until we can come up with a plan to beat them."

The crowd exchanged looks, and Lithia even heard a few laughs. What was wrong with these people?

A young man strode toward them from the main building, the Temple, as they called it. His hair was blond and short, and he was very skinny. He approached Brian and sighed, not the least bit worried about the dire news.

"Brian, you shouldn't have come back so soon," he said. "You know I'll have to arrest you."

"Nick? Where's Victoria?"

"Those Flyers you offered to unlock? Victoria already did. She took them to one of the Aratian farms on the outskirts. We'll have a feast tonight," he said.

A few cheers erupted from the crowd. Lithia felt sick to her stomach. Victoria had unlocked the shuttles. Their only bargaining chip was gone.

"How?" she asked.

"Using the unlocked Flyer you crashed into the hangar, Melanie and the other techs figured out how to reset the others," Nick said.

"Well, shit," Lithia muttered under her breath. Without the shuttles, they would not be able to evacuate the Ficarans to the Mountain Base. "You all figured out how to fly them rather quickly."

"We had directions for activating the AutoNav," Nick replied.

"Awesome." Lithia grimaced. She personally hated using autopilot functions, but the program would provide enough guidance for them to fly just fine, assuming standard conditions.

"Please come quietly, Brian," Nick said, softly so that only they could hear.

"You don't have to arrest me. I give you my word that I won't try to escape."

"Victoria would not take your word."

"But you are not Victoria. You're not blinded by your anger at the Aratians. Do you doubt that I want to help our people?"

Nick thought about this for a moment then nodded. "If you surrender your Flyer, I'll just confine you to the main hall."

Lithia bristled at this. "Brian, if they take our Flyer—" She clenched her fists at her sides. First, she'd been trapped on this planet when Dione and Zane decided to cannibalize the *Calypso*, and now she was stuck at this doomed settlement?

"It's the only option right now," he replied.

That wasn't true. They could still leave, maybe even take a few people who wanted to join them. Brian was looking at her with pleading eyes, and it hit her. She had come to evacuate the Ficarans, but Brian had come to save them. He wouldn't settle for rescuing a few, and she had agreed to help him.

"Fine," she said.

Brian turned back to Nick. "Deal. I do have one more thing to offer that will come in handy. If I'm confined to the hall, will you send me the key militia organizers? I would like to train them in using the communicators I brought."

This last part Brian said loud enough for the spectators who were nearby to hear, and Lithia watched the murmurs ripple through the crowd.

Nick glanced behind him and smiled, just barely. "Looks like I don't have much of a choice now."

He dispersed the onlookers, but one refused to leave. A beautiful girl with dark, wavy hair and blue eyes was arguing with Nick.

"No," she was saying. "I'm going to talk to him first. Then I'll move the Flyer."

Nick sighed and gave up. "Five minutes," he said.

The girl ran up and gave Brian a hug. "Brian, what the hell is going on? What were you talking about? Demons?"

"They're here. The aliens Dione told us about. Everyone needs to know the truth."

So Dione had met this girl already. Well, there was no time like the present.

"Hi," she said, stepping forward. "I'm Lithia."

"I'm Melanie," the girl said.

Lithia looked her up and down, both annoyed and impressed. This girl had unlocked the Flyers using only the program template from Nate, the shuttle Lithia had crashed here just yesterday. The Flyers had been their bargaining chip, though.

Melanie crossed her arms and turned back to Brian. "Another one? What happened to Dione?"

"She has something she needs to do," Brian said, avoiding Melanie's eye contact.

"Uh-huh. I knew that girl was too smart to bother with you. Brian, about the Flyers… Victoria didn't give me a choice. I tried to slow the work down, but there was nothing I could do."

"It's okay," he replied.

"So what's your plan?" she asked.

"I hand out these communicators," Brian said, holding up the bag that Nick had failed to confiscate, "and tell everyone what I know about the Vens, then hope that Victoria sees reason. If she gets back soon, we'll still have time to evacuate."

"Evacuate? But this is home. We'll defend it. The Aratians won't even attack us here."

"The Vens are nothing like the Aratians. What I've learned, what I've seen… I don't think we can do this alone," Brian said. "I need a favor. I need you to send Canto to the den."

Melanie folded her arms. "Planning your escape after all?"

"No, for Dione. She needs transportation."

Her jaw dropped. "You're sending Canto off with her? Are you sure you're feeling all right?"

"He'll be in good hands. Like I said, there's something she has to do."

Melanie titled her her head and looked back at Lithia. "How's your sick friend?"

"Bel? She's doing much better. Thanks," Lithia replied. Maybe Melanie was okay after all.

At that point, Nick began yelling at Melanie to take the shuttle. She rolled her eyes and stopped smiling.

"I'm coming! Fly it your own damn self if I'm moving too slow." She turned back to them and said, "I'm with you, whatever you need. I'll send Canto once I'm done."

Nick escorted them inside the Temple to the main hall. Brian settled himself on a little bench with his bag of communicators. She watched as the first curious Ficaran came and went before she took a seat beside Brian. Waiting for Victoria reminded her of the times she had spent outside the headmaster's office back at StellAcademy. There would be consequences. There always were.

***

The afternoon rolled by slowly. Groups of Ficarans showed up at regular intervals. Some wanted to hear about the demons. Brian told them, and he even explained, in detail, what they really were. As for whether or not people believed him, the odds were about fifty-fifty. It didn't matter, though, because everyone heard the important parts, the vulnerabilities of the Vens and their tactics, at least what little they were able to share. One old man stopped by, spit in Brian's face, then left without hearing anything he had to say. Luckily, most of the skeptics listened, even if it was just so they could scoff at him when he was done.

Lithia liked watching Brian explain the communicators to key Ficarans.While many of them were on the raid with Victoria, especially those in the militia, there remained those in charge of mundane tasks, like building management. Perhaps that was why the people he spoke to were so receptive. They weren't used to power, to having a voice, yet here they were, receiving long-lost Artifacts, as they saw it.

He did save a few for those he knew would return from the raid, like Victoria and Colm. Nick came back after a while to check in.

"Still here," Brian said, "as promised."

"Good," Nick said. "Victoria should be back soon. I just wanted you to prepare yourself."

"I appreciate it. Can I ask, did Victoria take all the guns?"

"No, she knew that this first raid would be a surprise, so there wouldn't be much resistance. All of the handguns are still here. She did take most of the Flyers though, to bring back as many supplies and provisions as possible from the Hub."

"Wow," Brian said. "An Aratian Hub?"

"What's that?" Lithia asked.

"The Aratians have a few large farms where everything goes for storage until it's brought into the settlement itself."

"Like warehouses where smaller distributors send everything so that it's easy to transport?" Lithia said.

"Sounds about right," Brian said.

"Don't they need those supplies, though?"

"They've got far more than they need, and we're on strict rationing. I doubt they'd even notice one Hub getting cleaned out," Brian said, bitterness back in his voice. He seemed to realize and added lightly, "Nick wasn't always so... lean."

It was hard to believe, but Lithia knew things had been tough for the Ficarans. In fact, if she had been the one to unlock the shuttles, she might have just given them all to Victoria. Then again, she had some personal issues with Aratian leadership.

A boy, maybe thirteen or fourteen, came running up to Nick.

"Nick, the demons, they're here! They're in the woods."

Lithia watched the color drain from Nick's face. This man was not a leader. He was a place-holder. She exchanged a look with Brian and realized he knew it, too.

Brian put a firm hand on his shoulder. "Let me help."

Nick's eyes went wide. "Victoria will kill me."

"Would you rather one of the Vens kill you? Please."

Nick hesitated and bit his lower lip as he thought. "All right," he decided at last. "Come on."

Brian and Lithia followed him to the weapons depot. Some Ficarans were receiving guns and ammo, but there were not many weapons to begin with. Victoria had most of them. Brian received a handgun, and Lithia received nothing.

As soon as they stepped outside, they heard it, or rather felt it. The low growl of a hundred voices, trembling through their already shaking bodies. The Vens were here. They were all going to die.

Lithia's heart was beating in her throat as she followed Brian to the crest of the wall. Melanie came running up, holding something familiar. Lithia's stun rifle.

"Here, Lithia, I though you might want this." It would be mostly useless, but Lithia thanked her all the same.

"And, just in case, take this, too." Melanie handed her a long knife. She didn't look forward to getting close enough to a Ven to use it, but it was better than nothing. She tested the edge, which was miserably dull, and hoped that the Vens would not get inside. She took that moment to regret not grabbing one of the machetes from the *Calypso*, and contemplated offering Melanie and Brian a ride out of there. They would never leave during an attack, though. This was their home. These people were family.

The growling rose into a horrible crescendo before cutting out completely. In the silence, the hairs on Lithia's arms stood on end. Somehow the silence was more terrifying than the growling, even in the light of the afternoon.

There were watchtowers at regular intervals around the settlement, protected by a wall made of sturdy pre-fab material. Lithia guessed it came from the colonizer, or maybe even the station. The towers the Ficarans had built were within the walls, but they provided a vantage point. Their biggest pitfall was their size. They could fit five men comfortably, ten at a squeeze. Lithia hoped there were enough towers to protect the walls.

The growling picked up again, and, restlessly shifting her stun rifle to her right shoulder, Lithia wondered what the Vens were waiting for.

5. DIONE

Dione was tired of waiting for Canto. They had been at the den for an hour, and every minute was the difference between life and death for the professor. Had Brian forgotten about his promise to help? She had already put her manumed back on and synced it with Zane's. All of the maps and info about Canto's commands were there, she just had no maximute. She had given Zane the machete and the stolen pistol. She might be able to use a stun rifle in a pinch, but she was not interested in carrying the pistol.

At last she heard the familiar sound of a giant dog crashing through the trees. His golden fur gleamed in a pocket of sunlight just before he reached the hideout. She reached up to scratch him behind the ears, and he yawned back in appreciation, revealing his large teeth. Beautiful as he was, she knew he could turn deadly if provoked.

Canto also came bearing gifts. Dione peeked into the bags balanced on either side and found that, along with some food for Canto, Brian had sent some ammunition for the pistol. *That was thoughtful.*

"All right, Zane, you ready?" Dione asked.

"He's huge." Zane looked a little pale.

"Yep. Come on."

Dione sang the mounting tune and swung herself up first, then waited for Zane to do the same. He hesitated.

She raised an eyebrow at him. "You a cat person?"

"I don't think I'm any kind of animal person."

"You never had pets growing up?"

"Pets aren't really standard on freighters, at least not for crew."

That was news. She didn't know his family had been crew on a freighter. "Oh, well, Canto is really smart. He's not going to hurt you. Plus, he's really soft."

Zane grimaced, but climbed on.

"We'll go slow at first, but I don't want to waste time. Professor Oberon has already been out there all morning alone." He was still alive. She wouldn't leave him again.

"Okay," Zane said. "Ready."

Dione sang Canto into a trot, using his harness rather than her voice to direct him. Even with Canto, it would take them most of the day to get to the professor's last-known coordinates. He couldn't possibly be there still, but they didn't have any other leads, at least until he sent them another message.

Zane was gripping her rather tightly, squeezing her ribs until they hurt. He kept sneezing, too, and with every sneeze, he involuntarily squeezed her harder. At least he didn't talk a lot. A conversation would have been difficult at the speeds they were going. He had been quiet on the *Calypso*, and he remained so now. Or maybe he just didn't want to talk to her. Things had been okay when they worked on integrating the charging matrix to power the Icon, but now that they were alone together, the silence was uncomfortable.

They still had a ways to go, but Dione needed a break. Her whole body was still sore from riding the machi two days ago, and she could feel the ache from riding Canto working its way into her legs. She sang Canto to a stop and let Zane get down first. His eyes looked a little red, and he sneezed again once he was back on the ground.

"Allergies?" Dione asked.

"I think it's Canto. I've never been around dogs before."

"Too bad that along with everything else, they didn't breed him to be hypoallergenic. I think I have something that will help." Dione rifled through her bag and produced a packet of pills. "Here. Take these. What was it like, growing up on a space freighter?"

"I got used to getting lost. Lots of places to hide in case the officers found you."

"Were your parents officers?"

Zane laughed. "No, they were just regular crew, but they were the best at their jobs. Probably should have been officers. They were certainly more qualified."

"So, how'd you end up at StellAcademy?"

"I overheard my parents talking about how it was always really annoying that some of the support systems were poorly calibrated. It made their jobs a million times harder and made the systems less efficient, but their supervisor wouldn't let them fix it. It was an easy fix, too."

"But that's stupid. Why would anyone refuse to fix something like that?"

"Because my parents were Level Two techs. Only Level Four techs were allowed to make these particular adjustments, and they never had the time. Anyway, while they were asleep, I sneaked out and made the adjustments. I was just finishing up when the

First Officer found me. He thought I was tampering with the ship and took me to the captain.

"I explained the problem and told him I fixed it. After he figured out that the supervisor had refused the fix, he called the guy in. Woke him up and chewed him out. He moved him to another position so my parents wouldn't have to fear retribution, and before he dismissed me, he handed me an application. He was a StellAcademy alum and was impressed that I was able to fix it, I guess. If there was any proof it didn't take a Level Four tech, I was it."

"And you got in. Did your parents stay on the ship?"

"No, the captain had them reassigned to work at the dock. I don't think they enjoy it as much, but they're doing it for me. I even got a little sister out of the deal." He smiled, but seemed sad to remember her.

"What do you mean?"

"There's not a lot of space allotted to crew on ships. A second child would have meant a pay cut, so they stopped with me. Now that they're planetside, the restrictions are lifted."

Dione tried not to imagine Zane's worried parents or his sister. "We'll get home."

"I know. I've always wanted to study jump tech. Couldn't ask for a better motivation than being stranded with no other way home."

"So you and Lithia are going to build a jump drive?"

"Unless you've got a better idea."

That was insane. Even though she had a newfound respect for Zane, she knew he couldn't do it. She looked at him, ready to explain how impossible that idea was, but then she realized he already knew. It was a lie he was telling himself to feel better.

She and Zane took turns wandering off to use the restroom. Neither was very hungry, though they had packed some of the rations Brian hid at the smugglers' den. Dione tried the professor's manumed.

"I still can't reach him," she said.

"His manumed might be completely shot by now," Zane said.

"Then how are we supposed to find him?"

Zane looked uncomfortable. He wiped sweat from his forehead with his shirt and then stretched his legs one last time. "If we can't find him, we could find the Vens that are chasing him."

"How are we supposed to do that?" Dione said. "Do we even want to do that?"

"I'd rather be the ones to find them instead of the other way around."

"Come on, we'd better keep moving if we're going to make it to the shelter Brian marked."

They were headed toward the river. According to his last known location, the professor was just on the other side. If you assumed that he was running from the direction of the Ven ships, that would put him somewhere in the red zone she had marked on her map. So much depended on his speed... and if he was even alive.

He's dead. You're too late. How could he still be alive? She and Zane climbed back onto Canto and in moments they were racing through the forest. They would find the professor. She would not leave him again. He was alive. She knew it. He had to be.

6. LITHIA

They had been waiting for hours. The tension in Lithia's neck and shoulders had turned into an ache. The sun had set, and it was getting dark. Where were the Vens? Where was Victoria? "We only have to hold them off until Victoria shows up with the shuttles. Then, evac," she said to Brian.

Brian gave her a knowing look. "We can only hope she agrees."

Of course Victoria would agree. It was the only thing that made sense, which she would see first-hand when she returned. Assuming they lasted that long.

Lithia was not worthy of a tower spot. She suspected if Brian's reputation hadn't been tainted by his collusion with Dione, he would be guarding the gate, but instead he was on the opposite side of the settlement, keeping an eye on the forest. Most of the defenders were concentrated at the entrance, which was flanked by two towers.

Without warning, gunfire erupted from the opposite side of the settlement, the side exposed to the open plain. Brian's communicator came to life, and a frightened voice spoke. Lithia couldn't be certain, but she thought it was Nick. "They're here, at the gate. They're trying to breach the tower. They're not stopping. Help us!"

"How many?" Brian asked.

"I don't know! Dozens!"

The defenders rushed to other side of the settlement, leaving a scant guard in the towers. Lithia saw the problem immediately.

"Brian, it's a misdirect. Most of their forces are still in the woods. They're luring us away!"

Brian cursed and took out his own communicator. "Nick, we need to hold here. Take a few reinforcements, but don't compromise the rest of the wall."

"Reinforcements, now!" was the only response. Lithia, who was near the base of the tower with others who did not have proper guns, could see men and women leaving the other towers. These troops, if you could call them that, were untrained. They were not supposed to be the ones on these walls, and Nick hadn't been trained for command. Brian shouted his warnings over the confusion, but armed civilians scrambled to the aid of those at the gates.

Most of the militiamen in Brian's tower stayed. A good thing, too, as it wasn't long before Vens burst from the tree line. Lithia saw that the tower to the right of Brian's now had a few vacancies, so she climbed up to join the others and get a better view.

The Vens rushed toward the walls in small groups. Melanie and Brian began to fire along with the others, but the bullets were not enough. Or maybe their aim was bad. In no time, the Vens were at the walls. The pre-fab material was strong, but the Vens sought out the joints. Were they trying to pry the walls apart? The defenders were firing, but most of the firepower was at the gate, along with the best fighters left in the settlement.

What were the Vens trying to do? Then she saw it. The towers were spaced too far apart. There was a place in between Brian's tower and her own where the angle of the wall blocked any shots they might take.

Lithia didn't know why—it was suicide—but she headed to that part of the wall.

"Brian, they're climbing in," she said into her manumed. The wall would have been enough to keep out humans, but Vens? Not even close. He didn't seem to hear her on the communicator. Even her ears were ringing a bit with all the gunfire. A few others who realized what was happening came to join her. Thankfully, they had guns. In no time at all, the first Ven had landed inside the settlement.

The Ven, green and hulking, was so much larger than the blue one she had seen in the cargo bay. Its overlapping plating gave the illusion of horizontal stripes. It extended its claws and growled, revealing sharp teeth. As it raced toward her, she did the only thing she could. *Retreat.* She fired a few times, but her stun rifle was useless. The long knife sheathed at her side would not stand a chance against the brutal club the Ven wielded. The Vens on the ship had not had weapons. She had not expected this.

Lithia sprinted toward Brian's tower, hoping she could get some cover fire, but instead she heard a scream. It was one of the Ficarans who had joined her at the wall. She turned to see the woman on the ground. The largest Ven she had ever seen loomed over her. Its bloody club was all the explanation she needed.

He raised it to finish the woman off, and there was nothing that Lithia could do. The Ven looked up at her, and Lithia was struck by how dark it was, so green it was nearly black. A bullet hit the shoulder of its raised arm, and it barely flinched. It growled in anger. Lithia turned her head away as it brought the club down. She couldn't watch. As she saw other Vens closing in, she ran. She had no means of defending herself.

Another scream meant another Ficaran down. This time when Lithia turned, the Vens were farther behind, and the black Ven was no where in sight. There were five of them, and they were slowing down after being shot a number of times. She saw one standing over a fallen Ficaran and immediately fired her stun rifle. Maybe it would distract the injured Ven, for just a moment, to give her a chance to move in.

When her shot hit, it growled. Apparently it did hurt. It bent over and bit the Ficaran, who howled in turn.

What?! Why now? There are only a few inside the walls, but they could easily overwhelm us. Where are the rest? If this was yet another misdirect, the settlement was screwed. Without Victoria and the trained soldiers who had the better weapons, they didn't stand a chance.

With horror, Lithia realized the other Vens around her were doing the same. They were biting as many Ficarans as possible. Soon, the bitten would turn against their own. The Vens had sacrificed a few of their number to sow chaos within the walls. Not a bad tactic when outnumbered. Still, Lithia thought it was overkill. Without Victoria and her trained fighters, the superior Ficaran numbers were meaningless. The Vens would figure that out soon enough.

Well, they had not expected Lithia. She focused in and got to work. While the Ficarans tried to take down the Vens, she directed her shots toward their bitten victims. They fell reluctantly, some even taking three hits before hitting the ground. They would wake up sore tomorrow, but they wouldn't be able to hurt anyone. She still ached from where Cora had stunned her last night.

Brian and Melanie found her as she was firing a final stunning shot at a crazed Ficaran man. There were no more Vens in sight, but the growling beyond had resumed.

"Come on, back to the tower," Brian said, a little too loudly.

More screams erupted behind them. A boy, no more than fourteen, was on the ground, being pummeled by a much larger woman. Lithia must have missed one. She fired, but her shot went wide. The woman was too far away.

"I need to get closer," she said, running forward.

"Wait!" Melanie said. It was too late. Another Ven had seen them and was heading their way. Lithia didn't stop advancing. She was still too far to make the shot. If she didn't, that woman was going to kill the boy.

She ignored the movement in her right periphery, the shots ringing in that direction, and took aim. The first shot hit the woman square in the chest. The second shot missed as the woman bent over, and Lithia sensed the movement on her right getting closer. She had to stop this woman now. She exhaled and took an extra fraction of a second to steady her aim. The third shot hit its mark, and the woman slumped to one side.

Lithia didn't get a chance to see if the pummeled boy was moving because in that moment, the Ven was on her. She dodged to the side, almost in time, but the Ven's club came down. Instead of smacking her in the chest, it crashed against her shoulder. Most of the power of the blow glanced off to the side, but her arm still throbbed with pain.

"Get out of there!" Brian said. Easier said than done. The Ven lunged again. She could see fluid leaking out of a few bullet holes, but they might as well have been microrounds for all the damage they had done. The Ven was fast despite its size, and she barely had the sense to draw the knife that Melanie had given her. The large, yet dull blade would not save her. They were far enough away from the wall by now that very few people with guns were nearby.

"Shoot it!" Lithia screamed.

"We're out of ammo," Brian said.

Lithia and the Ven circled each other, and Brian and Melanie inched forward. Maybe the three of them could take down the Ven together.

The growls from the forest turned to high-pitched screeches and every hair on Lithia's body stood on end. A warning. Something was coming.

Growing beneath the screeching was another sound. A familiar sound.

"Flyers," she said, never taking her eyes from the Ven. "They're coming back."

The Ven seemed to realize this, too, and knew it didn't have much time left. It lunged again, this time toward Melanie, who was not expecting it. Lithia flinched. This was an invitation to the Ven, who redirected its attention at her.

It seemed to realize that her weapon was useless and stopped holding back. It charged toward her. She scrambled backward. Just before the Ven swung down with its club, a shot rang out. It stumbled and dropped its club, though it was not dead yet. Lithia could see fluid leaking from a large hole on the side of its head.

Nothing she had seen at the weapons depot could make a dent like that. She looked up and saw a shuttle hovering far up in the air, the back open. She couldn't be certain, but the shooter's long, brown ponytail looked like Victoria's.

The Ven was moving toward Melanie, probably to bite her like so many others.

"Brian, help me," Lithia said.

She still held the knife, but it would be hard to get the right angle with it. Brian grabbed the Ven's club from the ground and aimed at the wound on its head. The Ven stopped its attack, allowing Lithia to step closer. Even though it was seriously wounded, Lithia was afraid to get too close to those claws. Brian swung again, and this time hit his mark. The Ven stumbled and fell to its knees. In the instant of vulnerability, Lithia shoved the blade up through its plates and into its brain, wiggling the blade to sever any neural connections.

Brian helped Melanie to her feet. They heard more booms ring out from the shuttles in the air. Some of the craft were so low that men were jumping out and joining the fray by the gate. *Maybe that's where this Ven had come from,* Lithia thought. If that was so, there might be more bitten Ficarans raging around the settlement.

Brian's communicator crackled. "They're retreating. Victoria's back! She's sent them running!"

As much as Lithia hated to admit it, Victoria and her people really had just saved them all. She pulled the knife from the Ven's back, wiped it in the grass, then sheathed it again. She kept her stun rifle ready in case they ran into any other frenzied Ficarans. Lithia had to stun several before they reached the gate.

When they arrived, Victoria and several of her soldiers were there, speaking with Nick. Lithia couldn't hear what they were saying over the rumble of shuttles heading toward the hangar, but Nick looked like he was going to wet himself while Victoria looked triumphant. Finally, the leader turned and addressed those present. A crowd had gathered, and Lithia recognized a few people who must have wandered this way from the forest side, just like she had.

"The raid was a success," Victoria began. "As I speak, our people are unloading supplies. And this raid was just the first. Tomorrow, we will go back out. These demons" —Victoria turned to Nick and corrected herself—"these *Vens*, whatever they are, will not destroy us. They are a distraction from the real threat. Did you see how they ran as soon as they saw the Flyers? They know that we cannot be beaten that easily. In light of our victories today, we will honor our fallen tonight. Food and drink are being brought to the square even now. We will take care of our wounded, and then we will celebrate what it means to be alive."

Lithia did not join the cheering crowd. She turned to Brian. "Is she freaking kidding me? A party?"

"It might seem strange, but in the face of death, we celebrate life every chance we get," Brian said.

"So you think this is a good idea?"

"I never said that. Just that this isn't unusual for us." He thought a moment. "Except for the fact there's actually food. Victoria doesn't know how much damage the Vens really did."

The crowd began to disperse, but Lithia and Brian were not lucky enough to avoid the woman's notice. Nick must have told her they were here, because she scanned the crowd until her eyes settled on them. She didn't send a goon after them. She just beckoned them over, and they complied.

"Brian, Nick told me you came back." Victoria nodded at Lithia. "Who's this one? I didn't catch her name when you all left me at the coast." She cocked her head and gave her a cold smile.

"This is Lithia. She saved a lot of Ficaran lives tonight, so before—"

"The Aratian prisoner who escaped," Victoria cut him off. "I've heard about you."

"Only believe the bad things," Lithia said.

Victoria raised an eyebrow. "You saved some of my people. Thank you. I also heard that you know the layout of the Aratian Temple."

So that's what this was all about. "Yeah, I got the tour."

"Here's my offer. I'll let you all join the celebration tonight, but I want all the intel you have."

"Why are you planning an assault on the Aratians when the Vens are attacking our settlement?" Brian said.

"Those Vens have only been trying to kill us for a day. The Aratians have been oppressing us or starving us for years, and I'm not going to give them a chance to find their bearings. Plus, after their defeat tonight, I imagine these Vens will look for an easier target. So, Lithia, do we have a deal? Your freedom, tonight and for the rest of your time here, in exchange for actionable intel on the Aratian settlement."

Lithia paused. "You grew up there. I doubt much has changed. The layout of the Vale Temple is probably just like yours. They all seem to be practically the same."

"I'm aware of that, but I don't need to know where the rooms are. I need to know who or what each one contains."

"Like where the Regnator sleeps?" Lithia asked.

Victoria's hard stare betrayed nothing. "We'll talk later. I need to see to the commemoration ceremony." She left them and headed toward the square where tables were being set up. Crates were being carried from the shuttles to the square, though some were taken straight into the Field Temple.

They were actually setting up for a party.

Brian shook his head. "That was too easy. She's planning something."

Melanie rejoined them. "Come on, there's some clean-up left to do. All those people who gotten bitten need to be moved."

"And restrained," Lithia added. "Just in case they wake up before the crazy Ven cocktail wears off."

"How many?" Brian said, his voice soft and serious.

"At least twelve dead, more wounded or stunned."

"I expected more," he said.

"So did I," Lithia said. "I guess we got lucky."

"Or these Vens aren't as bad of a threat as you claim," Melanie said.

Even Melanie was doubting her now. This wasn't good.

"Maybe," Lithia said, "but I don't think so. They've wiped out entire colonies." The Vens were deadly. She knew that. They were not easy to take down.

"How many Vens were killed?"

"Five," she said.

"And you're sure they're dead?"

"We did what you and Brian said. Severed the neural connections. The rest ran off."

That didn't sound like the Vens Lithia had heard about. "That's a lot of damage for a dozen Vens to do in such a disadvantageous position."

Melanie thought for a moment. "You're right. I hadn't thought about it like that. Why didn't they send in more?"

"I don't know, and that's what worries me," Lithia said.

7. CORA

Despite the long summer days, Cora arrived at the Aratian gates well after dark. Sam had shown her how to use the autopilot on the ATV, but she hadn't trusted it enough to relax and she certainly hadn't gotten any rest.

Her guilt had helped keep her awake. Lithia and Zane had lied to her. They had pretended to be working for the Farmer, the god who had created her people and brought them here. He was supposed to return. That was why she had helped Lithia and defied her father. If she could just explain everything, he would understand.

When the sentries opened the gates for her, she was surprised to find a small crowd waiting to greet her.

In another moment, she realized that the crowd was not there for her. It was the cavalry, assembled and making final preparations to leave. What had happened?

She scanned the men's faces, but before she could pick out her father, he stepped forward and usher her off to the side.

"Cora, you're all right," he said, giving her shoulder a squeeze. She could see the relief on his face in the soft light of the glowglobes, but it was gone in another instant, replaced by the stern mask she'd come to expect from Regnator Michael Bram.

"What happened? Was Evy with you?"

"Evy followed us," Cora said, fixing her eyes on the ground. "I thought Lithia was working for the Farmer. She had a communicator…"

Her father set his lips in a hard line. "Where's Evy?"

"She's still with them. She wouldn't come back with me. I tried. She wanted to stay," Cora said.

"And you let her?"

"I had no choice! Lithia took the medicine for the demon sickness. I had to bring it back. Wait—" She reached into the small bag where she had stored the vial in her escape. It wasn't there. "How?" She looked up at her father. "It's gone."

Her father frowned and leaned back. "Cora…"

He didn't need to scold her. Disappointment always cut deeper than wrath. She wasn't the one who was always running off into the woods, getting into trouble. Except for this one time. "I'm sorry," she replied, blinking back tears. "They won't hurt Evy, though."

"You don't know that." His voice shut down the justification she had been preparing on her ride home.

Michael looked over his shoulder. His assistant was approaching. "We'll talk when I get back. In the meantime, you'll need to explain to your aunt and uncle where Evy is. Go to them at once."

"Where are you going?"

"The Ficarans have raided one of the farms. They used the Flyers." Her father looked thoughtful for a moment. "Do you know how they got them working?"

Cora shook her head. "No, in fact, Lithia and the other outsiders had to escape from the Ficarans. They weren't working together."

"As far as you know, but they've lied to you before."

And you fell for it, Cora, you stupid child. Her father didn't need to remind her.

One of her father's cavalrymen approached, but waited at a distance. Her father summoned him with the slightest flick of his fingers.

"Yes?" he asked.

"Regnator," the rider said, "the men are anxious to get going, but Delia and Elijah have requested to see you before you leave."

"I'll only be another minute." Michael sighed. "Tell Delia and Elijah that their concerns will have to wait until I return. The demons they claim to have seen in the woods aren't the ones who attacked us."

Despite his command, a man and woman, clearly Delia and Elijah, approached unannounced. Delia spoke first. "That's not our concern. We have other suspicions about the demons. This is urgent."

"As is my mission. Take your concerns to Benjamin. He's my deputy while I'm gone."

Her father's assistant stood in their path and began to herd them away. Delia pursed her lips, and Elijah glared at her father. Cora didn't like it. She didn't like them.

Her father gave her one final look before returning to his men. "I expected more from you."

Cora blinked back tears.

Tomorrow, she would find a way to be helpful. To make amends to her father, and to everyone. She listened to the cavalry, a healthy mix of maximutes and machi, depart through the open gates until only the routine nighttime sounds remained, the laughing hoot of an owl and the persistent song of the bugs that Evy loved so much.

The ATV had been moved elsewhere while Cora had spoken with her father, and the gates were closing. Exhaustion began to overwhelm her as she made her way to the Temple. Her aunt and uncle might already be asleep, and she dreaded waking them to face the ire of her Aunt Amelia.

8. BEL

"Stop it, Daya," Bel said, half asleep. She rolled over, but the girl kept poking her. Classic Daya. So eager to start the day. "I'm still sleeping."

"Bel?" the girl said.

That voice was wrong. Bel sat up and looked at the girl. Not Daya. It couldn't be. Daya was dead, along with her parents and her brother Halen. The Vens had killed them all. This girl was Evy. Bel was on Kepos, the so-called garden planet, and she had almost let a Ven kill her a few days ago.

The thought released enough adrenaline into her bloodstream to wake her up completely. The others had tucked her into bed, then left. On the bedside table she saw her manumed. Zane must have fixed it. She tapped out a quick thanks to him, then looked up at Evy.

"How long was I asleep?"

"All day. It's dark out." That explained why she felt great. A full day of rest.

"Oh, I'm sorry, Evy. Did you find something to eat?"

"Yeah."

"What did you do all day?"

Evy grinned and came back with two clear plastic containers that she had found. Each contained some dirt, sticks, and leaves. Evy had spent the day bug hunting. Upon closer observation, Bel saw that she had poked a few holes in the top of each. She must have used a sharp knife, unsupervised. No parents to yell at her, though.

She remembered those days from her own childhood. Once she had used her mother's jam jars to collect critters from the lake near the colony. Her father had been impressed as she went through her finds with him. She had even managed to catch a scale bug. They were hard to find and nearly impossible to catch, but she had finally done it. When her mother came in, she was less than pleased. Turns out those jars had been set out because she was planning on making jam. Halen had helped her return all of her finds to the lake, even the scale bug, but she had washed the jars herself and refused to eat any of that batch of jam.

"What do you have there?" Bel asked.

"This is some kind of ant. I call them pincher ants because they really hurt." She pointed to a rather large ant pacing along the bottom of the container. "And there's a burrow bug. They dig down in the dirt, but you can see the outline of his shell." It took Bel a second, but she finally saw the outline where the bug was hiding. She'd ask to uncover it and get a better look later to see if she recognized it. She had some guesses as to its family and genus, but on this planet, anything was possible.

Evy still hadn't shown her the other container.

"What's in there?"

"I saved it for last. I've never seen it before."

With that, Evy produced a terrifying bug. It looked like it had a stinger. Its elongated abdomen pulsed in anger. Broad red stripes along its thorax warned of a painful sting.

"Be careful with this one, Evy," she warned. "I don't know what its sting will do."

"I know. I didn't touch it. It looks scary, but it's new. It's the first one I've found. I couldn't just leave it. I'm gonna call it a red-stripe stinger."

Sounded good to Bel. She inspected the holes on the tops of the containers. They were small. Even the giant ant wouldn't be able to escape through them.

"Just promise me you won't play with the red-stripe stinger until we figure out what he is, okay?"

"Okay. I already got bit by the pincher ant today, so I don't really want to get bit again anyway."

Evy held up her finger to show Bel her battle scar, a welt that looked like it probably still hurt. Bel had gotten a few bites of her own like that.

"Did you run it under cold water? That always helps me."

As Evy went to the sink to take her advice, Bel asked, "What's your favorite thing about bugs?"

"There are so many different kinds. You can never find them all. What about you?"

"I like their exoskeletons. I used to think they were inside out." Evy laughed at that, and Bel had an idea. "Evy, since you showed me your finds, do you want to see my collection? I only brought part of it with me, but I still think there will be a few new bugs for you to see."

Bel took her on board the *Calypso*. She expected to find her bugs a mess in her cabin. After all, there hadn't been time to put them away before the Ven attack, but she could probably piece together any that had fallen apart. It might be fun to have to find replacements for any that were damaged beyond repair.

So, she was surprised to find her bugs organized, or at least looking neat. Someone had come in and cleaned everything up. Zane. It had to be. He hadn't known how to organize them properly, but he had collected the ones that had fallen and broken, and put them back with the others. She smiled. He was thoughtful like that. He did things just to be nice. She noticed he was extra nice to her, but the thought made her smile fall. That would never work out. He would never accept that she couldn't be the girlfriend he imagined, even if a part of her wanted to.

The sound of small footsteps running up to join her helped her shake off the thought. She turned to Evy. "They're a bit of a mess because of the Ven attack, but this is part of my collection."

Evy stared at the cases. She seemed drawn to the more colorful bugs.

"That one is so pretty," she said, pointing to a bright green dragonfly with iridescent wings.

"You want it?" Bel offered. These dragonflies were everywhere at StellAcademy.

Evy could barely contain her excitement. "Really?"

"Yeah, I'll be glad to know it's going to someone who can appreciate it. Let's take these back inside."

Bel and Evy grabbed the cases that held her bugs and took them inside so Evy could examine them. Evy gingerly took her shiny, new bug and secured it in a small container. She pulled another one out of her bag and produced a black beetle.

"This is the biggest Cela beetle I've found. I want you to have it."

Bel inspected the beetle. Whatever it was, she didn't have one. "This is awesome. Thank you, Evy."

***

Between the bugs and needing some sleep, Evy wouldn't interrupt her now. Time to get to work. She wasn't looking forward to examining the dead Ven, but anything she learned from it could mean the difference between life and death. She was, however, looking forward to cutting it up, purely out of spite.

Zane had sent Bel a message while she'd been talking to Evy. He'd loaded some classified data about the Vens onto her manumed in case it helped. He'd apparently done a little bit of his own data-gathering when he was helping Lithia access the secured Alliance database, but Bel wasn't complaining.

After plugging her nose and throwing on some old clothes she had brought for fieldwork, she headed down to the lab Sam had indicated and got everything ready. She stared at the Ven, but its eerie dead eyes did not stare back. Something about those eyes bothered her.

Bel rummaged through the supplies Oberon had packed to find the gloves. *How was Oberon still alive? Why hadn't the Vens killed him?*

There were four Vens hunting him. There had been four Vens in the boarding party. Three to five Vens was the normal size for a hunting party. They were like specialized teams, and those teams would work in tandem. There had to be some reason the professor was alive, and figuring that out might be the key to saving him.

"First, though, time to find out why you're blue," Bel said. She put on her safety glasses and added a face mask, if only to reduce the power of its stench.

It smelled worse than she expected. She touched her face where it had cut a spiral into cheek, marking her. It was healing, but it still hurt. There would be a scar. Another reminder. Bel carved a jagged 'B' onto one of its arm plates. Now they were both marked. She pulled up all available information on Ven anatomy, including the new stuff from Zane.

There was one entry about juveniles. Apparently this one had been blue, as well. Pretty damning evidence, but she'd check a few other factors, too.

Raised bumps on the shoulders? No, but this Ven's shoulders were already turning green.

Significantly below average height and weight? Significantly? Who wrote this? That was an arbitrary modifier. Where were the numbers? This Ven was smaller, but it had been the biggest of the boarding party. Again, it looked quite close to full maturity, if that's what the green meant.

Underdeveloped fertilization sac? Again, the diagrams were not clear, and the description was vague. Though annoyed, she was glad to have a pass on checking that one for now. Maybe when Dione returned they could revisit it.

She didn't have a lot to go on, and despite her frustration with the vague information, she supposed whoever had written the report hadn't had a lot to go on either. The results of her examination were inconclusive, but the blue coloration seemed like strong enough evidence. She was pretty sure that Dione was right. She'd noticed Dione had a knack for these things. It was dangerous to make assumptions, but she wasn't writing a paper for publication. She was trying to survive, and she wanted to follow this train of thought further.

If these Vens were juveniles, why were they sent on board? Why not send actual warriors, who would have made quick work of them all? The stun gas never would have worked on larger, fully grown Vens, and that was the only thing that had given them a chance.

The Ven's open eyes with their narrow, rectangular pupils looked wrong to her. She glanced away and grimaced. She hated Vens.

They sent their children in. No, they were adolescents. The big one had already started turning green. That must have meant the Vens saw their ship as no threat. It was strange they would even attack something so small and pathetic, unless they needed an easy target. She had an idea. A first kill, to initiate the ones who were coming of age. She needed to call Dione.

"Bel, how are you doing?" Dione said when she picked up. "Is everything okay?"

"I'm fine. I think I figured out why the Vens were blue. I can't be sure, but I think you were right about them being juveniles. I started thinking about why they would send juveniles over to board us."

"And?" Dione said.

"It's a ritual. A first hunt."

"They didn't think we'd be much of a fight," Dione said, picking up her train of thought. "An easy win."

"Exactly," Bel said.

"That could explain some of the weird stuff I saw. The Vens were all watching some readouts, maybe monitoring the juveniles. Then when I was leaving, a Ven chased me to the airlock. It could have grabbed me, but it just stood at the door, like it couldn't follow. Maybe the adults weren't allowed to interfere."

"That doesn't explain why they didn't kill the professor," Bel said.

"I'm not complaining. I just hope we find him."

"Any sign?"

"No," Dione said. "We're about to stop for the night. Hopefully we'll figure something out."

"Good luck," Bel said, staring into the Ven's open eyes.

"Thanks," Dione said.

Bel was about to end the call when something clicked into place. "Oh my god!"

"What? What happened?"

The realization had hit Bel suddenly, like her brain had been working on the problem in the background.

"Dione, their eyes. They have rectangular pupils. Those are usually found on animals like goats that need to see in as wide a range as possible, to watch for predators. Predators usually have vertical slits to help them judge distance."

"Octopuses have them, too, and they're predators," Dione replied. "It's not that unusual, though I guess they're prey for larger animals, like sharks."

"You're missing the point. The redundant organs, the rigid plates covering their entire bodies, the rectangular pupils, all of it."

"No," Dione said. "You're not suggesting..."

"Yes, the Vens have a natural predator."

"Those adaptations could be vestigial from a time when they did have a predator."

"If something out there can kill Vens, I want to find it." Bel clenched her jaw.

Dione didn't answer for a moment. "Bel, if you're right, why would you want to find a predator so strong that it can kill Vens? What if it wants to kill us, too? Think about Marcan toads. They were introduced on Ulla Prime to control beetles that were decimating harvests, but they started eating local beneficial insects and pollinators."

Bel didn't have a good answer for that. "Sometimes it works. What about the fungal infection that killed off the invasive Balta moths back home?"

"That's an odd example," Dione replied. Bel could practically hear her thinking. "The introduction of the fungus was an accident, right? I swear I read that the intentional attempts to introduce the fungus failed. Years later, the fungus took hold, but it was an accidental introduction."

"The point I'm making is that it worked. The fungus resulted in a population collapse of the Balta moth. What if there's something out there than can cause a population collapse of the Vens?"

"When it goes wrong, it can get really bad. On Ulla Prime, they had to eradicate the toads, *and* they had to breed and reintroduce the beneficial insects," Dione said. "It's a good lead, Bel, but before we jump to conclusions, see what else you can find out."

Bel could tell she was making Dione uncomfortable. "Will do. And good luck, to both of you."

Bel ended the call. She wondered what the Vens were doing out there. Probably preparing for an assault on the Ficarans. She hoped Lithia would be okay.

"Sam, where are the Vens?" she asked to assuage her worries.

"They've retreated into the woods near the Ficaran settlement."

"Retreated? What do you mean retreated?"

"The Vens made an attack, but the Ficarans repelled them, based on the comms chatter." So Sam was using the communicators to eavesdrop. Their manumeds, too.

"Sam, why didn't you tell me?"

"Because there's nothing you could have done. I didn't see a point."

"Is Lithia okay?"

"Yes." Bel detected just a hint of hesitation.

It looked like she would be giving Lithia a call, too.

9. LITHIA

The wounded were all safely inside the Field Temple, and everyone else, including Lithia and Brian, was in the square.

A small stage had been erected at the head of the square next to some ugly, abstract statue. The platform was just high enough for the musicians on it to see above the crowd. Glowglobes lined the square. They emitted a yellow light so dull that Lithia wondered what the Ficarans fed them.

Victoria held up a hand, and the quiet chatter stopped almost immediately. Lithia couldn't help being impressed.

"Today was a day for victory, but victory always has a cost. Today, twelve of our brothers and sisters gave their lives, but they died free from Aratian oppression. They died good deaths. Their sacrifice has reminded us to live. Every day we live by our own laws is a day to celebrate. We can mourn their deaths, but first we must celebrate their lives, and in doing so, honor them. Honor what it means to be a Ficaran."

Victoria raised her hand into the air again, this time earning raucous applause from the crowd. That also seemed to be the signal for the music to start, though the beat was slow. A girl with a voice clear as water began a melancholy tune. Lithia was surprised to find that she knew the words. Grandpa Min used to sing it sometimes. It was a farewell to lost companions. After the first verse, the crowd joined in. The chorus of voices gave her goose bumps, especially when Brian joined in with the harmony. She looked over at him, but his eyes were closed.

Everyone around her was singing, and she felt compelled to join them. They were not her people who died, but the music moved her. She had fought alongside them, and her thoughts turned to the boy she had tried to save. What had happened to him?

Lithia closed her eyes and began to sing the chorus, interweaving her soprano melody with Brian's harmony. She might have her father's eyes, but she had her mother's voice.

Take the loaf and pass it 'round,
Then pour a glass to wash it down—
A toast to friends! A toast to blood!
We trees who all survived the flood,
Let's drain our cups; sate our roots;
Endure to bear tomorrow's fruits.

As she sang the last line, she opened her eyes to see Brian staring at her. At first, she was worried she had done something wrong by joining in, but he didn't look angry. He looked surprised.

When the song was over, the musicians picked up their beat without ending the song. The solemn elegy shifted into a more upbeat tune, and the people around them spun and stomped and began the celebration.

Brian led her away from the center of the square. "I didn't realize you could sing like that," he said.

"You're not bad yourself." Lithia grinned. "I can't believe Victoria didn't lock us up."

"We're not exactly free. We're confined to the settlement," Brian said.

"But she's letting us join the festivities."

He shook his head. "She's up to something. Threatening Dione didn't work. She tried the stick. Now, she's trying the carrot. Don't be fooled."

"Speaking of carrots…"

Barrels and boxes of food had been put out at the back of the square, along with ample bottles of juice, beer, and liquor. Lithia's stomach growled, but Brian had already beaten her to the buffet.

"So this is all from her raid today?" Lithia said.

Brian managed to say yes through a full mouth. After he swallowed, he filled his hands with more stolen Aratian provisions and directed her to grab a bottle of some brown liquor.

"Come on," he said, beckoning her to the edge of the square. She followed him to an out-of-the-way spot where they could still hear the wild strings and see the movements of the dancers. He sat with his back against a building, and she plopped down next to him.

He laid out a spread of dried fruit and bread and cheese. A simple meal, but to the Ficarans, a feast.

"I bet you don't get much cheese here," she said, chasing a swig of the liquor with a morsel of cheese.

"Nope. Not much alcohol either." He extended his hand, and Lithia put the bottle in his grasp. He tipped it up to his mouth, swallowed, and coughed.

Lithia laughed. "Did you know that it's illegal for me to drink where I come from?"

"Let me guess. You do anyway."

"On occasion. Dione never does, though."

Brian laughed and passed the bottle back. "Why does that not surprise me?"

After more food and a few more passes of the bottle, Lithia felt amazing. Somehow she was numb and tingly at the same time, and she could not only hear the music, but she also felt it.

Musicians were playing a lively tune that reminded her of ancient jigs. Every few minutes the song would transition, the beat would shift, and the eager dancers would adjust. Lithia just stood, staring. It was amazing.

"Do you dance?" she asked Brian.

He stood and brushed off his pants, offering her a hand up. "The real question is, do you?"

"I think I've had enough to drink to give it a try, though this dancing is not what I'm used to. It just looks so fun. Will you teach me?" She took his hand and gripped it tight. He pulled her to her feet, and her head swam with warm, fuzzy happiness.

"I'll teach you the basics."

There were enough people dancing in the square—and enough bottles going around—that she was not the worst dancer there. Brian taught her a few steps that followed the basic dancing principle of follow the leader. When he stepped back, she stepped forward, and vice versa. Sure, Brian was able to add more drama and flourishes to his moves, but with the music rising and falling all around her, she easily obeyed the rhythm. Though the other dancers showed no signs of growing weary, after a few songs, she had to excuse herself to find some water.

As she left, Brian found his friend Melanie and danced with her a few rounds. Melanie was on par with Brian's skill level, Lithia noticed, and the two swept around the square matching each other and transitioning seamlessly with the music. Lithia was mesmerized not only by their dancing, but by Brian himself. His flowing, dark hair, lose and free, those earnest eyes, his playful smile. She wasn't the only girl noticing him tonight. She gave a wry grin. She had met guys like Brian before, and under the right circumstances, they could be a lot of fun.

Mesmerized by the musicians and dancers, Lithia barely heard her manumed chime. It was Bel.

"Hang on, friend," she said, laughing. Lithia moved to the far edge of the square, away from the music.

"What is hap—" Bel began. "Is that music?"

"The Ficarans are celebrating their victory. Double victory, actually."

"Are you okay?"

"Yeah, Victoria raided some Aratian farm, came back with food and booze, then we beat the Vens, and now there's a party."

"Are you drunk?" Bel said. She sounded like Dione. Judgmental.

"I'm just relaxed," Lithia replied.

"Lithia, this isn't over. Today's attack was a test run. They were feeling you guys out, figuring out your go-to offensive and defensive moves. The Vens are going to come back. Maybe tomorrow, maybe the following day, but they're not finished. Whatever celebration is going on there, it's premature. You should be improving fortifications, checking weapons, and getting some rest."

"I've got a meeting with Victoria tomorrow. I'll let her know, but I doubt it will do any good. She's set her sights on the Aratians."

"You have to convince her, Lithia. Do you understand how important this is?"

"I'll do my best, but confirmation bias is a real pain in the ass. She doesn't think the Vens are a threat, and even I thought they gave up pretty easily tonight. Anything else?"

"Stop drinking. Get some water and go to sleep. Please."

"Will do," Lithia said, ending the call. She had found another bottle, and in order to appease Bel, she only took a small sip. *Last one.*

"Why wait until tomorrow?" Victoria said. "What did you want to tell me?"

Lithia didn't know where Victoria had come from, but she wasn't exactly in the mood to talk. She hadn't figured out the best way to convince her of what she needed to know. All the same, there was no time like the present.

"That the Vens will come back. In full force."

"We'll be ready. Tell me about your time with the Aratians."

"No, you won't be ready. Tonight was just a few dozen. Tomorrow, there will be over two hundred."

Victoria laughed. "Will they do more than sing in the woods?"

Lithia stared her down. "They will destroy everything you care about."

"I think I may have gotten to you too late," she said, eyeing the bottle in Lithia's hand. "What can you tell me about the security at the Vale Temple? If I want to minimize casualties and maximize hostages, where in the Temple should I go?"

"Huh?" Lithia was having a little trouble focusing on Victoria's words.

"Where are the girls' rooms?" Victoria asked.

"Top floor."

"Were there guards?"

"Outside the Temple and everywhere I went. Until Cora ditched them."

Victoria sighed. "I suppose that's good enough. Oh, and I'd ease up on that," she said, nodding to the bottle.

Lithia almost took another giant swig in defiance, but she remembered her promise to Bel. Well, it wasn't technically a promise, but somewhere deep down, she knew she'd already had more than enough. This Aratian stuff was strong. She made a rude gesture to Victoria's back as she walked away.

Lithia leaned against the nearest building, trying to process what Bel had told her about the Vens and what she'd just told Victoria. It wasn't working. Her brain. It didn't want to process these unpleasant thoughts. She could die tomorrow, according to Bel, when the real attack began. There was zero chance she'd be able to convince Victoria of anything she didn't want to hear. She didn't hear Brian approach until he was close enough to make her jump.

"Hey, you okay? What did Victoria want?" he asked.

"To get us all killed. She won't listen."

"What happened?" She saw the rapid rise and fall of his muscled chest, the sweet concern in his eyes.

"I think I figured out why Victoria let us join the festivities," Lithia said.

"Why's that?" Brian cocked his head to one side and smiled.

The world was ending, and he was so damn gorgeous. *Might as well.*

Lithia put her arms around his neck, tilted her head up, and paused just long enough for him to say no. When no complaints were made, she kissed him. She was not gentle. She pressed her body against his, feeling his heat, and turned him around so that his back was against the wall. There was no sweetness here, no romance, only desire and wandering hands.

Brian broke away. "I think you've had too much to drink."

"So have you."

Brian leaned back. Was he embarrassed?

"Dammit, Brian, really?" It was Melanie's voice.

Brian released Lithia and laughed.

"I don't see why you've got a problem, Melanie," he said.

"Can I talk to you for a minute, then?" she replied.

"Sure."

Brian walked off with Melanie, but Lithia could still hear them.

"See, this is why Colm punched you."

"You know me. Plus, she started it."

"And you're wasted. No alcohol for months and you have the tolerance of child. What happened with Dione?"

"Does it matter? If we can't convince Victoria, we're all dead anyway."

Lithia frowned. What did that mean? Did he have a thing with Dione? She hadn't said anything. Lithia could tell Dione thought he was attractive, but that didn't really mean anything. Dione thought almost every boy was attractive. If she spent half as much time following through as she did pining, she might have kissed more than that one guy back at StellAcademy, whatever his name was.

It became too difficult to focus on their words. In fact, all of her focus suddenly turned inward, on not puking. While Brian and Melanie argued, she found a private place, out of the way, and threw up. She came back, found the bottle of booze, and washed her mouth out with the alcohol. Anything to get rid of the sour vomit taste. Brian and Melanie were still at it. She should find some water.

She stumbled away. Yes, that would be good. Water.

10. DIONE

Dione's frown deepened. It was bad enough that it was already dark and they were no closer to finding the professor, but the memory of her conversation with Bel kept distracting her. The Vens might be prey. What would a Ven-killer even look like? How hard would it be to kill?

There was no point in worrying about something that probably didn't exist, though Bel brought up some good points. She had never noticed it before, but the Vens really did have a lot of defensive adaptations, which just happened to make them ruthless killing machines, too.

With Zane and the maximute, she had made it safely to the hunting shelter. She gave Canto some dinner and sent him to rest nearby. Like the smugglers' den, there were whistler trees not far off. Hunters probably made good use of them. The shelter was off the ground, up in the trees, and looked like it had recently been repaired.

"Do you think he's alive?" Dione said, the professor on her mind.

"It doesn't matter. We just need to find him," Zane said.

"What do you mean?"

"We can wonder all night if he's alive, but we can't know for sure. Tomorrow, we're going to wake up and keep looking."

Dione supposed he had a point. She had a habit of worrying herself sick over things beyond her control. The night before the Post-16 internship assignments were announced, when everything was already decided, she had spent half the night staring at her bedroom ceiling, reading and rereading all of the inspirational quotes that projected against her wall, wondering if she'd get to go to Barusia. The memory felt distant, like it belonged in someone else's life.

"I guess you're right," Dione said. "Let's get some rest."

***

It was still dark outside when Zane woke her. She checked her manumed. It was the middle of the night. Before she could speak, Zane put a finger to his lips. She sat up and listened. The whistler trees. She had no idea what had passed by. It could have been deer, or Vens, or a herd of large rabbits. She would never know.

Once the whistling had subsided, Zane spoke. "Vens. I think I saw one in the distance."

"You sure?"

"No, but I wouldn't be telling you if I didn't think I was right."

"Fair enough. You still want to follow them?" Dione asked.

"Want isn't the right word, but yes, I think that's what we should do."

"And if they realize they're being followed?"

"Canto can outrun them."

Canto could outrun them, but that was assuming they got the chance to run.

"Let's give them a bit more of a head start," Dione said.

"Just enough time to pack up. If they get too far ahead, we'll lose them."

The tracking went well for maybe an hour. The Vens had made no attempt to mask their tracks. Then, there was nothing. Dione hated to admit it, but she was relieved. She didn't like following the Vens and was still a little paranoid that they had looped around behind and were going to attack at any minute. Canto seemed relaxed, though, so her rational mind didn't think they were close at all.

Dione regretted not getting more sleep, but that couldn't be helped. Everything was still pretty dark, and she wanted to rest. Her legs were sore from the continued riding, and she could use another bathroom break.

In the early morning hours, everything looked gray as she wandered off to find a good spot. While she took care of business and the world slowly faded into color around her, she saw something that set her heart pounding.

It was one of those terrible red-veined flowers that belonged to the angler worm that had nearly killed Lithia. She hurried back to get Zane. He needed to know that he had to avoid them. This one looked smaller than the other, but that was not a risk she was willing to take.

She found him safe and sound near the maximute. When she showed Zane the flower, he tested it by throwing a rock. Its rapid reaction was enough to make him raise his eyebrows.

"Good to know," he said.

They ate an early breakfast, mostly in silence. Dione tried starting a conversation a few times, but Zane wasn't in a talking mood and kept his answers short. She thought that after everything that had happened in the Mountain Base the night before, things were okay between them, but he was still distant.

Finally, out of the silence, he said, "I have an idea for how to find the professor."

Dione sat up a little straighter and leaned in.

"I think I can send a burst to his manumed that will light it up on our GPS."

"You can just do that? Track someone using their manumed?"

"Only because I have admin privileges for the *Calypso's* network. This wouldn't work normally."

Dione raised an eyebrow. "The professor gave you admin privileges?"

Zane looked away. "Not exactly."

"I see," she replied. "So what's the catch? Why didn't you mention this earlier if it will allow us to track him?"

Zane sighed. "See, it will only work once. It will fry his manumed and he won't be able to talk to us at all."

Dione thought a moment. "I don't see any other options, though. Let's do it."

"There are two things. This will only work if his manumed isn't completely dead or destroyed. The other is, well, it will probably hurt him."

"What do you mean hurt him?"

"Like a little shock."

"How little?"

"Painful, but it's not going to kill him. Even if he's still in the river, the power supply in a manumed can't discharge at a high enough current to do any real damage."

"Good to know," Dione said. "If we get his current location and use his old location, we'll have two points. We can draw a line between them to get an approximate trajectory,

"He's not a bullet, Dione. He could change directions at any time."

"It's better than nothing. Maybe he's heading in a certain direction. I say we go for it."

Dione stretched her legs while Zane worked. His speed was impressive, and just thirty minutes later, he had the coordinates. They were right on the river, just a little ways downstream.

"So he's in the river? Should we follow the river then, or try to use the points we have to map a path?"

Zane was ignoring her, or thinking, while staring at his map.

"I think... he may be stopped there." Zane pointed to a spot on the map.

"Why do you think that?" Dione did her best to hide the irritation from her voice, especially since she was trying this whole new thing where she listened to Zane, but old habits were hard to break.

"Pull up your map. Look at that area. The ping wasn't exact, so we just know his approximate location. What do you see there?"

"The river," Dione said. There were a few dark spots on the map. What did that symbol mean? She checked the legend and realized the point that Zane was making in a roundabout way. "Caves. You think he's holed up in one of those caves."

"He hasn't gone that far from his original location. The Vens would have caught him by now, unless he found a way to hide. Or lost his manumed. That's a possibility, too."

"It wouldn't hurt to check the caves, and if we can't find him, we'll use the river as a possible trajectory and follow it."

"Sounds good to me."

Zane and Dione climbed onto Canto and headed off toward the caves. Dione tried not to think about the tight, closed-in spaces they would have to search. The confines of the *Calypso* hadn't felt like a space coffin. The ship filled her with a sense of freedom and possibility. Caves, though, were dark, small, and unpredictable. Who knew how big the next cavern would be? What if she got stuck and couldn't make her way out, forward or backward? Dione shuddered. She would almost prefer to face another Ven than go spelunking.

When she realized she would probably have to do both, her stomach flipped in uneasy knots.

11. LITHIA

Lithia hated everyone and everything, especially noises and sunlight and whoever was banging on her door.

She forced her sleepy eyes open, but had no idea where she was or how she got there. She was still fully dressed, except for her shoes. She took in her surroundings. Simple furnishings, sparse. The pillow smelled like Brian. This must be his room.

Who did you think would take you in? Victoria? All those friends you made last night?

The knock sounded again. "Yeah, come in," Lithia said.

Brian opened the door. He looked tired. There were dark circles under his eyes, and she imagined he had a headache, too. She had kissed him last night, that much she remembered. The dancing had also been pretty fun. The headache, though, was the all-too-real price to pay.

"We need to meet Victoria at breakfast. Here." He tossed in some Ficaran clothes—loose knee-length shorts and a more fitted top.

Her current outfit was a mess. Between the fighting and the dancing and the partying, she was glad for a change of clothes. "No time for a shower?"

"No, sorry. We let you sleep too long. Come out when you're ready." He closed the door behind him.

We? Who else was here? Lithia dressed quickly, leaving her clothes in a pile on the floor. She opened the bedroom door and found herself in the center of a small apartment inside a pre-fabricated housing unit.

"Is there time for the bathroom at least?" There were probably communal kitchens and restrooms. That's what colonizers would have had fifty years ago, right?

"On our way out," he said.

He was handing a spoon to an old woman. She was bone thin.

"Ma, you need to eat. Please."

"I'm fine. Not very hungry today. Why don't you have it?" The woman pushed back the plate.

"I'll have a ration at breakfast. This better be eaten by the time I get back." Brian pushed the plate back toward her and kissed her forehead.

"Okay, honey."

The old woman took a small bite, and when Lithia approached, she realized the woman was not as old as she appeared. In fact, she was probably in her forties. This was Brian's mother. Her skeletal frame and features added a decade or two.

Brian looked to Lithia, and she saw something there she had never seen before. Vulnerability. So much emotion. His mother looked like she was dying.

"Come on," he said. He didn't even introduce her, but she didn't blame him for that.

Lithia kept her voice soft as she followed him to wherever breakfast was. "What's wrong with your mom?" Maybe it was cancer.

"Ever since my dad left, she hardly moves. She won't eat unless Melanie or I force her. I don't know. It wasn't so bad at first, but it keeps getting worse."

"Maybe she's depressed. My cousin was never that bad, but for months she could barely get out of bed. Once my aunt got her on medication, she got a lot better. People don't realize how serious it can be."

"Well, we don't have meds, and I can't snap her out of it." Brian didn't look at her when he spoke.

That's because you don't just snap out of depression. Lithia kept her mouth shut, though. If they didn't have the meds, she didn't know what else might help. Homeopathy was not Lithia's thing. Her parents were doctors, after all. Her aunt probably would have had some suggestions. Once this Ven nightmare was over, she would look into it and see if there was anything she could do.

***

Lithia was allowed to eat breakfast before the interrogation. Apparently her contributions to the fight last night had been enough to earn her a ration. By the looks on everyone's faces, she wasn't the only one feeling a little hungover this morning. Victoria, however, looked fully rested and properly hydrated.

The moment Lithia finished her bread and fruit, Victoria escorted her and Brian to her office.

"I hear you two had fun last night," Victoria said. Lithia didn't blush. She didn't care what Victoria had heard. "I wanted to follow up on our conversation."

"What conversation?" Lithia asked.

Victoria smiled so smugly that Lithia wanted to hit her. "I'm not surprised you don't remember. You told me where the Regnator's family sleeps."

For a moment, Lithia felt guilty. She vaguely remembered talking to Victoria now.

"I'm sure I did, but it doesn't matter."

"And why's that?" Victoria asked.

"Because we'll probably all be dead before you can act on that intel." Lithia might have forgotten about talking to Victoria, but not her conversation with Bel. "I want to tell you what I came here to say. You were gone yesterday when we got here."

Victoria leaned back in her chair and crossed her arms, but she didn't say anything. Lithia was about to enter full truth mode.

"You call them demons, but the Venatorians are a race of aliens. Hundreds of them landed here just two days ago, and they've already attacked your settlement."

"Nick filled me in," she replied. "I don't have much trouble believing that the Farmer lied to us when he called them demons, but we repelled them easily, and we'll do it again. The Aratians are the true threat to our wellbeing, and I don't need an outsider telling me what to do."

Lithia was frustrated, and her head pounded. How could Victoria just believe the Vens were aliens with no push back, yet still believe they weren't a threat? "Just think about it. How many Vens actually attacked last night? A few dozen, split into groups. They got inside your walls and caused havoc. This place is not safe."

"This is our home. We'll continue to defend it, from Aratians and Venatorians alike."

"The Vens don't want a truce. They don't want to force their ideology on you. They want to kill every single one of you."

"I could say the same of the Aratians. There's no dealing with them. Enough of this. Tell me what you know about the defenses of the Vale Temple," Victoria said. "How did you escape? I've heard rumors of secret entrances."

"Please just listen to her," Brian said.

"You need to evacuate your people. There is enough room at the Mountain Base, Temple, whatever," Lithia said. "The Vens were just testing your defenses last night. It was a trial run. Tonight, they will attack in full force. Think about it. How many Vens did you actually kill? How much ammo did you go through? I assume you have a way of producing more, since you still have ammo after all this time, but between your raids and the Vens, will you have enough?"

Victoria's clenched her jaw and stared at them. That meant no. They did not have a way to manufacture bullets. Lithia raised her eyebrows, but said nothing.

"The Vens are gone, but I'll be taking added precautions before today's raid."

"You're leaving again today?" Lithia raised her voice. "You can't be that stupid! If you take the Flyers, everyone here will be screwed. At least evacuate some of the people too young or too old to fight."

Victoria nodded to someone behind them. Lithia hadn't heard anyone come in.

"Thank you for your concern, but we've got things under control," Victoria said.

"I'm not staying here. The Vens are going to come tonight and kill us all."

"I can't let you leave. You know too much. In a few days, once we've taken over the Vale Temple, I may let you leave. Despite everything, I've been told what you did for my people during the attack. Don't cause problems, and I'll repay the debt by letting you go."

"You're sentencing us all to death," Lithia said.

"And you're being dramatic. Like so much of what the Farmer told us, these demons were a lie. He made them sound more dangerous than they are, all so he could seem more like a god. Last night proved that. We'll take care of the Vens once the Aratians have been dealt with."

"Victoria, please," Brian began, but she cut him off.

"Enough. Colm, lock them up. The Cell." A large, muscular man stood Lithia up. Another man did the same to Brian.

"Your people will die tonight if you do this," Lithia said.

Victoria paused, her fingertips spread across her desk. "Is that a threat? Is your friend selling our secrets to the Aratians?"

"No! God, you're such an idiot." In a flash, Victoria was in her face. Lithia thought she was going to slap her. Instead, Victoria punched her in the gut. Lithia coughed. "You should try that on a Ven, see how many bones in your hand you break."

She braced herself for the second punch, but it didn't help much. She groaned and kept her mouth shut. Another hit and she'd probably vomit.

"Don't overestimate my patience," Victoria said. "Tomorrow morning, once we've returned, you'll see."

Tomorrow morning we'll all be dead.

Colm took her manumed and Brian's communicator, and led them upstairs to a room with nothing more than a window, a bathroom, and a metal-framed bed. Brian slammed a hand on the door as it closed and locked, but Lithia was already at the window. It looked down on the square below.

"At least we'll have a good view," she said. She could almost taste the bitterness in her own voice. People were out in the square, cleaning up from the night before. They seemed relaxed and happy. Or maybe it was just her imagination. "And a private bathroom. How luxurious."

"That's because we won't be leaving here for days." Brian looked defeated.

"You okay? I'm sure that people won't think you actually deserve this. They must realize Victoria's insane."

"It's not that," Brian said. He was silent for another minute. "They're going to die. They don't have to, but they'll die. We should have started taking people yesterday, one trip at a time. All Victoria can think about are those damn Aratians. Argh!"

He started banging on the door again, yelling at the guard to let him out. He was going to hurt himself at this rate. Lithia was trying to find the words to calm him down when two swift knocks from the other side of the door interrupted Brian's rhythm.

"Brian, please. I don't want to hurt you."

"Jared, you know me! If the Vens, the demons from last night, attack again, we're all dead. Last night we barely withstood a few dozen. Tonight they're coming back in full force."

The guard, Jared, was not convinced. "Victoria's left more of the weapons and experienced guards. She's taking a smaller force this time. She's only going to one of their larger farms tonight, not a Hub."

"So there are still Flyers here?" Lithia said.

"I don't know," he said. "I'm not supposed to talk to you. Just stop struggling."

She turned to Brian. "It sounds like she kind of listened to us."

"But it won't be enough, will it?" Brian said.

"If we can start evacuating people…"

At that moment, a small group of Flyers rumbled across the sky, heading north into Aratian territory. At least Victoria had considered the Ven threat. It wouldn't be enough, but Lithia thought it was a sign of progress. She and Brian would have to figure out a way to escape and start the evacuation with as many people as possible. Some had to believe them. The people who were out fighting last night, they had to know how dangerous the Vens were. A few extra guns and experienced fighters would not be enough.

The shuttles, though. Those she could work with.

12. DIONE

"On the left," Zane said.

Sure enough, when Dione looked, she saw the eerie bloom of an angler worm. Another point for Zane, bringing his score up to two. Even though it wasn't the most exciting game, it did break up the monotony. Considering Brian had never seen one until a few days ago, it seemed strange that they had seen three in one morning. They were pretty deep into the woods by now. Maybe he hadn't come this way before.

They were nearly to the spot where the professor had been just a few hours ago, according to the burst Zane had sent to his manumed.

They were still a good distance away from the coordinates, but they could already see they had a problem. Vens. They were patrolling the section of the river where the professor's last known location was, but Dione saw no evidence of a cave.

"I guess this means he's still here," Zane said.

The Vens knew the professor was in the general area, but not his exact location. Maybe Zane was right, and the professor was still here somewhere.

Two Vens with scalloped edges along their plates, females, were down near the water's edge. The river pooled in this area, the result of a natural dam that slowed its flow. The other two were on the opposite bank farther up, pacing, or searching, Dione didn't know. They were females, too. One was painted with the same spiral design that was carved into Bel's cheek.

It was all making sense.

"I'm not one hundred percent sure, but I think these are the mothers of the Vens we killed on the ship," she said.

"Why do you say that?" Zane asked.

"These Vens have the same markings as the ones that boarded the *Calypso*. See that spiral? It's the same design as on Bel's cheek." Dione knew he hadn't forgotten that. She couldn't remember all the other symbols, but the three nested rectangles looked familiar. The ones along the opposite ridge were far away and hard to see, but Dione thought she recognized the bisected triangle that one of the blue Vens had displayed, but she couldn't make out or remember the other design.

"So the mothers of the Vens we killed are hunting the professor? Why not just kill him for revenge?" Zane said.

"I don't think the Vens only like killing. This is about more than that."

"Don't like killing? Tell that to Bel."

"No, I mean, the killing isn't really the part they enjoy. They like winning. They like to conquer. They might not see it as murder. What if it's just about the victory to them?"

"Then why are four Vens hunting one man? I thought they liked challenges," Zane said.

"If they are the mothers, maybe they couldn't decide who would get to kill him, so they're working together. That claim must override their normal rules."

"Then why didn't the adult Vens come over and attack when you and Professor Oberon killed the boarding party?"

Dione paused, thinking. She had often wondered why they hadn't sent more Vens. At the time, she had been too occupied to worry about it, but afterward, it bothered her. She had come up with another idea.

"I think it was some initiation ritual, and they couldn't interfere while the juveniles were attacking. We thought they were all dead when we boarded their ship, but the last one was still alive, stopping them from joining the fight." She couldn't prove any of this, and it would make for a weak scientific paper. Small sample size, not reproducible, and horribly biased and anecdotal, but she had to try and make sense of what she had experienced, even if her hypotheses only lasted until they were proven wrong by their next Ven encounter.

"And how does this intel help us?" Zane said.

"I don't know," Dione said. "Maybe we could find a tracking squirrel and set it on them. They run into the water and drown. They're not strong swimmers, right?"

"Tracking squirrel?"

"Like a trained, aggressive skunk with the stink dial turned up to a thousand."

"Huh. Any other animals around here that are maybe a little bigger and scarier than could distract them long enough for us to find the professor?"

"No, not that I've seen." Dione hadn't noticed or heard about many predators on Kepos. No big cats or bears or hippos. She would like to see a hippo crush a Ven's insides through its plates, though, and she said that as someone who hated hippos.

No large animals. It was strange, really. You would expect terraformers to create a balanced ecosystem, complete with apex predators, something to keep the other animal populations in check. She supposed there were probably some predators around, like birds of prey or larger fish. There had to be some predators in the forest. Nothing had attacked them, except…

She kicked herself for taking so long to figure it out, but that's what she got for thinking of it as a plant, even though it was an animal.

"Zane, I haven't seen any predatory mammals, except maximutes, but how far back was the last angler worm you spotted?"

"Maybe ten minutes, why?"

Dione grinned. "Are you a fast runner?"

***

Dione was waiting for Zane to signal he was on his way. According to the plan they'd hurriedly made, once the Vens on the opposite bank had gone out of sight down the river, Zane would get the attention of the two Vens patrolling the water's edge on his side. They would chase him to where she was waiting, trap ready. He would just have to reach Canto before they caught him. Should be manageable.

This was why Dione's heart skipped a beat when she heard the gun shot. That was not part of the plan. Had Zane needed to defend himself? That pistol might be enough to kill one Ven, if they were lucky, but not four. Dione hesitated for a few moments, waffling between staying put and sticking to the plan, or running back to help Zane.

She began to move when he called over her manumed, his breathing heavy. "We're on our way. They didn't want to chase me, so I had to shoot one of them."

"I assume it's still alive?"

"Yeah, I missed."

"All right, I'm still in position. Remember the song to send Canto to a safe distance?" They had decided they didn't want him too close in case things went badly.

"Yes, got it."

The minutes Dione stood waiting were agony. She was afraid to blink or even clear her throat for fear of missing the early signs of their arrival. Soon she heard the unceremonious snapping of twigs that meant Zane was getting close. She hoped it was Zane. *Please let it be Zane.*

"They're right behind me," Zane said as he ran up to Dione, careful to watch his step. She had her machete out. A Ven came hurtling into the clearing and charged right for them, but before it could reach them, it stopped, unexpectedly jerked back. Its foot was caught in something. *By* something. The angler worm.

A few days ago, an angler worm had been large enough to pull Lithia's thin frame all the way into its hole. This one was smaller and the Ven was bigger, which meant that the Ven was only up to its thigh on one leg. Having one leg free gave it a huge advantage when it came to leveraging itself out of the hole. The Ven struggled and growled.

"Where's the other one?" Dione asked in the uncertain respite.

"I don't know. It was right behind me."

The trapped Ven pushed against the ground, trying to free itself. "We've got to take this one down while it's still immobilized."

Dione watched her own footing. They had picked an area especially dense with angler worm flowers to increase the odds of a catch, and it had paid off. Dione threw a rock at the nearest and most threatening flower, just so she wouldn't have to worry about it. It disappeared underground. Now, she could concentrate fully on the Ven, the one with three nested rectangles.

She thought the Ven would be more restricted and lower to the ground, but its size meant that it was still upright and fighting back. Zane was at its back trying to slide his machete in between its plates to reach those vulnerable neural connections. She was staring it in the face, trying to keep it occupied with jabs from her machete. It was a hacking weapon, not a stabbing weapon, so she aimed for the places where the plates overlapped, hoping to injure it slightly.

It was not very effective. Zane wasn't having any luck either. Once she thought he had it, but he had hit the wrong plate junction, and his machete stopped just a few centimeters deep.

"Should I shoot it? I could probably hit it at this range," Zane said.

"The gunshot would give away our position," Dione said.

"I think all this growling already has." As if on cue, the Ven let out a shrill howl.

"All right," Dione said. The Ven looked like it was making progress in its battle against the angler worm. "Anything to slow it down."

Dione got out of the way, and Zane fired two shots. The first hit it in the neck, and the second missed, because it writhed in pain. Or anger. Dione still had no idea what those facial expressions meant.

The Ven sank a little deeper into the hole. One more shot from Zane, this one to the head, slowed it significantly. The Ven began howling again, and Dione just wanted it to be quiet. By some miracle, the other Ven was not there yet. Dione saw her opening and took it. She shoved her machete into the Ven's open mouth, bringing her close enough to feel claws scrape her right shoulder, but they didn't go deep.

Finally the Ven collapsed, giving Zane the opening to sever the neural connections. The Ven was finally dead. The angler worm continued pulling.

"I'm not sure how I feel about feeding this thing," Dione said.

"I doubt it will be able to pull the Ven down anyway," Zane said, reloading the pistol.

"Never underestimate nature."

A growl echoed through the forest, but it was not a Ven growl. It sounded like a dog. The frightened growl was followed shortly by a whimper.

Dione's head jerked up. "Canto! It must be the other Ven. Come on."

They two ran off through the trees in search of the maximute, before it was too late.

13. DIONE

Dione and Zane followed the sounds of Canto through the woods. When they crashed into the right clearing, they found Canto and a Ven squaring off. The Ven seemed put off by the hugeness of the maximute, and both creatures looked worse for wear.

Canto had a nasty scratch down the side of his face, and the Ven, the one with the spiral, seemed to be limping.

"We've got to help Canto," Dione said.

Upon their arrival, Canto gave a gentle *boof*, as if in warning. She had never heard Canto be so vocal before. He didn't bark or growl while they rode him.

"We're here to help," Dione said. Three of them against one Ven. These were the best odds they'd had yet. The Ven let out a piercing howl, almost like a challenge. She and Zane attacked from either side while Canto swatted at the Ven with his giant paw. Somehow the wretched creature managed to dodge most of their swings and jabs, rotating its body at just the right moments to avoid the brunt of the attacks.

Finally, Canto got a solid smack in with his paw, knocking the Ven down. Before Dione could rush in for the kill, Canto snapped up the Ven in his mouth and shook vigorously. The Ven struggled and clawed wildly, but Dione heard the cracking noise of bones and plates breaking.

Canto was a freaking beast, and she had not realized it until now. He might be beautiful, but he was a far cry from the gentle dogs back home. He dropped the Ven on the ground and yelped. Dione looked to the Ven, and guessed it was dead, but Zane moved in to make sure. Then Dione looked to Canto. Had the Ven tasted so bad he would yelp? Or maybe he had cracked a tooth?

Canto approached, turning slightly, and Dione immediately saw. Deep horizontal gashes crossed his back and bled into his golden fur. He turned his head in distress, but clearly couldn't see his injury well. It probably hurt a lot.

She rubbed his neck. "It's okay, Canto, we'll get this fixed up."

How the hell was she supposed to do that? They didn't have any medical supplies that would help him. She didn't want to send him off alone, even to safety. What if he was too weak to make it?

Canto lay on his side and panted. Dione stared at him, running through possible scenarios in her head. Suddenly, though, his ears perked up and he was growling again. He got to his feet.

"Zane," she said, but he cut her off.

"The other two Vens. They found us."

This was not good. The final two females with the spiked circle and the bisected triangle, had entered the clearing.

Canto did his best to look menacing, but he also looked very tired. His panting was loud, and Dione worried that he wouldn't be able to fight. If he couldn't fight, she and Zane were screwed, too.

She realized her own fatigue at the same time her despair set in. All of the running and hacking and jabbing had worn her down. Her right shoulder stung where she had been scratched, but her wrist especially ached from bracing herself against the inevitable resistance of Ven plates.

She cycled through their options. They could flee, but Canto was in no shape to carry them, and they would not be able to outrun the Vens for long. They had to fight, though they would lose.

Could they somehow do both, retreating slowly back to the angler plant? It had worked on the first Ven, but she worried that a Ven corpse sticking out of the ground would either spook the others or enrage them. Maybe Canto had enough fight left in him.

The Vens focused their attention on the maximute, as if they knew he was the real threat, that the pitiful humans standing nearby would be easily killed afterward.

One charged, and Dione lunged with her machete just in time to make him dodge, forcing him to veer from his attack vector. Immediately the other raced forward from the other side. Neither Dione nor Zane were close enough to stop it. It would land a blow on Canto's unwounded side.

A hair-raising howl pierced the air. The Ven stopped and turned. Two giant dogs sprinted into the fray. The dark brown one at the front didn't slow down, but charged head down at the Ven closest to Canto. The Ven flew backward and struck a tree.

Wild maximutes. They must have heard Canto's cries and come to help.

The other maximute, a lighter chestnut brown, snapped at the standing Ven and got a clawed hand to the face. He yelped and retreated backwards, but managed to swat back at the Ven. Everything happened so fast after that. Dione didn't see what happened to the Ven the first dog attacked, but she did watch the second Ven get dismembered, limb by limb, like a chew toy. The maximute made it look as easy as pulling the legs off a bug, but there was no way a human would be able to replicate that Ven-killing method.

The sounds of battle faded to the heavy breathing of all five survivors.

"I think they're dead," Zane said.

Dione nodded. Now to assess the damage. She approached Canto, but the dark brown maximute growled at her.

Dione held up her hands in a useless, human gesture of peace. "We're his friends."

Canto let out a few gentle barks, and the wild maximute stopped growling, but stayed close to Canto. The chestnut maximute licked Canto's face right where the Ven had scratched him. The dark brown one was licking the other scratches along Canto's body. Canto whimpered, but once he was done, he did the same for the chestnut one.

Perhaps maximute saliva had healing properties, or at least did something to reduce the risk of infections. Dione was fascinated. At any rate, she was glad someone could help Canto, because she had no idea what she and Zane would have done. Her next thought was to call Brian. He might have some insights or advice where Canto was concerned.

Zane called over to her from beside the dismembered Ven. "I severed the neural connections on the other Ven, but this one, well…"

It had been decapitated. Pulled apart.

Dione nodded. "I don't think even a Ven can survive that."

***

While they rested, she monitored Canto closely. The maximutes seemed to be doing the same, judging by the soft, grumbling sounds all three were making in turn. Once they were satisfied that Canto was okay, the wild beasts each gave him one final lick, then trotted off into the forest. She wondered if Canto had met them before, perhaps on his way to or from a rendezvous spot. She would ask Brian when she called.

She put off the call for several more minutes, worried that he would blame her for this, too. When she finally got up the nerve, there was no answer. She tried Lithia, but her manumed was off.

"Lithia and Brian aren't answering," Dione said, the first sign of anxiety hitting her voice. "I guess Victoria didn't like the evacuation plan."

"I'll call Bel. Maybe she's heard from them," Zane said.

He put Bel on speaker. She was able to tell them that Lithia and the Ficarans had survived a Ven attack last night, but she hadn't heard from them this morning.

Dione couldn't believe it. Lithia and Brian could have been killed. "Why didn't you tell us the Vens attacked!?"

"There's nothing you could have done. I didn't see a point in worrying you. Have you found the professor?" Bel said.

Dione looked to Zane to back her up, but he didn't seem all that bothered. She sighed. "No, but we got the Vens that were hunting him. We think," she said, "that he's hiding in a cave system on the map, but his manumed's blown."

"Are you sure? He said it was broken, but maybe he'll get it working."

"No, it's blown," Dione said. "Some trick Zane used to get a location."

"Then you'd better get to that cave system."

"We're going to need someone to come get us afterward. Canto's injured. He's doing okay, but he can't carry three of us back to the Ficarans."

"I wouldn't send you back there anyway. The attack last night was a ruse. Now that they've seen the defenses, they'll make their real attack."

"They still have time to evacuate," Zane said.

"I just don't know if they will. From what Lithia told me, Victoria seems more interested in stealing Aratian supplies than dealing with the real threat."

Dione clenched a fist. "What? Are you serious?"

"Lithia was a little hard to understand, but that's the gist of it. She was going to try to convince her this morning. If you can't reach her, I imagine it didn't go well."

"Then once we find the professor, what are we supposed to do?"

"Find shelter and hope the Ficarans change their mind," Bel said. "I don't think I can fly the *Calypso*, and even if I could, I definitely can't find a place to land in the woods. She's too big."

"Fantastic. Let us know if you find anything else useful."

"I'll take another look at the Ven body, but I want to go through some of these logs Zane found, too. Good luck."

"We'll tell Professor Oberon you say hi," Dione said.

Things were not going as well as she'd hoped, much less how they'd planned. The Ficarans should have evacuated by now, but instead they were off raiding farms, doing exactly what she feared they would do with the newfound technology, and Brian and Lithia were out of contact.

As much as she wanted to take a break and rest, she couldn't risk losing the professor. Canto was curled up, not quite asleep, breathing shallowly.

"Zane, will you stay here with Canto? I don't want him to exert himself. I'm going to go find the professor."

"On your own?"

"I think the worst of the threat is over," she said, gesturing to the Ven corpses that littered the ground. "Plus, I can't stand the smell here any longer." Vens were nasty in every conceivable way.

"You're right about that," Zane said, wrinkling his nose. "Once Canto feels a little better, I'll take him down to the river. He probably wants to wash the Ven taste out of his mouth."

Dione gave the maximute one last pat on the head and headed back, toward her professor's last known location.

14. CORA

Cora woke up late. She lay awake in her bed for a while, dwelling on her father's disappointment. He should have been angrier with her. Yelled at her. Maybe he would when he returned in the evening, when he wasn't within earshot of his men.

Tomorrow was the Matching, a tradition started by the Farmer himself. During the ceremony, young women and men would be paired with the goal of improving the genetic diversity of the settlement. Pathetic Ficaran raiders would not keep her father away, and even if he was still upset, she wanted him to be there for her Matching.

Besides, she had meant well when she helped Lithia escape, but Lithia and Zane had tricked her with the communication devices. Lithia looked so much like her that she'd been sure it was a sign, but Lithia had somehow faked her DNA and appearance. They were not related. It wasn't possible. Lithia was an alien, just like she claimed the Vens were.

No, she wasn't really an alien. Her uncle's DNA analysis couldn't be that far off. She came from somewhere else, though. Cora was tired of thinking about it. She would help her aunt make the final preparations for the Matching. Aunt Amelia had not been pleased last night by the news that Evy was still at the Mountain Base. She blamed Cora, even though she knew how stubborn Evy was. She got dressed, asked around, and soon, she found her aunt.

Cora noticed the bags under her aunt's eyes. She looked tired. She and some of the other women were sitting at a long table, fashioning wreaths from fresh-cut flowers. Their fingers poked, pulled, and twisted flower and stem into position in a mindless rhythm, like background music for their soft conversation. They deftly wove together the pink, orange, and blue flowers, some large and vibrant, others with thick clusters of tiny blooms.

"Good morning, Aunt Amelia," Cora said.

"It's hardly morning anymore, child," Amelia said, not looking up from her work.

She was still mad about Evy. Last night Aunt Amelia had asked about her cousin. Cora showed her aunt the mark on her wrist where Evy had bitten her to escape. She had tried to bring her back, but apparently not hard enough.

Aunt Amelia was probably just upset with Evy. Cora studied the streaks of gray in her aunt's hair and the curve of her frown lines and wondered how much of it was age, and how much of it was Evy. Aunt Amelia was not very old.

"How can I help you prepare for tomorrow, aunt?"

"Help? And what's inspired this sudden change?" Amelia said. One or two of the women at the table smiled, but the others pretended not to hear.

Cora couldn't think of a clever response, but took a seat at the table.

Her aunt finally smiled and looked up. "Tomorrow is your Matching. You do not need to help, though we would welcome an extra set of hands here."

"Certainly," Cora said.

"Watch the others, and when you are ready, begin on your own, at your own pace."

Cora took up one of the frames, a tightly-woven net of twine tied into a circle. The garlands would be placed over the couples as they were matched, so each was quite large.

The woman next to her worked quickly but carefully, pink, blue, orange, pink, blue, orange. Color rather than type of flower seemed to dominate the pattern.

"Aunt, what do these colors mean?"

"The pink comes first, for health, the blue, for fertility, and the orange is for joy in your Match."

"And the garlands are to join us together in marriage," Cora said.

"Yes, child," Amelia said.

Cora watched a bit longer before joining in. At first she found it calming, but soon her hands grew tired. Then her brain grew tired of the repetitive movements. Her eyes began to wander, and her hands slowed their labor. She caught sight of someone peeking from behind the doorframe. She could recognize his golden hair and laughing blue eyes anywhere.

Will! He was back from his inspections.

"Aunt, may I be excused?"

"Yes, child, go on," Amelia said. "After nearly twenty minutes of demanding work I'm sure you need a break."

Cora was too excited to care about this final jab from her aunt.

***

Cora walked with Will through the market. She bought a few *pollas*, then they hiked up to the overlook of the city, a ledge deep enough to be safe but small enough to give her butterflies if she looked over the edge. It was not higher than the Temple, but the other buildings were easily in view. They sat far back on the ledge, and Will put his arm around her.

"How were the inspections?"

"Better than expected," he said. "Jackson got his plow working again, somehow. The other farmers had good yields. This will be especially important after the raid on one of the Hubs."

"What?" Cora said. "It was a Hub? They told me my father was out because of a raid, but they never said it was a Hub. I bet his cavalry will get them in no time." Her father's cavalry was extremely well trained. "How could they even manage to raid a Hub?"

Will looked concerned. "They haven't told many people, Cora, but I thought they would have told you. Don't share what I'm about to tell you, but the Ficarans found a way to unlock the Flyers. They used them to clear out the Hub yesterday."

Cora felt sick. This was all her fault. She had helped Lithia and Dione and that Ficaran Brian. This must have been their plan all along. Cora blinked back tears.

"What's wrong? I'm sure your father will be all right."

"I know, it's not that," she said, wiping the tears from her eyes.

"Is it tomorrow? Are you worried about the Matching?" Will said.

"No, not at all," Cora said, smiling at him. "I can't wait for us to be matched."

Will smiled at her and squeezed her into a hug.

"Are you sure we'll be matched?" he said.

"Of course, it's the only thing that makes sense. I just know it."

"But…" Will hesitated, "Have you seen the Matches? Are you certain?"

"Of course I haven't *seen* the Matches, but I just feel it. We are the perfect match, so how could we not end up together?" She watched his face fall. "You don't think we'll be together?"

"I hope for it, but we have no way of knowing if our genes will make the best pairing. And that's all the Matching is. It's emotionless. This is why we're discouraged from making attachments before the Matching."

Cora grabbed his hands and squeezed. "Have a little faith. This will work out. I promise."

The Farmer would see how they felt and bring them together. After all, it had brought her aunt and uncle together, and they had been in love before their Match.

From their vantage point, they could see, rather than hear, the commotion at the gate. The cavalry had returned. The auxiliary machi riders stopped just inside the gate, though it looked like a few were riderless. Some riders were shouting, and others were running, carrying men toward the hospital. The gate, usually open during the day, closed behind them. Cora inched as close to the cliff's edge as she dared, trying to figure out where the maximutes were. The machi would never have outpaced them, and her father would be on a maximute.

"Come on," Cora said. She needed to get down there and figure out what was happening. She and Will hiked back to town, but by the time they got to the gate, the riders had cleared out. Without a word, Cora led the way to the stables.

One of the machi riders was feeding his mount. He didn't hear them come in.

"Where are the maximum riders?" she asked.

He turned, startled. He had bags under his eyes, but he looked about her own age.

"They're still on the hunt," he replied.

"Then why were you sent back? Why are you not still helping my father? Why is the gate closed?"

"Our machi never stood a chance. He sent us back with the wounded because—"

"I don't care if she's the Regnator's daughter," one of his fellow riders, a dark-skinned, muscular man, interrupted. "We were ordered to keep quiet. You'd do well to obey."

"I'm sorry," the young rider said, though Cora couldn't tell where the apology was directed. He turned away from her, so she glared at the man who had interrupted.

"I will not forget this," Cora said, her face growing hot.

"Please, remember. My name is Theo. You may have use of a man who can follow orders someday." He bowed his head slightly and returned to tending the machi.

Will touched her arm and gently guided her from the stables, worry apparent on his face.

"While you were talking, I was counting empty stalls. We had over two dozen machi trained for the cavalry, but I only counted eighteen."

"You think the rest are what, dead? And their riders?" Cora said.

"I don't know, but we did see at least one person carried to the hospital wing. I'd better go see if Benjamin needs help," he replied.

Will squeezed her hand before heading toward the Temple. Cora stood alone and confused outside the stables. She could see a few extra guards on watch by the closed gate.

Had the Ficarans done this? Had Lithia helped them kill the machi? Cora grimaced. If they harmed her father, she would make sure they paid.

15. BEL

Bel had been listening to Samantha's logs all day. She wasn't paying full attention most of the time, and she had fallen asleep more than once.

Most of the logs were detailed records of Sam's experiments and methods, along with her findings. Apparently she had used bird genes to get maximutes and machi to understand certain tunes from birth. The analysis parts were interesting, but mostly speculation, leaving off with ideas for further experimentation.

It was the personal logs that Bel found the most compelling. She felt a little awkward listening to them while Sam could hear, but she never injected commentary. Bel wondered what it was like for Sam to hear them, now that she was trapped as a not-so-artificial intelligence in this base.

Bel was preparing to go back down and take another look at the Ven when a log titled "Jameson's nightmares" began to play.

It was easy enough to create a new species. The real test was viability. Could it reproduce? Could it survive in the world? One of the other head scientists made a bet with Jameson. Told him he couldn't make this creature or that species cross. Nothing lit a fire under Jameson like a challenge.

As the result of one of these bets, he created this horrible creature that served no benefit to colonial life, which was our primary research objective. It grew flowers that were traps, that would pull down prey to its digestive system. Somewhere between a plant and an animal, it was a monster. We hid it away far from the research bases. We didn't want it interfering with the other species.

Things just went downhill after that. When no one reprimanded him, he unshackled his imagination. Until then, I hadn't realized how much darkness there was inside him. Still, I trusted him.

At some point, we stopped asking why, more concerned with the what and the how. Some nasty stuff came out of that. His creations took a strange turn. He exceeded his quota for new species far more easily than the rest of his colleagues, so he had plenty of time to think up new terrors.

Bel paused the playback. How many of these terrors were out there? Could they hurt her friends?

"Sam, explain. Where are these creatures? Are Zane and Dione in trouble?"

"No, none of those monstrosities are in the inhabited area, though I'm ashamed to say that I helped him," the AI said.

"But that plant sounds a lot like the thing that attacked Lithia," Bel said.

"That's not possible. No specimens were ever released anywhere in the research zone."

"The research zone? Where did you release them?"

"Somewhere far away."

"Not far enough," Bel muttered under her breath.

There was a pause before Sam replied. "Sometimes it's hard to know where the line is until you've crossed it."

16. DIONE

Dione was back at the spot on her map where the professor was. In theory. He could have dropped his manumed in the river. He could have moved once he saw the Vens leave. Or he could be hiding in one of the caves, as Zane had suggested.

Might as well look around.

The river was partially blocked here by a wall of earth that provided a natural dam. The dam hadn't been there long. She could tell by the grass growing under the water. Well, it hadn't grown there. It had grown on the riverbank, then been covered as the dam caused the water level to rise. If the water level didn't drop soon, the grass would probably die. In addition to the wall of mud, a few downed trees blocked the rest of the river. They caught debris, like leaves and branches, and added to the effect until most of the water flow was blocked. No wonder the water level here had risen.

On the opposite side, the bank turned into a wall of steep rock, covered in shallow-rooted grasses and vines. The water here was mostly calm, though she didn't know what lived in the river. She wished she could call Brian and ask.

According to the map, the professor was across the river. Dione hesitated, but decided that she would rather be immodest than walk around in wet clothes all day. She removed everything but her underclothes, thankfully dark colors, and jumped in.

Even though the dam had slowed the current to a near standstill, every stroke was terrifying. Eventually she decided to swim on her back, because her eyes kept seeing phantom monsters just under the surface.

As soon as she reached the other side, she pulled herself onto the bank, shivering as she searched for a cave entrance. The warmth of the sun began to dry her out, but she still hadn't found anything.

This was so stupid. She had no idea what she was doing. Here she was, wandering around the river, hoping a cave entrance or the professor would suddenly pop up out of nowhere.

After twenty minutes of cold, half-naked searching, she settled on another possibility. One she had been keeping from her thoughts, because she didn't want it to be the case.

What if the cave entrance is underwater?

Dione felt claustrophobic just thinking about it. Still, her manumed was top of the line. Sweatproof, waterproof, damage resistant. Her uncle had wanted her to have something that would work, even in the marshes of Barusia, where she would never get to start her research. Luckily, it had a strong light. As much as she didn't want a clear view of the underwater scenery, and as gross as opening her eyes in the river would be, she didn't see any other choice.

She didn't have to look long. There it was, just under the water's surface. She came back up, feeling simultaneously hopeful and apprehensive. She would have to swim into an underwater cave and hope that somewhere down the line it opened up into a place with air to breathe. Granted, the entrance was fairly large, but what if it got smaller as she went along? What if she got stuck?

She went underwater for one more look and saw something else. Though black, its manmade shape stood out against the rocks it was wedged between. With a little effort, she worked it free.

Dione surfaced and climbed onto a nearby rock with her prize. A boot. She was certain it belonged to the professor. She didn't want to, but she had to check the cave. The professor could be in there, alive but injured. He needed her help. How could she get to him?

After looking up some stats on her manumed, she decided she should be able to hold her breath for about a minute and a half, maybe a little longer because there was more oxygen in the Kepos atmosphere. She would start a timer and swim forward until she hit forty seconds. If she hadn't reached an air pocket by then, she would turn back.

Satisfied with her plan, she turned on her light, started the timer, and headed down. She didn't hesitate at the entrance, but went straight in. She blew out a few bubbles, just a few, but the burning in her lungs was unbearable. The searing pain bled out from her chest into her muscles, and all she saw ahead of her was darkness and water.

She was going to die. The blackness ahead overwhelmed her senses. For a moment, Dione couldn't move, but then she sprang into action. There was enough room in the cave to turn around, but her hair snagged a rock as she did. When she pushed her arms down to propel her forward, she met with resistance. More bubbles escaped from her lips, more than she intended.

A moment later she was free and kicking furiously in the direction of the light, her insides burning, her lungs pulsing in agony. The only relief was releasing more bubbles, which she did. They zoomed upwards. She was out of the cave.

She kicked with everything her legs had and pushed water down with her cupped hands. She broke the surface with a desperate gasp and kicked over to the warm rock, keeping her head above water. She glanced at her timer on the way and realized she had only been underwater for a total of forty seconds. The whole ordeal had been her proposed forward movement time.

Dione no longer thought she could hold her breath for a minute and a half. She was not going to make it through the underwater cave. No way.

She called Zane. "How's Canto?"

"He seems okay. He ate some food, so he can't be feeling too bad. I think we could meet you. Find the professor?"

"Not exactly. I found the cave entrance, but it's underwater. I can't hold my breath long enough to swim through. Maybe you can try? Can you hold your breath very long?"

"I grew up on a spaceship. I can't swim."

"What?"

"I can generally manage not to drown, but I can't swim, like, actually swim."

"Oh, right."

He sounded incredulous. "I can't believe you actually tried it, though. That was a stupid thing to do. What if you hadn't made it out? Sounds more like one of Lithia's plans."

"Are you calling Lithia stupid?"

"No, I'm just saying that you're not Lithia. What's a smarter solution? That's your thing, right?"

She could hear the sarcasm in his voice, but tried to ignore it.

"All right, I'll keep working on it. I'm at the part of the river that's been dammed up."

"We'll be there soon."

Dione looked down and realized she was still in her underwear. It was drying out surprisingly fast, and for that she was thankful. She planned to be fully clothed by the time he arrived.

Just in case, she sent him one last request before ending their conversation. "Give me a heads-up when you're close."

***

Dione, back on the riverbank and fully dressed, waved Zane over the moment he came into view with Canto. Canto headed straight for the riverbank and started lapping up water. Dione smiled. He had to be thirsty after everything.

"I think I figured it out," she said to Zane. "You were right. I was trying to brute-force my way into the cave, but I know out how to remove the obstacle."

"Wait, did you just say that I was right?" Zane asked.

"Yeah, and if the professor's in the cave, I'll say it again."

"So what's your brilliant plan?"

"Unblock the river," Dione said.

Zane looked at the mountain of dirt blocking the current, and Dione could see the doubts forming in his head.

"Dione, I don't think that's gonna go easily."

"It doesn't have to. Not all of it. Hear me out."

She walked him closer to the water's edge.

"If you look at the ridge damming the river, you can see plants and small trees growing on it. It's been there for a while." She pointed to the underwater grass. "But if you look down here, this grass has only been covered for a few days. It's still alive, meaning that the reservoir isn't always this high. Something changed recently. That fallen tree? It's still got leaves. I think it fell during the bad storm a few days ago, right before Lithia got kidnapped."

He shook his head. "I still don't see how we're going to move the tree."

"We might not have to. That tree isn't doing all the work. It's catching everything that's being washed downstream. All the branches and leaves that got knocked down into the river during the storm. It's like cleaning out the strainer on a kitchen drain. If we remove enough of the small debris, I think the water level of the reservoir will go back down. Maybe even enough for me to get through the cave. All I need are some air pockets."

Dione got back into the water, leaving her StellAcademy tank top on this time. The leggings, though, she removed. She focused on the area that seemed to have the most debris, grabbing leaves and branches, then tossing them to the other side. After a time, she felt the pull of the water grow stronger against her legs.

"It's working! I can feel the current moving along through the branches." She pulled away an especially leafy branch and, before she could react, the increased flow of water pinned her against the hole she had made. She was trapped.

"Zane!" she cried, frantically moving her arms to keep her head above water. "I'm stuck."

"I can crawl out on the log, try to untangle you," Zane said.

She bobbed beneath the surface, just for an instant, and in her panic choked on the silty river water.

Dione coughed. "I'm not caught in the branches. It's the suction from the water."

"Delta P," he nodded. "Change in pressure."

Dione had read about it before. What was the solution? She was trapped in such an awkward position that she really had to work to keep her head above water. It was exhausting. She didn't know how much longer she could keep it up.

By dislodging that piece of debris, she had lowered the pressure in the area, and the velocity of the water had increased. The faster moving water had trapped her. She might be able to struggle enough to get herself free, but she might make things worse. She wasn't actually forming a perfect seal against the the water flow. There had to be other small openings in the dam. They were just too small. Creating a larger opening, however, would reduce the velocity of the water pinning her.

"Zane, start clearing another opening on your end. Climb out on the trunk. Don't get in the water!"

"Already on it!" he said. She couldn't see him from where she was, but he'd apparently already figured out the solution. She heard splashing, which she assumed was the sound of debris being thrown downstream on the other side of the dam.

He was doing his best, but her arms in their perpetual struggle were getting tired. She had to take a break. Dione put her face down in the water and stopped struggling, relaxing her body as much as she could.

"Dione! Dione!" She could hear Zane's cries even though they were muffled by the water.

She lifted her head suddenly above the surface. "What's wrong?"

"Thank god. I thought…"

"Just resting my arms."

"Then blow some damn bubbles next time."

She had forgotten about that. She put her head back in the water and blew bubbles slowly. A few more of these, and she was back to keeping her head above water.

Finally, she felt the water's chokehold loosen. She kicked away as hard as she could toward the shore. Canto was there, pacing at the water's edge as if he was nervous. When she climbed out, the maximute nudged her with his nose and gave her a lick before leaving her to a sunny spot on the bank.

Zane kept removing debris, tossing it to the other side of the blockage. Her successful rescue aside, they still needed to lower the water level.

"You okay?" he asked.

"I'll be fine. Thanks, Zane."

After a little more work, Zane crawled back to the bank. They waited. It was surprising how quickly the water level dropped.

"Look!" Dione said. There it was, the top few centimeters of the cave entrance. The water level looked like it had stopped falling, but it was enough. She could make it this time. If only her mind would stop focusing on that suffocating darkness.

She inched back into the river and shuddered once the water reached her waist. Professor Oberon needed her help. She ignored the earthy taste of silt that lingered in her mouth and picked her way to the half-submerged cave.

It wasn't that bad, once she got going. She was able to keep her head above the water most of the time. When the ceiling of the cave dipped below the water level, Dione held her breath and kicked her way to the next air pocket. After that dip, the cave opened up into a larger cavern, about the size of the cockpit on the *Calypso*. Small holes in the ceiling let tiny spots of sunlight through. The ground seemed completely dry. This area had not recently drained.

One of the tiny spotlights landed on something dark blue. The professor's uniform. Dione gasped. He was here. He was actually here.

"Professor Oberon!" she said, rushing to his side.

The professor coughed. "Dione? How—"

She cut him off, speaking into her manumed. "Zane, I've got him. You were right again. Thank god." She turned back to the professor. "Are you hurt?"

"My shoulder's not much use," he said. "Where are the Vens? I'm sure they'll find us soon. You and Zane need to get out of here."

"They're dead."

"But there were four of them." He looked down at his arms, and Dione followed his gaze. There were four Ven symbols cut into his arms, recognizable despite the dirt and blood.

"All dead. I'll tell you about it once we're on the riverbank."

"I don't think I can swim back out. I barely made it in here before I passed out. Adrenaline's the only thing that kept me going."

She shook her head and gave him a weak grin. "We drained the reservoir. If you can hold your breath for just a few seconds, and swim enough to keep your head above water, you'll make it. Plus, we've got some food. You'll feel better once you eat something."

He sat up with some struggle. "You know, I never underestimated you before. I don't know why I bothered to start now."

"I couldn't have done it with out Zane." It was true. He had saved her life. Dione guessed it didn't really matter if he liked her or not. He'd done what was necessary, and she was grateful for that.

She guided the professor back to the bank, and a joyful Zane helped get him onto the shore. The professor lay there, shivering despite the warmth of the day, eyes closed. His skin was dull and covered in goosebumps. She was painfully aware of her bare legs in the broad daylight.

"Zane, can you give him some food and warm him up? I'm going to call Bel." She held up her leggings, and he seemed to understand.

She walked off into the woods to a safe distance. "Bel, we've got him. The professor is okay," she said, removing her wet underwear and replacing them with the dry leggings. She removed her tank top to wring it out. Water poured from the fabric.

"That's great! What's that sound? Are you... going to the bathroom?"

"Nope, I'm going commando. Have you heard from Lithia? Can she come get us?"

"I haven't heard anything. Dione, I'm worried. I don't think the Ficarans will evac, and she and Brian aren't communicating with us. I think they're being detained."

"There's no way we can get back there any time soon. Canto's hurt, and the professor should really get some rest. He's been through a lot."

"The Vens are going to attack again, I'm sure of it."

Sam's voice cut into their call. "Don't forget about the Ven beacon. It needs to be disabled as soon as possible."

Dione wrinkled her brow in thought. "It's not far, but at the pace we'll be going, it will still take us a while."

"Then make the most of the daylight. I cannot stress enough how important it is to disable the signal," Sam replied.

"It never ends, does it?" she sighed and put her damp top back on.

She signed off, the joy of finding the professor wearing off quickly as she realized how much there was left to do. She looked around on the ground, making sure she hadn't forgotten anything, when she caught sight of a small, white pebble, smooth and flat and wet. It must have been stuck in her tank top.

A sign of good luck. She slipped the coin-sized rock into her pocket and headed back to Zane and the professor.

17. LITHIA

Brian had stopped banging on the door hours ago and had taken up residence on the bed. His eyes were closed, but Lithia knew he wasn't sleeping. She was staring out the window at the square. The cleanup was long over and everyone was getting back to work. Lithia stared at the statue. What she had imagined to be modern art last night turned out to be a part of a spaceship welded to a plinth. Odd.

The back of the square was lined with waist-high posts. At first she had wondered what these posts were for. Then a boy, maybe thirteen years old, rode up on something like an elephant-horse. He tied up his mount and hurried inside the main building holding something.

"What is that animal?" she asked.

"Machi." Brian hadn't even turned to look at her.

"Ah, Cora told me about them. They are strange-looking." Even from up here she could see its elongated snout curling around something on the ground. Probably scraps of food.

She looked at Brian who still hadn't moved. "I wish we could see the tree line from here." She could see the canopy, but not into the woods where the Vens would be gathering.

When he remained quiet, she started in. "So, Brian, about last night…"

"What about it?"

"I'm sorry if that kiss crossed a boundary."

He laughed bitterly. "It doesn't matter. It's too late to change anything now. Just drop it."

Lithia thought about saying something else, but she had never seen Brian like this. She didn't even know how to describe it. Fragile? He seemed like he was on the verge of breaking.

Brian sat up and spoke in a low growl. "I can't believe I'm locked in this room, and in a few hours, aliens will be inside the walls killing everyone I know and love. I'm trying to figure a way out of this."

"Don't take it out on me," Lithia said, crossing her arms. She wasn't the one who organized last night's celebration. She wasn't leading the Flyers on another raid. Those were Victoria's mistakes. "Can't Melanie free us?"

"Victoria's probably got someone keeping an eye on her. If she can help us, she will."

"Good. Because we need to start taking the people who will leave in the Flyers. I imagine a lot of the people who were on the walls last night would be happy to come with us."

"We can't get out of here," Brian said. "We're locked in and guarded." He was right. Lithia had seen the lock on the door. It was an electronic lock with a key pad. Not only did they not have the code, they were on the wrong side of the door.

Speaking of which… Lithia heard voices on the other side of the door for the first time in hours.

"Please, just five minutes. I want to thank them," an unfamiliar voice said.

"I can't let you in. I have orders." That was the guard, Lithia was sure.

"Five minutes. You can lock me in there. My mother sent me. Please."

The guard took a moment to reply. "I can't guarantee your safety."

She exchanged a look with Brian. This was their chance to escape.

"When he's leaving, we make our move," Brian whispered. Lithia nodded and relaxed for a moment. The door opened and the guard looked surprised to see them at the back of the room, Brian on the cot, Lithia by the window.

Lithia's gaze shifted to their visitor whom she immediately recognized as the boy who had ridden his machi into the square a few minutes ago.

"Roy, what are you doing here?" Brian asked. The boy called Roy stepped into the room and the guard locked the door behind him.

"I wanted to thank you. You saved my little brother last night. Our aunt was bitten and nearly killed him. He's badly bruised and has some broken bones, but he's going to be fine."

Lithia remembered. That woman who had been pounding on that boy. "I'm glad he's okay," she said.

"Brian," Roy said, lowering his voice and speaking more urgently, "Melanie's got a plan. She's already getting groups together for the Flyers."

"She's going to evacuate against Victoria's will?" Brian said.

"Some people have been pretty vocal about wanting to leave. Others have joined in," Roy said.

"A perfect time to be divided," Lithia said.

"Well, Colm hasn't figured out our plan yet. Once everything is in place, Melanie will come for you."

"What about everyone else?" Brian asked.

"We'll come back for them. We have to remove the most vulnerable as soon as possible."

The guard knocked on the door. "Time's up. Let's go."

Roy headed back to the door.

"Do we wait for Melanie?" whispered Lithia. If they were going to try and make a break for it, they needed to get into position now.

Brian frowned. "We wait. Don't want to screw up her plan."

The door opened, Roy left, and the lock clicked back into place when the door closed. They were still trapped.

"Then it's my turn on the bed," Lithia said, sprawling out on her back. She hoped Melanie would come soon.

∗∗∗

Lithia must have dozed off, because when Brian pounded his fist against the window, she bolted upright, disoriented. It was almost dark outside.

"What happened?" she asked. Brian didn't need to answer. Lithia could hear it. Gunfire.

In just a few strides, Brian had reached the door. "The Vens are here, Jared. Let us out. We can help. We have to help."

Jared didn't respond. The only answer Brian got was footsteps thumping away down the corridor. Their guard was joining the fight, leaving them trapped in this room. Lithia wasn't eager to join the fight, but she felt a responsibility to the people here. She had to help. She could hear screams mixed in with the gunfire now.

"What now?" she asked.

Brian clenched his fists so hard they trembled. "Nothing we can do. We wait for Melanie." Lithia tried to read Brian's face, but she couldn't. He sat on the floor next to the door, but she went to the window. She wished she hadn't. The Vens were already inside the walls. Ficarans were running through the square, talking into their communicators, trying to organize.

Soon, she saw her first team of Vens. Some they bit, but others they killed effortlessly. She saw one Ven go down, but the others avenged him. They were heading toward the Temple, toward them.

Lithia watched from the window until she heard gunfire coming from inside the building. Brian stood up. She heard footsteps pounding down the hallway followed shortly by the click of the lock on their door.

Brian pulled open the door just in time to see a monstrous Ven eviscerate Jared. Brian cried out and took a step forward, but he was unarmed. They both were.

Lithia looked around the room for anything they could use as a weapon, but there was only one piece of furniture. She tore the thin mattress from the bed, leaving only the frame. "Brian, the bed. Get that side. Like a shield."

Thankfully, he understood. He grabbed the other end, and with the legs pointed away from them, they faced the Ven.

"If we can switch places with him, we can get to the hallway, then lock him in," she said.

"We need to be fast. More will be coming."

The Ven stepped into the room, and at first, it tried to move around to get to them on the other side of the bed. In no time they were in position, their backs to the door, the Ven fully inside the room. They inched backward toward the exit, but the Ven must have sensed what they were up to. Arms extended, it rushed them, pushing on the center of the bed, forcing them back until Lithia and Brian were pinned to the wall on either side of the door.

The bed pressed hard against Lithia's chest. She gasped for air, but it was like her lungs weren't working. She tried to take deep breaths, but the Ven kept applying pressure. She couldn't breathe. Brian was struggling against the bed, but with no success. She couldn't help him.

Panic set in and filled up her rib cage, like an overinflated balloon that pressed outward, like it would break her open. She struggled and flailed, but it was no use. She still couldn't breathe or talk or scream.

As soon as it had come on, it was gone. The pressure released. Lithia sank to the floor, waiting either to breathe or die. She tried to inhale, but nothing happened. She felt like a fish out of water, silently opening and closing her mouth with each failure.

"What happened to her?" Melanie's voice.

At that moment, Lithia finally rasped in a breath, then coughed. She took a few deep breaths before responding. "Knocked the wind out of me."

Brian helped her to her feet, and she glanced over at the Ven. One of the Ficarans was severing the neural connections with a wooden sword. Cora had called it a *pila* blade when they were stealing the shuttle. Protruding from the Ven's forehead was a metal rod.

"What the——?" Lithia began.

"Harpoon gun," Melanie said, holding it up. "Thought it might come in handy." She dislodged the harpoon from the Ven, reloaded, and glanced up and down the hallway. The other three Ficarans nodded at Lithia in greeting. They all had handguns.

"Here's your stun rifle, manumed, and a long knife," Melanie said. She handed Brian a *pila* blade.

They all hurried out of the Temple and into the town. Melanie spoke as they moved.

"Several groups already evacuated on the Flyers that Victoria left behind. We got the coordinates for the Mountain Temple. Sam's directing them—she contacted us through the communicators. That was certainly a surprise. They'll come back soon."

Not soon enough, Lithia thought grimly. They should have started this hours ago.

"My mom?" Brian asked.

"She was in one of the first groups," Melanie said. "We've been sending people to the hangar to wait for the next group."

Melanie was already halfway down the stairs that led to the hangar when someone started screaming over her communicator. Lithia was too far behind to make out the words, but Melanie stopped in her tracks and responded. "Where are you?"

Melanie apparently understood the garbled response because she dashed back up the stairs, directing the others to follow. Lithia and Brian kept pace with her as she explained.

"The other half of our team was getting more people out of the apartments. The gates are the hot point right now, but they ran into Vens raiding the houses. They'll have a lot of vulnerable people with them."

Lithia did not want to run back into the Ven-filled town, but she didn't have much of a choice. Part of her thought that this was a stupid idea. They would all die out in the open. The other side of her, the side who liked to play the hero in their holo games, knew she had to help these people. This was her fault. She couldn't forget that.

Lithia saw bodies. So many bodies. Most of them were human, though a few Vens lay among them, absolutely riddled with holes. *This could have been prevented.*

The thought made her angry. Stubbornness. Ego. All of it got in the way. She knew firsthand. These were her flaws, too, and it made her hate Victoria even more.

When they entered the next street, two men charged toward them.

"Where are the others?" Melanie yelled, but they didn't reply. Their eyes were unfocused.

"Ven-bitten. They're Berserkers," Lithia said, aiming her stun rifle and firing. Each man took two hits before falling.

Melanie knelt next to one of the unconscious men. "They were part of the group we sent. We'll get them on our way back. The others must be up ahead." Melanie called over her communicator, but received no answer. She put one hand on her hip and wiped the sweat from her forehead with the other.

"Do you know where they were checking? Going for family?" Brian asked.

Melanie snapped her fingers. "The Bear Complex."

"The what?" Lithia asked.

"Look at the doors," Brian said.

Lithia obeyed. She'd been too distracted by the Berserkers to notice it, but all the housing units had images painted on their doors to distinguish them. A lily, a rodent of some kind, a bug. She didn't see any bears, though. Melanie was already leading the way through an alley to another row of buildings.

The chaos that had felt distant only moments ago was now before her eyes. The screaming got louder. They were running toward the gunfire. On the ground was a door painted with a bear standing upright on its hind legs. Lithia presumed it belonged to the building that had a gaping hole for an entrance.

She looked down at her knife. This was not going to go well.

As soon as she entered the building, she could smell the blood. It was dark despite the glowglobes. She couldn't hear anything. The Vens should be making more noise than this.

"Split up. Look for survivors," Melanie muttered. The complex had housed four families, so the six of them split into teams of two. Brian and Lithia took the lower left apartment and two of the Ficarans took the lower right. Melanie and the other Ficaran headed upstairs.

After a thorough search, Brian and Lithia returned to the base of the stairs. They'd found no one, but the others had found a family hiding across the hall.

"Let's head upstairs and help Melanie check the other apartment," Brian said.

Lithia nodded, but didn't say what was on her mind. If there was still a family hiding here, the other team had probably never made it. They were more than likely dead.

Lithia gagged when they reached the top of the stairs. She had never seen so much blood in her life. One of the families had tried to escape, and had been cut down at the top of the stairs by the Vens. Lithia heard Melanie's voice coming from the apartment on the right.

"It's not safe outside, but it's not safe in here either. We've got to go."

Lithia couldn't hear the response, but she could hear Melanie getting frustrated.

A call came from downstairs. "Vens in the street! We need to move."

Brian raced past the grisly scene into the apartment, leaving Lithia at the top of the stairs. There was crying, then a shrill scream, but Brian reappeared dragging a young woman behind him, followed by Melanie and the other Ficaran, along with several children.

Lithia ran ahead of them. One of the Ficarans downstairs was glancing around the corner of the doorframe, motioning for the woman to quiet down. Brian put a hand over her mouth, but that only alarmed her into another high-pitched, albeit muffled, scream.

That was all it took to attract unwanted Ven attention. The Ficaran popped out of the doorway and began firing into the street. Melanie and her team swept into action.

"Lithia, stay with them," Melanie ordered.

Lithia was about to object, but she got it. Someone had to keep these people relatively calm, and she was the least armed of them all. It made sense. She knew it made sense. It still bothered her how relieved she felt to be out of the fray. Then she came to her senses. It would only delay the inevitable. The sobbing woman was too loud. Lithia slapped her hard across the face.

"Get a grip and shut up. You're going to get your family killed."

The slap seemed to shock her into silence, right before she threw up at the base of the stairs. She was quiet after that.

"Stay here," Lithia said. She was going to look out into the street, see if she could do anything to help.

Out in the road, there were three Vens. Three against five, but her friends were surrounded. The Vens absorbed a few shots, then all charged inward at the same time. There was nothing Brian and the others could do but dodge. It became clear that the Vens were expecting this. A Ficaran fighter dodged the Ven that headed straight toward her, but didn't see the one coming from the other direction. It struck her in the head with its club, and she fell to the ground. Lithia watched for movement, but the woman didn't stir.

Lithia looked around the street. There were other bodies. It was hard to tell in the dull yellow light of the glowglobes, but... yes. There. Two buildings down, a dead man, his handgun on the ground near his outstretched hand. Lithia sprinted for it.

It wasn't until the weapon was in her hand that she stopped to wonder how much ammo it still had. It looked like the Ven closest to the Bear Complex had been momentarily distracted by her break, and had opened its position to keep an eye both on her and the four remaining fighters. It was just enough to give Brian and the others the chance to fall back into a more favorable position. They were no longer surrounded. They each took a few more shots, except for Brian, who had only the *pila* blade, but clearly they were trying to conserve ammo. Lithia joined them and took two shots of her own. Both found purchase, but barely they made a difference in the Ven she hit. One of the men had managed two head shots in the same Ven, enough to disorient it. Another Ven charged, but Melanie sent it reeling backward with a bolt from the harpoon gun.

Unfortunately, she had only hit it in the shoulder, and it looked angry at this new wound. The others did, too. Even the disoriented Ven looked like it was about to rip them apart.

At that moment, Melanie's communicator came to life. It was Colm, calling a retreat. Then Lithia heard the shuttles coming in overhead, and she felt cautiously hopeful. Victoria was on her way back.

It had been enough last night to send the Vens into a retreat. Maybe they would get lucky again.

A shrill growl, impossibly loud, rang out through the town. The three Vens before them joined in before rushing off into the darkness.

"What just happened?" Melanie asked.

"They're retreating again," one of the fighters said.

"I don't think so. We need to go now. Victoria might buy us enough time to get out of here," Lithia said.

They herded the two families out of the complex and retraced their steps. They picked up the two Berserkers she had stunned earlier. They had reached the edge of the square when Melanie stopped them.

"Victoria set down a few Flyers in the square, but it looks like most of the Vens came here, too," she said. "It's impossible to get inside the Temple. We'll have to go around."

Lithia remembered well how the hangar opened up from the back of the Temple, but it was a long way down. The closer they stayed to the Temple, the steeper the incline. Further out, the slope was gradual, but there were more people and more Vens.

She peered ahead into the square and took a few steps forward as Melanie and Brian argued about their plans. The lighting here was better than in the streets, and the omnipresent Vens were a terrible rainbow of green interspersed with Ficarans. There were many more Ficarans. Lithia grimaced when she realized that was true of the fallen bodies as well. On the opposite side of the square, Victoria and Colm were fighting back to back, holding their ground in front of one of the remaining Flyers as Ficarans flocked inside. It wouldn't be long before they joined in the retreat.

That's when Lithia saw him. A monstrous Ven, his sharp teeth bared, claws fully extended, his straight-edged plating black as tar.

he was the same Ven from last night, and he seemed to be staring at her again.

Lithia tightened her grip on her stun rifle. The Ven moved purposefully in her direction as if he remembered her. In the lighting, she got a better look at him. His plates looked thicker than most, and she noticed a small pale spot on his chest, lighter and greener than the rest of him. The scar from an old injury? What had broken straight through Ven plating? She stood paralyzed for a moment before stepping back.

"Lithia, behind you!" Brian's voice broke her out of her daze.

Two Vens had found their way behind her, separating her from the rest of her group.

Dammit. She was such an idiot. How did she let this happen?

Another team of Vens was closing in on her friends and the families they had rescued. Their options were evaporating.

"Go! I'll meet you down at the bottom," Lithia shouted.

"You can't take them by yourself," Melanie said.

"I know. I'm not going to try to fight them. I just need to dodge them. Go, before it's too late."

"Melanie, take them to the hangar," Brian said. "We'll be right behind."

Before she could tell Brian to get the hell out with the others, the black Ven was on her. She wasn't ready for him. The two Vens at her back at least seemed to be there to keep her contained rather than to attack, because her dodge was sloppy, putting her directly in their path. Around her, the Ficarans were disappearing into Flyers, leaving more Vens unoccupied. Most ran off into the town, but some stayed to besiege the final Flyer.

Focus. You don't need to win. This isn't a fight. This is an escape. Get to the edge, and gravity will do the rest.

Brian didn't seem to have the same plan. He was trying engage one of the Vens at her back. By himself.

The black Ven attacked again. This time her dodge took her in the right direction, but he gave her no time to recover before moving again. He was fast. How could something so large be so fast?

Brian cried out in pain. She turned. He was still standing. Just a scratch.

Another mistake. She was caught unawares, and the black Ven charged, swinging with all his strength. He would have hit her straight in the chest if something hadn't hit him first.

A bullet.

Colm. She couldn't believe it.

He fired again, this time at the Ven fighting Brian. The Ven fell at once. This was their chance. Before the black Ven could recover, she sprinted toward Brian, taking a moment to glance down at the fallen Ven. Colm had hit it straight in the eye. Effective. There was no time for gratitude. Colm was inside the final Flyer, and the door was closing.

She hit Brian, who was stationary, at a run and the two stumbled over the edge, tumbling and rolling a good part of the way down.

Lithia groaned. Her body felt like one giant bruise, but there was no time to lose. Shuttles were leaving the hangar, one after the other. They needed to be on the next one.

Lithia was dismayed to find that the hangar was practically empty. Just a few shuttles remained to take the Ficarans away. There were a few people arguing with one of the soldiers. Now that Lithia and Brian had arrived, Melanie ran up to join the conversation.

"These are for the soldiers. Victoria's orders. We can take you and those four," the soldier said, gesturing to the two fighters and the two unconscious Berserkers. "The other Flyers will be coming back for a second run."

"There won't be a second run. If we don't all get out of here now, we'll die," Melanie said.

"I have my orders," he said. He tightened his grip on his gun. That wasn't a good sign.

"Fine," she said. She turned to the two fighters. "Take the other two and go." Each fighter supported one of the unconscious men and dragged them on to the shuttle.

Melanie threw up her hands and stalked away.

"Melanie," Brian said, waving her back towards him.

"Don't even start," she said as she marched up. "I'm not leaving you here."

"But—"

"We're getting out of here together." There was a finality in her tone that reminded Lithia of Dione. Melanie was a true friend.

"What about that one?" He nodded over toward a battered-looking shuttle in the corner.

"That thing is as likely to crash as fly," Melanie said. "I needed more time to fix it."

"So you're saying it's fifty-fifty?" Brian said.

"I'm saying we need to be on one of those working Flyers," Melanie pointed back toward the well-guarded shuttles. "We could try the stables, but the maximutes are gone, I'm sure, and the machi, too. We could try on foot…"

"That's suicide. Maybe Victoria's Flyers, in the square…"

"We'd never make it. What is she doing?" Melanie asked.

Lithia was already heading over to damaged shuttle. She could not believe that this mess would fly, until she saw its designation. *N-8*.

"Hello, Nate. It's good to see you." Lithia smiled. It wasn't much, but it was something. And she could work with something.

18. LITHIA

Lithia scrolled through the battered Flyer's systems. Things didn't look so bad. *Nate, you are wonderful. I may just name one of Dione's unborn children after you.* The Ficarans had done a good job of prioritizing system repairs.

Stabilizers were fine, but high altitudes were still out of the question. Navigation was completely shot. She wasn't sure how they would make it back to the Mountain Base, but really, anywhere but here seemed like an improvement.

Lithia was feeling downright optimistic until she realized why Melanie had been so skeptical. Nate's thrust was just barely in the green. Minimal power. She wasn't even sure she could get them off the ground.

She had tuned out most of the chatter behind her, but when she turned, she saw the back of the shuttle was full of others the soldiers had turned away. One passenger was holding a crying baby.

Every single one of them was more weight.

"Listen up," she shouted over the din. Much to her surprise, all the noises, except the steady cries of the baby, softened. "Everything that's not essential needs to go. That means that unless it's breathing, you throw it out the back. Weapons, personal items, storage containers—all of it. Unless we lose a serious amount of weight, we're not going anywhere."

One of the fighters looked down at his gun, as if debating whether it counted. Brian got to him first.

"When we get into the air, you won't need it. Toss it," he said.

After that, everyone began tossing or sliding anything they could out the back. It was like Lithia's closet method of cleaning—where she would shove all the mess out of sight—just without the closet.

She fired up the engines. This was going to work. They were still too heavy, but just by a hair. They could make it.

At that moment, Roy, the boy with the machi, ran up to the shuttle.

Lithia groaned. "There's no room. We're too full as it is," she said.

"There's plenty of room," he said. She could understand his confusion. There was indeed plenty of space, but even the sixty kilos he weighed could trap them on the ground.

"See if the soldiers will take you. They must have room for one more," Brian said.

"They've all left. The Vens are right behind me, please!"

Brian turned to Lithia. The question was in his eyes, but he wouldn't say it out loud.

The answer was no. It had to be no. She could hear the Vens' growls growing closer. They had to leave. They couldn't afford any more weight. They might all crash and die as it was.

Instead of answering him, Lithia turned and took them up before Roy could jump on and doom them all. There were a few gasps of protest, but no one did anything to stop her. They wouldn't.

Lithia flew them out of the hangar, trying to blink away the image of Roy, his bright, blue eyes and blond hair, his mouth open in fear.

Fear. Roy reminded her of her little brother, not because they looked anything alike. Her own brother had dark hair and dark eyes, just like her own, but she couldn't shake the thought. She imagined leaving her own brother to the mercy of the Vens.

You could have made room. You could have found a way.

But not in time. She knew that she had made the right choice. At least, she would keep telling herself that until she believed it.

She felt tears well up in her eyes, but refused to let them fall. She didn't cry, and she wasn't going to start now, not when she had more important things to do like keep this shuttle in the air.

She saw others fleeing across the plain on foot and on machi. She also saw the dark green bulk of Vens chasing them. This is what the Vens lived for.

She could keep Nate airborne for a while longer at least. They had made it off the ground, but the shuttle was heavy and flying low. She had worried about the navigation, but that was irrelevant. They were slowly losing altitude. They were not going to make it to the Mountain Base, and she had ten, maybe fifteen minutes, to figure out the best way to crash. For the third time in just a few days. It was not the skill she had planned to improve this trip, but it certainly kept coming in handy.

"Brian," she said. She looked at him and could see the agony spread across his features. He felt responsible for Roy, too. "Brian, focus. We're losing altitude. Where should we land?"

"What?"

"We need to land somewhere. Preferably not on trees. The thrusters are failing."

"Go back to the plains, then."

"It's a Ven killing ground! I won't go back there."

"There's nothing else. The Aratian plateaus are too far, and also not a good idea. Can you find a clearing?"

"It's too dark, and the AutoNav isn't working, so I'd have to do it by sight."

Brian though a moment. "The lake."

"Yeah," she said sarcastically, "these things don't land on water. They sink."

"We're almost over the lake, just hover over the water near the shore. It'll be deep enough we can jump in, then swim to the shore."

"I guess that could work. Can everyone swim?" Lithia asked the group.

At that moment, the baby wailed. She had forgotten about the baby. From the look on Brian's face, so had he.

"We'll figure it out," he said.

***

The lake was easy to find, like a change in the texture of the dark. She thought she'd seen a clearing or two but couldn't be sure, and she really didn't want to crash.

When she began hovering over the water, it was about a three meter drop. Brian urged people out. The bolder ones went first, and as the shuttle dropped, little by little, others took the plunge and accepted guidance to the shore.

There were only a few people left when Nate hit the surface and began to sink. The woman with the baby hurried out to where another man was waiting to help her swim while keeping her baby above water.

Finally it was just Lithia, Brian, and a girl who didn't know how to swim.

"Roll over onto your back, push your belly up, and lean your head back, and I'll swim you in. You should mostly float in that position," Brian said.

They all went out out together, just in time. Lithia swam away from the sinking shuttle, but soon found herself being choked by something. An arm.

The girl was not following Brian's directions. Instead she was grabbing on to Lithia, who probably could have kept both of them afloat if the girl weren't panicking and flailing all over the place.

Lithia's head plunged underwater, and she struggled back up for air. She gasped another breath before being pushed under again, deeper this time. She was not going to make it back up.

She could bite the girl, but that might not work. As she sank deeper, she noticed the grip around her neck loosen. That was it. She needed to go the one place this girl did not want to be: underwater.

Lithia put all of her effort into swimming down, and sure enough, once her assailant realized that she was not headed in the right direction, she released her. Lithia was able to swim away and pop back up to the surface.

"Brian, do you see her?"

"No," he sputtered. "She went under. I couldn't get her."

She heard him take a breath and go underwater, but she knew he wouldn't be able to see anything. She tread water, waiting, trying to see anything beneath the black surface.

After what seemed like forever, Brian reemerged with the girl. By the time they reached the shore, the girl was coughing.

"Are you all right?" Melanie asked when they slogged ashore.

"Yeah," he said. "Did everyone else make it?"

Melanie nodded. "A few are gathering firewood. My communicator is working, and there's a Flyer that will come get us."

***

They had barely started the fire when the shuttle arrived. The pilot was a little heavy-handed with his maneuvering, but he was good enough to fly with the AutoNav. There were a few others already on board. Some had blood on their clothes and faces, and Lithia couldn't tell if it was their own blood or not. A few were crying.

As each of her own crew found a place to sit or stand, water pooled under them, and she could hear teeth chattering. She shivered, and Brian reflexively put his arms around her. His warmth was dulled by the water's chill, but it was warmth all the same.

She didn't like it. She felt like he was trying to comfort her, keep more than the cold at bay. His embrace felt like an apology, full of regret, and she didn't want that. She pulled away and approached the copilot.

"You came from the settlement?" she asked.

"Yes," the copilot replied.

"Did you go in the hangar?"

"Yeah," she said, "but it was overrun with Vens by the time we got there. We found a few survivors in the fields."

"When you were in the hangar bay, did you see any bodies?"

The copilot was silent a moment before answering. "Yes."

"Did you…" Lithia wasn't sure she could get the question out. "Was a there a blond boy with blue eyes there? Named Roy?"

"He was already dead when we arrived."

The memory of Roy's face as she flew off flashed in vivid detail across the walls of her mind. The fear. He knew what would happen.

Lithia returned to her seat. *You could have saved him. He didn't need to die.*

19. LITHIA

Lithia was so lost in her thoughts that Brian had to shake her out of them when they arrived at the Mountain Base.

The scene that met them was chaos. Armed men and women shouted and ran to and from the shuttles. Somewhere, a small child was crying and screaming for his mother. Lithia wondered if his mother was still alive. Some carried guns, some carried the wounded. She could smell the sharp, iron scent of blood. There were pools and splashes of it on the landing area.

The people on their shuttle were mostly unharmed, but when another shuttle landed roughly opposite them, she could see that was an anomaly. The survivors in these second- and third-wave shuttles had not gotten out in time.

A woman ran out first, screaming and clutching a limp child. She ran to another woman who ushered her inside. Others followed, and she felt Brian tug her in their direction. That was not where she wanted to go, but her headstrong voice of dissent was not there. There were no words.

"I'm going inside to see what I can do," Melanie said, tears in her eyes.

"All right," Brian said.

Many of the injuries were serious. Though survivors walked or limped off together, guided by other Ficarans into the mountain, several stayed put until makeshift stretchers dotted with blood could be brought over. One man's leg looked like it had been severely broken by a Ven club. Another man looked like he had been shot.

"What happened to him? That's a gunshot wound," Lithia said.

"Friendly fire?" asked Brian.

"Ven bit him. He went crazy. I—we didn't have a choice," said the soldier who was holding a scrap of fabric to the man's chest.

"I know. You did the right thing," Brian said.

When the next stretcher arrived, Lithia and Brian lifted the man onto it and helped carry him while the soldier kept pressure on the wound.

Inside, the main atrium had been converted into a hospital. They were met by a severe-looking woman. One glance at the stretcher and she directed them down a hallway to the area for critical cases. They moved the patient into some sort of office with just a few other wounded. One was already dead by the looks of it.

A bearded man met them and spoke in a brusque voice. "We'll take it from here."

"I'm staying," said the soldier, still applying pressure.

"Fine," the man said. "You two, go."

Lithia hesitated, but Brian pulled her away. "Come on, let's see what else we can do," he said.

"Yeah." It was all she could manage.

They returned to the atrium to find Bel and Evy passing out blankets and food.

"Lithia!" Bel said, running over, followed closely by Evy. "Thank the void. Turn your damn manumed back on." Evy said nothing but hugged her, wrapping her tiny arms around Lithia's waist, burying her head in her stomach. Evy shouldn't be here. She shouldn't have to see this.

Lithia turned her manumed on. She hadn't even checked in when Melanie returned it to her in the cell. Something about hearing Bel's voice snapped her out of the daze she had been trapped in. Or maybe it was Evy's warmth. "What's going on? Who's organizing it all?"

"Sam, mostly. She's guiding the medics and creating a catalog of survivors and where they're staying. Her consciousness or whatever can only be in one place at a time, though. Victoria had a chat with her and agreed, I think mostly because she is too busy coordinating the rescue efforts."

"Sam," Brian said. "My mother, Bethany Caldwin, where is she?"

"Apartment B24," Sam replied.

"I'll be back. I just need to check on her. See her with my own eyes."

Without another word, Brian sprinted off toward the stairs.

"Sam, how many survivors accounted for so far?" Lithia asked.

"I have only cataloged the ones who have been moved into the apartments. Everyone still outside or in the triage and hospital areas have not been counted."

"Okay, how many in the apartments?"

"Two hundred and fifty-four." Her heart sank. Brian had told her there were over six hundred Ficarans, but there were definitely not three hundred people upstairs and outside.

"That's it? How many are in the hospital area?" Lithia said.

Bel answered. "A lot of people are running around the main floor. It's just a preliminary number."

Lithia began shivering. She was still wet from the lake, and she felt so numb.

"Get changed," Bel said. "Sam has a few people going through all the clothes and sorting them by size downstairs for the refugees."

Refugees. The word hit her. The Ficarans were displaced. Homeless. Refugees.

Wars had refugees. *This was war.*

***

Lithia received fresh clothes from some tired Ficarans who were gathering and cataloging a variety of supplies. Clothes in hand, she ducked into the apartment they had all shared a couple of nights ago. She needed a moment alone to change and get her bearings.

As she peeled off her wet clothes, someone came out of the bathroom. It was Brian. He looked startled to see her, half-naked in the living room.

He looked at her for a moment in confusion before turning. "Sorry, I didn't realize you had come in."

"It's fine. I thought you were with your mom." Lithia put each leg quickly into the shorts she had been issued.

"I checked on her, but she's sleeping. I didn't want to bother her."

Lithia pulled the loose-fitting shirt over her head. "All dressed." He had also changed into dry clothes. She hung her wet clothes over the back of a chair and looked at him. She couldn't imagine what he was feeling. He looked broken.

Lithia wrapped her arms around him, and he hugged her back. She rubbed his back in a soothing motion. He felt warm, and took the chill from her cold, damp skin. Boys were always so warm. This hug was nothing like what she had felt last night when she had put her arms around him. There was no fire, no lust. This was comfort. This was an apology. This was friendship. Nothing more.

"Lithia, that kiss last night... it's not that I don't find you attractive, but there's someone else."

"No need to explain. It was fun, but it won't happen again."

He nodded. "I want to go back out and look for survivors."

Roy's face flashed through her thoughts again. She hadn't saved him, but she would save others.

"Let me come with you," Lithia said.

***

Victoria was outside on her communicator with someone, directing people this way and that. "There's a team on their way already," she was saying to the person on the other end.

Brian looked like he was ready to punch her, but when Victoria saw them she waved him over. Lithia couldn't decide whether to try and hold him back, or punch her herself. Luckily it didn't come to that, because Victoria spoke first.

"I'm sorry," she said to Brian. "I should have listened to you."

"Yeah, you should have. Do you know how many people are dead? Do you? Because it's all on you." Brian was shouting, and Victoria let him. "We told you. We warned you! We gave you a plan that could have saved everyone, but you let your hatred of the Aratians blind you. This blood is on your hands."

"I know. A true leader accepts responsibility for her decisions. I accept responsibility. I made a mistake, and our people, the people that I love just as much as you do, are suffering for it. I will not make the same mistake again. I have no energy to waste on self-pity, though, not when I can save a few more lives." Victoria turned her cold stare on Lithia, who blazed with anger. "Just remember that I'm not the one who led the Vens here."

"No," she shook her head furiously, "you don't get to pin this on me. It was just a matter of time before the Vens found you. Sam wouldn't have been able to protect you forever. Be glad that we were here to help you. Without us, you'd all be dead. No Flyers, no information about the Vens, and another full Invader class vessel on its way."

Lithia had said the words, and on some level she knew they were true, but deep down, she believed Victoria. She blamed herself. They had come to this planet because of her, because she had these coordinates. Even though all her research led her to believe this was an uninhabited planet and her grandma had not come here, she had been wrong. Maybe if she had told Dione about her search, her friend would have seen something she missed, some sign that this planet was home to so many people.

"And for those reasons, I'm letting you live," Victoria said. At that moment, her communicator came to life with Colm's voice. "Victoria, I've found them, but the Vens are in pursuit."

"Keep moving," she ordered him. "I'm sending someone now."

"We're going," Brian said.

"Fine," Victoria said. She called over a few other soldiers. "Take that Flyer." With Sam's help, they would be able to find Colm using his communicator. "Colm was searching for a group that made it to the woods. It's a large group, Brian. Bring them back."

Energized by her seething anger and regret, Lithia hopped into the copilot seat, ready to go.

20. DIONE

"Is that a Bolma tree?" Professor Oberon pointed at a large tree oozing thick, dark sap.

Dione smiled. She was glad the professor was feeling better after some food and rest. Lithia had called in the middle of the night. She was okay. Brian was okay. They needed rest, but would come get them later in the day once things at the Mountain Base settled down. Meanwhile, she, Zane, and the professor, along with Canto, would be heading toward the Ven distress beacon.

He approached the tree and inspected it. "It's been grafted!" He turned back to Dione and Zane. "What is this place?"

Professor Oberon had not been in much of a talking mood yesterday, so they hadn't explained much to him yet.

"This is a garden planet called Kepos," Dione said. "The scientists who worked here created and manipulated species for use in terraforming, but about fifty years ago, they were evacuated when the Vens showed up in our part of the galaxy."

"Why evacuate the…" Professor Oberon paused as realization sank in. "We're outside the Bubble, aren't we?"

"Yes," Dione said. "There weren't a lot of options after the attack. There was a tracer, and we couldn't go to an inhabited planet. Lithia thought this place was abandoned."

The professor raised his eyebrows, but he didn't ask how Lithia got the coordinates for a planet outside the Bubble.

Dione told him about Bel's infection, how the anti-parasitics were on the planet, and the ensuing conflict with Aratians, Ficarans, and even Samantha. She touched on the mythology of the Farmer and Architect, and through it all, his frown deepened.

"So one of the scientists brought all these people here to control them, and the other scientist killed him and uploaded her consciousness into a computer to defend the planet?"

"Basically," Dione said. She left out the part about Miranda Min. That was not her secret to tell, and she doubted Zane would say anything. Lithia could tell him if she wanted.

Dione scratched Canto behind the ear. His wounds had scabbed over and didn't look infected. She imagined they would leave nasty scars, though. Dione had forgotten to mention Canto's injuries to Lithia when she called, so Brian would probably not be happy when he saw Canto. He had trusted her, and now Canto was injured. He had blamed her for the Vens, and now he would probably blame her for what had happened to his beloved maximute.

Apparently Victoria had used the shuttle Lithia crashed to start the others, and because of that, there were not enough shuttles to evacuate everyone in time. Lithia had left out the details, but they had been running rescue ops all night, looking for survivors. Dione should have been there to help, but she was too busy making up for another mistake.

Now that they had found the professor, though, things were looking up. He would know what to do.

Dione led the way toward the beacon, so lost in thought that by the time she noticed them, she had nearly tripped over them.

Two bodies. A man and his machi. They'd been in the wrong place at the wrong time, it seemed. The Vens had probably killed them while searching for the professor.

The others stopped behind her. Professor Oberon put a hand on her shoulder and gently urged her away, but she couldn't move. She recognized the man. He still had a black eye, healed to a grim shade of yellow, from where Brian had punched him. He had been the man foraging, and his machi, dead beside him, was the one they'd stolen.

Dione knelt and struggled to wipe away her tears with no sleeves. Was this her fault? Was this man out in this area because of her? Had she thrown off his schedule and forced him to ride into harm's way?

If she hadn't gotten to the Field Temple, and then to the Mountain Base, so many more Vens would be here. She had to think of that. They would have been doomed for sure. At the time, she hadn't realized any of that. She had just wanted to save Bel, and she hadn't cared about what happened to this man.

Now the universe had put his corpse, and his machi's, in her path. A reminder that her choices had consequences.

"Dione, what's going on?" Professor Oberon asked.

She couldn't explain it. She was too upset. Too ashamed. She longed to tell Brian. He would understand, but then it would be his burden to bear, too, and she wouldn't do that to him.

She brushed away a few more tears, then got back up. There was no time to bury them, and Dione didn't know what Aratian funerals were like, or if they even had them. Instead, she took a handful of earth and sprinkled it over each body. There was no prayer in her heart, but she felt the universe listening to the chaos of her thoughts. *I'm sorry, I'm sorry, I'm sorry.*

"Dione?" the professor asked. The question was an invitation to talk, one she refused.

"Let's go." She avoided eye contact with Zane and the professor, leading them away from the bodies. "We need to find the beacon." She continued in silent contemplation for the next hour, walking close enough to Canto that every so often, she could reach out and give his fluffy, golden neck a reassuring pat.

***

Zane tripped over the first piece of debris, but Dione caught him. It was dark green, just like the hull of every Ven ship.

"Well, we're in the right spot," he said. "Now we just need to find the source of the distress beacon."

They passed a large section of the scout ship, but Dione couldn't see any bodies. With a long-dead human, the flesh decayed to leave behind yellow bones. She wondered what a decades-old Venatorian corpse looked like. She hoped she would find out, and then grimaced at the thought. Where had that idea come from?

"I wonder what happened to the Vens who didn't survive the crash?" she said instead, coming out of her daze.

It was Sam who answered through her manumed. "Jameson burned all their bodies. He didn't know as much as you do now, but he knew they didn't always stay dead."

"Holy crap, Sam, are you always listening?" Zane said.

"No. Actually, it's hard for me to split my consciousness. I think a normal AI can do it easily, but it's a human limitation I wasn't able to fully shed. I just started listening minutes ago. You're close."

The professor knelt down to study the ship, perhaps the Venatorian glyphs on the wreckage. When Dione approached, she saw something else entirely. A few neatly stacked rocks. The top rock had a symbol carved onto it, a spiral inside a triangle. She had seen it before, on a tree, when Brian was leading them to the Forest Temple.

She took a step closer and saw something stranger. Recently cut flowers. Three gaping orange blossoms lay at the base of the pile.

"What is that?" Dione asked.

"I'm not sure. A shrine?" Professor Oberon replied.

"A shrine to the Vens? That makes no sense," Zane said.

"These stones are smooth," Dione said. "They came from the river." She reached into her pocket and brushed her thumb over the surface of her own river rock.

"Whoever did this spent time moving them," the professor said. He had come close as well, and frowned over the stones. "And these flowers are fresh. Probably a day or two old."

"That's when the Vens came," Dione said.

"Do you think it's for the Aratians who died fighting them? That would make sense," Zane said.

Dione took another look at the shrine. Something seemed off. "This symbol, though. It has to be Venatorian." She glanced at the scabbed-over cuts on the professor's arms. "Why put a Venatorian symbol on a memorial shrine for dead Aratians?"

"It's a bit strange, but not completely unheard of," the professor offered.

"I've seen this symbol before," Dione said. "Carved onto a tree when we first got here. I thought it was a trail marker or something. But it's too Ven."

Zane stepped forward. "Let me see."

He removed the engraved rock from the top of the pile and inspected it. Dione noticed another carving on the other side. It was worn but legible, despite being written years ago.

"Zane, flip it over," she said. "There's something written on the other side."

"What does it say?" Professor Oberon was just as curious as Dione.

"*The Farmer lies.*" Zane read. *"Do the demons tell the truth?"*

The hairs on Dione's arms stood on end. "They mean the Vens. Who would do this?"

"Who do you think?" Zane shot back. "It has to be the Ficarans."

Dione furrowed her brow. The Ficarans did hate the Farmer, so it made sense.

"I think the better question is why," Professor Oberon said. "Why would someone create a shrine to so-called demons?"

Dione thought a moment. *The Farmer lies.* "Because they might be telling the truth. Whatever that means. Think about it. If the Farmer is a liar, then you can't trust anything he says, including his warnings about the Vens."

"But the Vens killed some of the colonists. You'd have to be crazy to worship a Ven," Zane said.

"Maybe, but there's usually a reason behind a person's actions, even if it's a bad reason. Humans are amazing at justifying their actions," the professor said.

"Yes, we are." Dione looked down and felt the knot of guilt in her stomach tighten. It had developed days ago, and though she could forget about for a while, it eventually constricted again.

***

As it turned out, the beacon was easy to find. Finally, something easy. It was larger than Dione expected, but she supposed it was attached to some other ship component. This was more Zane's area of expertise. In fact, she was coming to realize he was kind of brilliant.

"Zane, how did you end up qualifying so low? For the internships, I mean," Dione asked. After the plant experiment fiasco on the ship, she had looked up his ranking. Now that she had gotten to know him a little better, she didn't understand.

"I never turn in homework."

Dione gasped. "Why?" She had forgotten her homework once. It had been such a stressful experience that she had never let it happen again.

"Better things to do. Like learn."

Dione looked to the professor, who was smiling. "So he didn't do your homework either?"

"He did the practical assignments. Read up enough to figure out how to do them. I don't know if he told you, but he was working on some modeling programs to predict what we would find on Barusia based on past data. His project wasn't hands on like yours and Bel's, but it would have been a great tool."

"I didn't know, Zane. That's really cool." Dione meant it. She had played around with some existing programs, but she didn't have the skills to create something that complex. Yet. Maybe Zane could teach her when they got back home.

Home. It hit her hard in that moment. They were so far away, without a jump drive. She probably wasn't going home again.

The professor saw her blink hard, and she hoped he wouldn't say anything to make her lose her composure. One reassuring word, and she'd be bawling. Zane was busy at work on the beacon.

"Did Zane ever tell you how he got the open spot on this trip?"

"No, how?" She just wanted the professor to keep talking. She couldn't handle a moment alone with her own thoughts right now.

"I borrowed this beautiful, antique harmonophone from Headmaster Halloway and, I don't know what happened, but it stopped working. I was trying to fix it when Zane came in. He took one look at it, and figured out what the problem was. The regulator."

"When a harmonophone breaks, it's always the regulator," Zane said over his shoulder.

"Well, if I had broken it, Halloway probably would have fired me. Or at least moved my office to the basement. When I realized Zane didn't have an internship placement, I talked him into it."

Dione smiled at the professor. Here was a man who really got what it meant to be a teacher. Dione was easy. She played by school rules. Yet somehow he had found a way to give Lithia and Zane these unique opportunities to bring their talents to the program in unconventional ways.

***

Zane had been pulling wires out of the beacon for nearly twenty minutes, so when he turned and asked if she could help him dig out another access panel, Dione leapt at the chance. Finally, something she could help with.

"Sam, are you there?" Zane said.

"Yes, but the beacon is not yet disabled," Sam replied through his manumed.

"I know. I can't find the active connection. I can see where you severed the first beacon linkup, but I have no idea what I'm looking for."

"Can you just cut everything?" Dione said.

"Maybe," Zane said. "Sam, why were you so precise when you did this the first time? You only focused on shutting down the flow of energy from the power source to the transmitters."

"I didn't know much about the technology or what would happen, so I interfered with as few systems as possible."

"Hmmm." Zane was staring at the beacon. "I have an idea. Dione, get back."

"What are you going to do?" she asked.

His reply was to take the gun from the makeshift holster on his hip. When he aimed at the beacon, the professor said, "Why don't you let me? I'm sure I'm in enough trouble already without letting you shoot things."

"Well, I tried conventional problem-solving methods first," Zane said.

"Sorry for the confusion," Professor Oberon chuckled, taking the gun from Zane's outstretched hand. "I didn't mean we weren't going to shoot it. I just meant *you* weren't going to shoot it."

Dione and Zane moved back to a more-than-safe distance. Canto, who had been curled up into a giant, fluffy ball, stirred next to Dione, ears perked.

The professor took a few calculated shots.

"Sam?" he called back to them.

"The beacon is still active," she said.

He fired a few more shots.

"The signal has stopped," Sam said.

"You got it," Zane said, and that was that.

Dione laughed. It was so anticlimactic. No giant explosion, no dramatic music. The beacon looked the same, except for several large holes smoking in the exposed control panel.

***

When Lithia arrived in the Flyer, Dione was surprised to see Brian with her. He looked tired, but still beautiful. His hair was wet, probably from a shower, and it went all the way to his shoulders. He wasn't smiling at her like he had when they first met. He had the shuttle, and his people, many of them at least, were safe. Why would he come with Lithia to retrieve them?

Canto. Of course.

Brian went straight to his maximute. "Brian, I tried to call when it happened, but Canto was hurt," Dione said. As if in response to his name, or maybe the sight of his master, Canto came bounding up to Brian, licking his face.

"Hey, boy, looking good," he said, rubbing the dog's giant nose. "What happened, tough guy?"

Brian was clearly talking to Canto, but Dione answered, wringing her hands as she did.

"There were Vens, and he killed one, but it scratched him. Then two more Vens showed up, but some wild maximutes came and helped, too."

"Wild maximutes?" Brian asked, giving her a puzzled look for just a moment. He turned back to Canto and smiled. "Or were they old friends?" Canto licked his arm in response.

"What do you mean?"

"When our food stores got low," he explained, "we couldn't keep very many maximutes anymore. We had to release most of them into the forest so they could hunt for their own food. I'd bet those maximutes that came to Canto's rescue used to be Ficaran."

Dione hadn't thought about the extra resources needed to care for machi and maximutes. She wondered how Brian had secured rations for Canto. Probably by smuggling, and he needed Canto for that. She continued her story.

"After the fight they licked him, and I think it helped heal him, because he looks a lot better today. I'm sorry, Brian." *For everything. I'm sorry.*

"I know," he said. "Canto's gonna be fine."

He looked her in the eyes for the first time since the Vens had landed. Really looked at her. She couldn't read his expression. It was heavy with sadness, or maybe guilt, but none of it was directed at her. She was beginning to feel uncomfortable, but she couldn't break his gaze. He was studying her, though she didn't understand why.

At that moment, the professor stepped in between them and extended a hand.

"I'm Professor Elian Oberon."

"Brian Caldwin."

"Oberon!" Lithia said, running up and embracing him. When she finally released him, Dione got a good look at her. She couldn't place it, but something seemed wrong. She knew her best friend.

When the professor took the copilot seat, though, she had to settle for talking to her later.

Dione strapped into a seat along the side, and Zane settled in across from her. Not that she could see him, because Canto was still standing in the back of the shuttle. Brian sang him into a lying-down position and buckled in on her side of the shuttle, leaving one empty, awkward seat between them. He nodded to Zane, who nodded back. That communication was all they needed. Zane closed his eyes.

Dione looked once more at Brian, who was staring hard at nothing, and then closed her eyes as well. Despite the welcome reunion, no one seemed in much of a talking mood.

21. DIONE

The Mountain Base was a completely different place from when Dione had left it. When their Flyer returned, there were so many shuttles on the landing pad that there was barely any room left to set down.

Canto had been especially glad to leave the shuttle. Brian followed to find a place for him. Zane took the professor to see Bel, who was busy cataloging supplies for the refugees.

Alone at last. Dione turned to Lithia, but before she could ask, her friend shut her down. "I don't want to talk about it."

"Well, I'm here when you do." Dione examined Lithia's crossed arms and clenched jaw. Yep, classic signs that she just wanted to be left alone. "I'm going to go to the *Calypso* and change," Dione said.

"Okay," Lithia said.

The landing pad was a mess. Dione could see patches of dried blood. Every face she passed looked grim. She dreaded going inside the building. Things here were worse than she had anticipated. While she had been out in the woods facing down four Vens, the Ficarans had taken on the rest of them and lost.

Her cabin was undisturbed. Dione put on a clean StellAcademy uniform. As she changed, she heard something clatter to the floor. The river rock. She picked it up and put it in her pocket again.

After she changed, Bel called to tell her they were all coming to the *Calypso*.

The professor's arm was in an improvised sling, his cuts were bandaged, and his head wound had been cleaned. He had a new manumed, or rather, an old one. Probably a backup. Bel looked much better, and Evy was practically her shadow. Zane and Brian followed, talking softly, and Lithia came in last.

They all sat in the common area. There were not enough seats. None could be brought over, since all the chairs were bolted down, so Dione took a seat on the floor. Evy joined her.

She stared up at the professor, but he looked lost. It was disconcerting, really. He always had the answers, or at least the right questions.

The professor seemed to feel all eyes on him, because he spoke first. "I know you all expect me to have a plan, but I don't. Zane caught me up on the details of the charging matrix, and he's right. There's no way we can reintegrate it into the *Calypso*."

"We're stuck here," Lithia said.

"We owe it to the colonists to help," Bel added. "Not just because it's the right thing to do, but because if they fail, we're doomed, too."

"I have practical self-defense training," Professor Oberon said, "but no military training. Certainly nothing on the scale of addressing a colonial assault, even though this is not a large colony. I think the best thing we can do right now is share everything we know, and come up with a plan."

Dione really wished he would just tell them what to do, but he had never been that kind of teacher. In class, it was because he wanted students to figure things out for themselves. Now, it was because he himself didn't have the answers. Dione realized she had been holding her breath, and she slowly exhaled. Trial and error were their only options, but there was no doubt what "error" meant in this case. Error meant real-life consequences. Mistakes meant death.

Bel spoke up. "Oberon, I want to—" She broke off at the sound of footsteps. Dione's back straightened and her heart picked up its pace, but with relief, she realized that it could not possibly be a Ven. Sam would have warned them.

It was the next worse thing, though. Victoria and Colm. Brian tensed, and next to him, Lithia stood up, her eyes as dark as Dione had ever seen them.

"Get out." Lithia's voice was low, almost a growl.

Colm stepped forward to respond, but Victoria held up a hand. "I'm here to listen."

"It's a little late for that," Brian said.

"I'm not asking for your forgiveness or approval. You all seem to have more information about this threat than I do, so I'm looking for your help," Victoria said. She turned toward the professor, sensing the other adult in the room. "I'm Victoria, the leader of the Ficarans, the people in this Temple. And this is Colm."

"Elian Oberon," the professor said, extending his hand. Victoria gave it a brief shake.

She turned to address everyone. "The current number of survivors cataloged by Samantha is four hundred and fourteen. There may still be survivors in the woods, but we do not expect to find many more." Victoria paused a moment as if the words were painful. "There were six hundred and ninety of us. I knew the name of every single person in my settlement. I feel our losses keenly, and I don't need to hear it from you all. Don't forget, you brought these... aliens here."

"So you believe us—that they're aliens?" Dione asked.

"The Farmer lied about so much, even you have more credibility in my eyes," Victoria replied.

Dione glanced at Zane and the professor, but neither of them reacted. She recalled the words carved onto the rock at the Ven shrine. *The Farmer lies.* Could there really have been Ficarans who worshiped the Vens? She doubted it would matter now that the Vens had destroyed the Field Temple.

"I don't care if they're demons or aliens," Victoria was saying. "You're still the ones who led them here."

"They would have found you anyway. It was inevitable," Bel said.

"And who are you?" Victoria said. Dione could see her looking down on Bel, judging her small frame.

"I'm the one helping Sam organize your people. I'm a survivor of a Venatorian assault, and I was a refugee, just like you are now." Bel stood, and despite being a full head shorter, she looked rather intimidating. "The Vens would have found this place again, just like that scout ship found you all those years ago. Sam was hiding you, but it was only a matter of time. Consider yourself lucky we showed up."

Victoria scoffed, but Bel pressed on. This time, she spoke to everyone.

"I lived on the Dappled Rim with my family. There are a lot of planets out there, and ours was on the wrong side of the Bubble. My parents knew about the danger, but they didn't want to move. They were descendants of the original settlers, and they didn't think the Vens would come to their small farming colony. There was no reason. We had a comfortable life, but little of value."

Bel paused and took a deep breath. Zane reached out and squeezed her hand. Dione suspected that he was the only one who had heard this story in full before.

"The Vens don't need a reason. They aren't here for your land or resources, not beyond resupplying. The Alliance, our government, would have gladly traded them what they needed. My colony would have traded with them. They attacked us because they enjoy fighting. They enjoy killing. They enjoy stalking their prey."

Victoria was silent, and Dione was surprised to see her listening so carefully.

"We had warning. We thought it was a pirate ship at first. Pirates want an easy raid. Put up a strong resistance, leave a few crates of supplies where they can get them, and they'll take it, call it a victory, and then leave. Vens are not pirates. They are hunters. They didn't want our supplies. They wanted our lives, and they took them.

"Most of the colonists prepared to make a stand when they came, but my brother and I were in the cellars with my mom. It was safe enough from pirates. I don't know how she realized what was happening, but she told us to hide in the cold storage room, then ran upstairs to find my sister. My brother didn't listen. He hid me and ran off after my mom."

"It felt like forever, but my mom finally came back. My brother was behind her, bleeding from his arm. I didn't realize it at the time, but it was a bite mark. He wasn't himself. I watched him—"

Another pause. Bel closed her eyes for a moment, reliving the horror in her memory.

"He killed her. I hid inside one of the carcasses in cold storage until I could barely feel anything. When I came out, I saw my brother's body. Some other Ven had sliced him open like it was nothing."

Bel took a breath.

"Ever since, I've read everything I could about the Venatorians. The truth is, the Alliance isn't interested in stopping them. They've got their damn Bubble, and anything outside isn't their problem. The Vens get what they want and leave all of the protected outposts alone, for the most part, so the raw materials keep coming in, and the Alliance doesn't have to expend resources fighting the Vens. The Vens still get to kill people. Everyone wins, except the ones who die."

"Why didn't we hear about this on the vids?" Dione said.

"The Alliance keeps a lot of intel to themselves. No need to alarm the populace with the death of the criminals who thrive outside the Bubble. That's how they paint us, so that people like you don't care if we die."

That wasn't fair to say. Or was it? Bel was right, though. She hadn't cared, because she hadn't known. But all that would change. She would talk to her father when they got back. If they got back. There had to be something he could do. There was no way he knew about this.

"So how do we fight back?" Brian asked Bel.

"There's no avenue for talks or peace or surrender. The only way to stop them is to kill them all. Every last one. I'm sure you killed many of them last night, but the death tolls were disproportionate. They have redundant organs, a degree of regenerative capabilities, and their plating makes hand to hand combat a death sentence. Ballistic weapons are our best bet. Stun weapons are basically useless, though we only have the one rifle," Bel said.

"When we were in the woods, maximutes seemed to do a good job of killing them," Dione said.

"The Aratians have a lot of maximutes. We didn't have the resources to keep many," Victoria said.

"Bullets work," Colm said.

"That's true, but how much ammunition do you all have left?" Bel said. "My colony was not equipped with enough weapons to kill the Vens fast enough."

"We have a healthy supply of bullets," Victoria said, "but we'll have to go back to the Field Temple to retrieve them."

"I'll send patrols to see when it might be safe to go back," Colm said.

Dione shook her head. "Until the Vens have been taken care of, this is the safest place for your people. We have the high ground, and the Icon will prevent them from flying closer. They're grounded, and after what Sam did to their other vessel, they know it."

"They're just having too much fun killing people to care," Lithia said.

The professor had been quiet since Bel told her story, but now he spoke. "Where are they going next?"

"Some teams will continue to hunt any Ficaran survivors, but they know the next big target is the Aratian settlement. From what you've told me it's the largest population center," Bel said.

Dione involuntarily looked to Evy, who had grabbed Bel's hand. "You can't let them do that," the girl said.

"We're going to find a way to help them," Lithia said.

"Can I go back home now?" Evy said.

"You can go back home whenever you want," Bel said. "You are not a prisoner here."

Dione watched Evy's chin wrinkle and braced herself for the tears. She hadn't seen Evy cry since they found her in the Forest Temple days ago. It struck her how amazing it was for a ten-year-old to be so independent. Because of it, she had forgotten that Evy was probably homesick.

Bel led Evy away to get some fresh air.

"The only chance we have is to work with the Aratians," Brian said, looking directly at Victoria. "Without our weapons, they may not survive."

"I will not put any of our weapons into Aratian hands," she said.

"Well, you'll have to figure out something, because if the Aratians fall, they're coming here next," Lithia said.

Victoria frowned. "I'll negotiate with Michael, but I'll do it here. That's why I need your help. I want you to bring him back."

"So you want us to bring the Aratian leader back here?" Lithia raised an eyebrow. "How's that gonna work?"

"I'm sure you'll think of something," Victoria said. It sounded like an insult.

"Victoria," the professor said, heading off the argument. "What can you tell us about Michael?"

"He's cruel. We grew up together, and he can only deal in absolutes. Right and wrong. Black and white. He can't see my people for what we are, humans. He thinks that we are all criminals. He's impossible to deal with, which is why my people are starving. The only way to solve this problem is to kill him," Victoria said.

"That doesn't sound like a very good plan. Who is his successor? Would that person work with you if you had just killed Michael?" Professor Oberon asked.

Dione went cold. What was the professor saying? It sounded like his only concern with killing someone was that it would create ill will.

"His brother Benjamin would succeed him until his daughter Cora could take proper control. Benjamin is at least reasonable. Show him evidence, and he might listen."

"I doubt Benjamin would cooperate if you killed his brother. Murder aside, your plan is illogical," the professor said. Dione relaxed as she saw what he was doing, showing Victoria that even if she thought killing Michael was fine, it was still a bad plan.

"You have a compelling hostage right outside," Victoria said all the same, referring to Evy.

"She's not a hostage," Lithia said. "Drop it." There was a true darkness in Lithia's voice that Dione had never heard before.

"We have the Flyers," Colm said. "A display of force might persuade them."

Dione had heard enough. "Are you people idiots? I know you hate the Aratians, and you may even have a few good reasons, but the Vens will kill you all unless you find a way to work together. You have to make a deal or a trade or a truce. You have weapons, they have numbers and a strong defensive position. Give them some guns, for void's sake."

"Absolutely not. The guns are the only things that have kept my people safe from them all these years," Victoria said.

"Then send in your fighters with guns. You saw what the Vens can do. This threat is bigger than the Aratians. At least they don't want to kill all of you," Dione said.

Victoria stared at her hard for a moment. "There are some fates worse than death. Ficaran guns will stay in Ficaran hands. Colm will go with you. He'll come find you in an hour. Michael and I will negotiate here."

"I can't imagine how this could go wrong," Lithia said, glaring at Colm.

Victoria nodded, and Colm scowled. Dione realized he was not happy that he had to go along. She wished he wouldn't. This would be a volatile situation no matter what, and a brute like Colm would only make things worse.

Victoria and Colm left, and soon after, Bel and Evy returned.

"So that's it? Our plan is to negotiate peace between two groups that hate each other with no bargaining chips?" Lithia said.

"All we need is a temporary alliance," Bel said. "After the Vens are dead the Aratians and Ficarans can go back to hating each other."

"I don't want that. These people are nice, even though they've lost so much," Evy said. It was then that Dione realized that she had been in the thick of it all with Bel, getting the refugees settled.

"I don't want that either, Evy," Brian said. "I think that if you go back and tell the truth, and keep telling the truth, you can make a difference."

"I can talk to my uncle and father," Evy said, "but they don't usually listen to me."

"It can't hurt," Bel said. "How are we going to get Michael to agree to negotiations?"

"Hostages. We need to leave collateral there," Lithia said.

"Do you trust Victoria to honor a truce so much that you'll stay behind?" Bel said.

"Nope. That's why we'll give them Colm," Lithia smiled, proud of her brilliant plan. "Two birds, one stone."

Dione still felt like there was another angle. Reason. There had to be an avenue for reason instead of threats. Instead of human insurance. What did the Aratians value that she or the Ficarans could provide? Suddenly, it hit her.

"Genetic diversity," she said.

"What about it?" the professor said.

She stood up. "That's what the Aratians value more than anything else, or at least what their leaders value. They've been working on preserving and enhancing genetic diversity as much as possible, to the point of oppression. If too many Aratians die, they will lose a piece of their diversity. I think it might be enough of a worry for them to come to the table."

Everyone was silent for a moment, considering her words. It sounded stupid, of course, but this was a bizarre world they had crashed into, and when one thought of it like that, her plan just might work.

"If they really cared about that, why do they shoot us on sight?" Brian asked.

Dione thought for a moment. "Are you sure they do?" she asked. "Remember those captured Ficaran techs? They were using them to make repairs."

"They only shot Nadia when she tried to escape," Lithia said, frowning at the memory.

Brian said nothing.

"I think you may be right," the professor said. "Even if they don't value Ficaran lives, they must realize that they need to work with them in order to preserve their own."

"It's worth a try," Bel said.

Zane nodded. "I'm in."

"I'm driving," Lithia said.

"I'm going to stay here," Bel said. "I've been working with the Ficarans and Sam, and I think I can do the most good by staying put."

"Then I'll go with Lithia and Zane," Dione said.

Brian turned to her. "I'm not going to the Vale Temple. I want to stay here and see what I can do to help."

"I understand," Dione said. She was a little nervous, but also relieved. She didn't want the Aratians to hurt Brian.

He got to his feet. "Come on, Evy, I'll help you get your things." The two left, leaving only the four StellAcademy students and their professor.

"So, Oberon," Lithia said, "any other thoughts?"

"We can't figure this out for them. Even if we get them to cooperate, there are no guarantees. The Vens might be too powerful. I'm out of my element here, but we'll provide a forum to talk."

"And if the talking fails?" Bel said.

"Many more people are going to die," he said.

22. CORA

Cora woke up earlier than usual. Today was it. The Matching. She just knew that she would be paired with Will. After all, the original Farmer's granddaughter should get the best match, and Will was the best for her. She looked out the window at the assembly area. Giant, colorful blankets of blue, pink, and orange had been laid down for the crowds to sit on later as they watched the Matching.

Despite the early hour, many people walked around, enjoying the holiday. The market was open, and people from the farms on the outskirts were already milling around. She hoped her father had returned with the rest of the cavalry in the night.

She wanted to go out and wander around the town on her own, but there was so much to do already. At least she didn't have to pack. As the Regnator's daughter, her Match would be moving in with her. How strange it would be for Will to live here in the Temple.

Her aunt would be coming soon to help her get ready for the day. In the morning, she would parade through the city with the other girls, followed by the new mothers from the Matches of the previous two years. At midday, she would share a meal with her own family. For most of the girls, this would be the last meal with their family for weeks. After the Matching they would have dinner with their husbands and new family, and move in with them that night.

As the Regnator's daughter, Cora would have a special ceremony in a few weeks before her new husband moved in with her. Cora stared out the window, daydreaming about what it would be like having Will around the Temple. He seemed worried about today, but Cora knew the Farmer would want them matched. She knew that her uncle wouldn't make a mistake.

She couldn't wait anymore. She would see if her aunt was awake. She walked down the hall to her aunt and uncle's room, and paused at their door, listening for movement. Voices! They were awake. Cora prepared to knock, but stopped once she heard her father's name.

"The runner who came said Michael and the cavalry were pursuing the demons," Ben said. "Everything is on lockdown right now. I can't send someone to look for Evy."

Cora's breath caught in her throat. First the Ficarans, now the demons. She should have known the Ficarans wouldn't pose a challenge, that something else was keeping him. This must have been what Theo was ordered to keep from her.

"But you're the First Geneticist," her aunt replied.

"All the more reason I have to stay here. We have to trust that Evy is okay. If Cora says Evy wouldn't come with her, we have to believe she's not in immediate danger. She's a stubborn child, but she's not stupid."

"*You* believe it, then. I'll worry for the both of us. Are we still holding the Matching today?" Amelia said.

"Yes. Cora will be disappointed that Michael isn't here. So will the other girls whose fathers are still out with the cavalry," Ben said.

"Or worse," Amelia chimed in.

"But we have to maintain our traditions. I won't delay the Matching."

"Then we continue on. Ben, will you tell me—"

"No," he said. "I cannot disclose the Matches until the ceremony, even for our niece."

"She has expectations, and I don't think she realizes that she may not be matched with who she expects," her aunt replied.

"If you're worried, talk to her."

"Very well. It's a sacrifice all of us must make, even Cora. That's what makes us Aratians. Honor and duty, a lesson we all must learn. I'll go wake her."

Cora rushed as quietly as possible back to her room. Her father wasn't back yet, she thought, but it was only morning. He might still return, despite what her uncle had said. Even demons were no match for Michael Bram. When her aunt arrived a few minutes later, she was pretending to sleep.

She heard Amelia mutter under her breath, "Of course, she's still asleep." Then she felt a rough shake of her arm.

Cora made a big deal of yawning. "Good morning, aunt," she said.

"Good morning, child. Time to prepare for today. I'll send for some breakfast."

"I'm not really hungry," Cora said.

"Well, you need to eat something. How about a polla? They're your favorite, right?" Amelia said.

"Okay."

Cora showered, and when she came back out, breakfast was ready, delivered straight to her room. It was a feast. There were pollas, but also red and yellow berries, a fresh floral tea made from pink blooms that reminded her of early spring, and porridge boiled with sucra leaves that gave it an aromatic sweetness.

Seeing it all made Cora's stomach rumble. Perhaps she was hungry after all. Her aunt had already begun eating. Cora, dressed in clean sleeping clothes, sat across from her and dug in. Her aunt always ate slowly, but soon, Cora realized she had paused mid-meal.

"Yes, aunt?" Cora said, in between bites. It was probably about Evy. She felt a pang of guilt, but Evy had not wanted to come with her. She had tried. It wasn't her fault.

"It looks like Evy won't be here for your Matching. The city is on lockdown." Her aunt didn't try to hide the bitterness in her voice. "Your father also won't make it back today." This last sentence was meant as a jab, but Cora was ready for it. She remained calm, much to her aunt's surprise. Her aunt was helpful, sure, but this wasn't the first time she had tried to needle a reaction out of Cora.

"I understand. He's doing the Farmer's work."

Amelia raised an eyebrow and continued on. "I wanted to talk to you about one more thing, child. I know you've been spending time with that boy—"

"Will," Cora said, smiling at the thought. She couldn't help herself.

"Yes. It's highly unlikely that he will be your Match. You need to start coming to terms with that now, rather than during the ceremony. Any unfavorable reaction would be unbecoming of the Regnator's daughter."

"Don't worry, aunt, I have faith that the Farmer has chosen me the only suitable Match," Cora said.

"The Farmer doesn't always work in the way we think. Sometimes he sends us adversity. Even now, your father is paying for your indiscretion. The demons have returned."

Cora clenched her spoon a little too hard and paused when it was about halfway to her mouth. She was about to be matched, and still her aunt treated her as a child. "Aunt, do you warn me because you were unhappy in your Match? What indiscretion of yours prevented you from bearing my uncle more children? Perhaps you didn't have enough faith."

Amelia pursed her lips, opening them only to have a sip of tea. After a moment, her features relaxed into a saccharine smile.

"Well, we all learn the truth about the world one way or another. Some of us would rather take the bruises than allow another to soften the blow. Finish up. It's time to get you ready."

Cora realized she should have been nicer at breakfast once her aunt began brushing her hair. Each stroke of the brush felt like it was tearing hair out. She wished her mom were alive. Clara would have been gentle. That's what everyone said about her, at least those who liked her. The others called her mother weak. Cora heard them when they didn't realize she was listening. Even the Regnator's daughter was ignored in the bustle of the marketplace.

Her aunt would not let her brush her own hair despite her polite requests. When the twisting and braiding and pinning part came, Cora was in tears. This must be why hair was always done before makeup. Her aunt might be enjoying this torture, but when she was matched with Will, she would have the upper hand. One day, she would wield the power of Regnator, and her aunt would be sorry.

Amelia had finished with one side of her head, and just as Cora was wondering how she would survive the other side, a woman summoned Amelia away to begin her own preparations. Another woman, this one quite old, came in to take over. Before leaving, Amelia said, "Happy Match Day. I'll see you at the luncheon."

"Thank you, aunt." Cora wouldn't be alone with her at the luncheon, at least. Her uncle would be there, even if her father was still gone, thanks to those awful liars. Rotten Ficaran spies. They still had Evy, too. Cora felt a little sad to realize that her luncheon would just be her and her aunt and uncle, but it wasn't so bad. Again, she remembered that she was lucky enough to get to stay in her father's house after her Matching. Her official Matching ceremony would take place in a few weeks. Her father would certainly be back by then.

The old woman approached her and smiled, sending a ripple of wrinkles across her face and filling her eyes with warmth.

"Hello, grandmother," Cora said, lowering her head in respect. Though her biological grandmothers were dead, women of a certain age became the grandmothers of all.

"Hello, child," she said, running her fingers through Cora's hair on the unfinished side. The woman's touch was much gentler than Amelia's, and Cora relaxed a bit more.

The woman held up a few sections of hair, and Cora saw her gnarled hands with their swollen joints. She doubted that this woman would be able to match the precision and tightness of her aunt's side, but as the woman began twisting and braiding, Cora was amazed at her speed and skill. Of course, she had probably done this dozens of times.

"How many daughters have you made ready for the Matching?" Cora asked.

"Seven," she replied. Cora widened her eyes. That was a lot of daughters. The woman continued, "But I also prepared my three sons. It is not easy for the men, either, and they do not have the warning that we women do."

Cora had never considered that. She had known all her life when she would be matched, but the men never knew when, or if, they would be chosen as suitable matches. That could be a little scary.

"How many Matches did you have?" Cora asked. This woman had probably had two. That would explain the large number of children. Cora wanted to know what it had been like, to be married to your first match, but to have obligations to your second.

"Three," she said.

"Three?! I didn't know that was even possible," Cora said, twisting her head back to look the old woman in the eye.

"Sit still, child," she said, dropping the section of hair in her hand to start again. "It no longer is. And one day, soon, there will be no second matches. We won't need them anymore. And one day, the Matching may not even exist, at least not as a way to choose partners."

"What do you mean?" Cora had never heard her uncle talk about this, though he didn't like to discuss his work in front of her and Evy.

"Those who left, those who became the Ficarans, they didn't like being told who to marry. They refused to be matched. While many called them selfish and dishonorable, they were just impatient. Short-sighted. We have the Matching to protect our genetic integrity. It's not about breeding out physical traits, it's about preventing genetic illnesses. They are a danger to our population because we are so few. But once our numbers grow, once the gene pool is strong enough and large enough, there will be no need to mandate matches, just as we no longer need third matches, like I had."

"You sound like you pity the Ficarans."

"I do. We shouldn't hate them. They are our blood."

"They keep attacking us! How could you say that?"

"With ten children, don't you think it likely that a few joined the Ficarans when they left?"

"So you have children who left us?"

"Many my age do. My own daughter mutilated herself, so that she would never be able to bear children. She thought that was her only escape. Then the Architect showed her another way, and Victoria was gone."

Victoria. A chill swept through Cora's body. "The leader of the Ficarans is your daughter?"

"Yes, child, keep your head still." The woman had worked more quickly than her aunt, and her hair was almost done. "It is my hope, and the hope of many my age who are still alive, that one day, we'll be able to heal the divide. We have always been more patient than the younger generation, but I fear my patience may outlast these old bones."

The old woman put the final pin in place, and Cora admired the intricate pattern of braids and coils. Everything was becoming real. Today, she would be matched.

"Blessings upon your Match, child."

"Thank you, grandmother," Cora said. She hesitated, trying to find more words to say, but the old woman was gone, replaced by a young pregnant woman with a large belly. The new woman applied makeup to her face and eyes, but said little when Cora questioned her. She seemed tired or busy, and had no time to give Cora any insight or advice in regards to her condition.

Cora dressed alone, in brilliant billowing pants of gold and brown, with a simple white shirt. It was almost time to report to the main hall of the Temple where she would wait with the other girls and make final preparations for the parade.

She hesitated for a moment on the threshold. She felt a little sick. Was it excitement? Fear? All of a sudden, the certainty she had felt just hours before was draining from her. Victoria had harmed herself to avoid the Matching. Hundreds had rebelled and fled. Why was she only questioning this ritual now? No, the Ficarans were wrong. They were selfish. They did not believe in the Farmer and his vision. They did not respect the process. She would honor her responsibility in the Matching, and marry Will. If she was given a second match, she would honor that responsibility, too.

Cora headed to the main hall downstairs, confident in her future.

23. DIONE

Dione and Professor Oberon were the only ones left on the *Calypso*. Lithia and Evy had gone to get a shuttle ready, and Zane had followed Bel into the Mountain Base. Dione finally had a moment alone with the professor, and she needed to say something. But the words kept getting stuck.

"Dione, is there something you wanted to talk to me about?" Professor Oberon's voice was gentle and patient.

"I'm sorry," she said, blinking back tears. "On the Ven ship, I thought... I thought you were dead. You weren't moving, and there was so much blood."

He put his hand to the back of his head where his wound was still healing. "Dione, you can't blame yourself. If you had stayed, we'd both be dead, and so would the others. You gave them a chance to escape, and somehow, me, too."

"What do you mean?"

"You probably noticed the Vens hunting me had the same symbols as the blue ones that boarded the *Calypso*. I don't understand it all, but I think they were hunting me for retribution. It's strange, because they don't seem to have the same ritual for adults who are killed in battle. It's almost reassuring that they hold the lives of children sacred, too."

Dione had never thought about that. The Vens seemed like a monolith to her—all the same, all violent, evil, irredeemable—but they had to have hierarchies or social structures, surely, and culture. No. Curiosity had its place, and this wasn't it.

"They're monsters," she said, emphatically.

"Maybe. Certainly from our point of view. I'm not condoning their behavior, but I'm asking why. Why are they doing this?"

"Maybe it's how their culture operates, or there is some biological imperative within them to kill. Who cares? They almost killed you. They killed hundreds of Ficarans. The sooner they're all dead, the better."

The professor thought a moment. "I think what you're saying is that this question doesn't matter right now, because we're all in danger, right?"

"I guess so," Dione said.

"What if understanding their motivations helped us defeat them?"

Dione said nothing. She was torn. This was not the time to study the Vens, unless it could be done at the same time she was killing them.

"I think that survival is our number one priority," she said.

"I won't tell you to show them mercy or spare them. They won't spare our lives. Just don't let your anger blind you to opportunities to understand, because those opportunities may save your life. They may save the planet."

"Bel has been studying the one we killed on the ship. She has a hypothesis," Dione said. "She was making observations about the Ven's physiology, and she noticed a pattern. The Vens have a lot of the adaptations of prey: the thick plating, the rectangular pupils, the appearance of being dead while regenerating tissue."

The professor furrowed his brow. "She thinks they're actually prey."

"What if they're not nomadic hunters roaming the galaxy for prey? What if they are fleeing something more terrible?"

"That's a troubling idea. More terrible than the Vens?" The professor considered the proposition for a moment, then shook his head. "For humanity's sake, I hope you're wrong."

Dione looked down. "I'm sorry."

Professor Oberon put a hand on her shoulder. "Never apologize for asking questions. Without scientific questions, we'd never get any answers. I think that this Ven hypothesis is worth investigating."

Dione stood up to leave, but hesitated.

"Yes?" the professor asked, sensing her unasked question.

"Do you think we can make it out of this?" She needed to hear him say the words.

"I do. And I'm not just saying that. If we can get everyone on the same page for long enough, I think we'll be able to stop them. The Vens thought they would have another Invader class vessel full of soldiers from what you've told me. They are at a greater disadvantage than they planned, but for some reason they won't back down. They have no problem fighting until the end, even if every last Ven dies. We don't know why. Another cultural quirk, perhaps."

"That's stupid of them."

"So it seems to us, but they must have their reasons."

"Thanks, professor," she said. He looked tired. "Get some rest. We'll need you later."

He chuckled. "You know, I should be panicking right now. Four of my students are running around this planet in the middle of a Ven invasion."

"You're not panicking?"

"Oh, I'm panicking, but I also see what you've done so far without me."

"We've screwed everything up," she said.

"You did the best you could under the circumstances. I believe in you, Dione. I believe in all of you, because you are some of the most capable students to come through StellAcademy." Professor Oberon put his hands to his temples and winced.

"You need to get some rest," Dione repeated.

"Unfortunately, you're right. I don't think I can come with you. Wake me if there's anything I can do."

Dione helped the professor to his cabin, then entered the base to prepare for their trip. Bel sent her to search the basement for communicators. Sam had barred most Ficarans from entry, worried about what they might get into or find. Bel didn't warn her that Brian would be here, too. He was sitting with his back against a wall, eyes closed. A box of cleaning supplies was on the floor next to him. He looked exhausted.

"Need any help?" she asked, startling him.

Brian jumped. "Dione?" He looked up at her, his eyes bloodshot. She wasn't sure if he had been crying, or if exhaustion was weighing him down.

Her heart ached for him and his people. "I wanted to say I'm sorry. After the Vens landed, I was overwhelmed. And then the professor was alive, and... I didn't know what to do. I should have been there with you."

"You don't need to apologize. There's nothing you could've done that would have changed things."

"I thought you blamed me for the Vens."

"I know it wasn't your fault. Not really. I was just focused on saving my people."

"So we're okay?"

"Yeah." Brian paused for a moment and looked at her. "You know, you remind me a lot of my father. He questioned everything, and I forgot that. I let my anger at the Aratians take over, and that's not what he would have wanted. Even though he's lost, I feel like I've found a piece of him in you."

Dione didn't know what to say. Brian stepped closer and tucked a piece of hair behind her ear. She leaned in to kiss him, but he took a step back. Was she misinterpreting things?

"What's wrong?"

"It's… nothing. Just promise me you'll be careful. You can't trust the Aratians."

"I thought you were warming up to them," Dione said.

"Just because we need to make a deal with them doesn't mean we have to trust them."

Brian's communicator came to life. It was Bel. "Brian, did you find those cleaning supplies? What's taking so long?"

"Yeah, I've got them. On my way." To Dione he said, "See you when you get back." With a kiss on the cheek, he left.

She didn't understand. She knew she shouldn't take it personally, but his rejection consumed her thoughts. Something was going on with Brian. And Lithia, she wasn't the same either. What had happened at the Field Temple?

Dione gathered up the remaining communicators to bring to the Aratians as a peace offering. Their manumeds had been enough to convince Cora that they were working for the Farmer, so maybe these communicators would help them negotiate.

A message from Lithia appeared on her manumed: *Time to go.*

24. BEL

Bel was busy organizing welcome baskets. At least that's how she tried to think of them, but the welcome felt hollow. When the Ficarans came to her, stained with tears and blood, a stack of clean clothes and some soap, with directions to the shower, felt almost callous. Each face was a mirror for her own pain. How could she tell them they were lucky? Lucky to be alive. Fortunate to have a friend or a family member to put a steadying hand on their shoulders.

Bel had nothing. No, that wasn't true. She had the memories, good and bad, and she was grateful for those, once the nightmares had stopped. Her throat felt tight, but she knew she wouldn't cry. Not anymore.

"Hey."

Bel jumped a little and turned to see Zane. His deep blue eyes pulled her out of her dark thoughts. Without thinking, she pulled him into an embrace and didn't let go. She leaned her head against his chest and felt his chin rest gently on top of her head.

She let go, and as nice as the hug had been, she immediately regretted it. He would probably read into it. How could he not? They'd been getting closer and closer, but she'd always kept a necessary distance to protect him. To protect herself. Even if he understood, he wouldn't be interested. He wouldn't be willing to make that sacrifice.

"What's up? Did you come here to help?" She smiled at him, and he quickly pushed the look of confusion from his face to smile back. She almost sighed with relief. She was afraid this might be the moment he brought it up. "I'm sorting the clothes based on size."

"I'm going to the Vale Temple," he said. He picked up a shirt, checked its size, and folded it before setting it on the top of the medium stack.

"I know, I was at the meeting," Bel said.

"I'm going to stay there, I mean. I know they plan to offer Colm as collateral, but I'm going to volunteer."

Bel's pulse quickened. "But why would you do that?"

"I dug up some spare parts. Based on what I've learned from Brian and Evy, I think I can fix some of their tech. Their Artifacts are broken, right? What if those Artifacts can help us fight against the Vens? They might not even know what they have."

"I think the sentiment is nice," Bel started, "but it's not safe. I don't trust the Aratians. I don't even really trust the Ficarans."

"We don't have a lot of options."

"It's too risky. Wait until they've reached an agreement, at least."

"Sometimes we have to take risks, and this is a risk worth taking."

His voice gave him away. He wasn't talking about becoming an Aratian prisoner anymore. He was looking directly in her eyes. He was talking about her. Before she realized what was happening, Zane leaned in and gave her a short kiss on the lips.

He looked at her expectantly, like the kiss had been a question, and he was looking for the answer. Was the answer supposed to be another kiss? Bel had no idea. She had never kissed anyone before. She had never wanted to kiss anyone before.

That's how she had figured it out. While all the other girls were talking about dating boys, she had been searching for new additions to her bug collection. It had almost been a point of pride for her to be above their obsession. It wasn't until she came to StellAcademy, and even the most brilliant girls, like Dione, still let themselves get distracted, that she began to realize that she was different.

"Zane, I… I don't… I'm sorry—" she began.

She hadn't finished her thought, or figured out what to say, but Zane already looked defeated.

"It's okay, I shouldn't have—"

"I care about you, Zane. A lot. But there's something you need to know about me," Bel said. Her chest ached with everything she had been holding back. "I'm asexual. I can't be your girlfriend. Or a proper girlfriend anyway."

"What do you mean?" Zane said, confusion again furrowing his brow.

"I mean, I'm not interested in sex or other stuff like that." She felt like a freak. Here she was admitting that she was completely indifferent to the things teenagers were supposed to think about constantly.

"How do you know? Have you ever?"

"That was my first kiss, and I just know."

"But when you hugged me just now, I thought… I'm sorry, I misunderstood. I didn't mean to—"

"I'm asexual, not aromantic. I still want relationships, and hugging, and maybe even kissing. I don't know. I'm still figuring out my boundaries. I just don't want to lead you on."

Zane thought for a minute. "Wait, are you saying that you like me?"

"Of course I like you. As more than a friend."

"Then let's figure this out," he said. He held her hand, but tentatively, still uncertain.

"You did hear me when I said sex was off the table, right?"

"Yes, and I can't promise that will never be an issue, but for now, it doesn't matter. You matter, Belen, and if you're willing, I want to give this a try. If it doesn't work out, at least we'll know."

Bel was still terrified. She had expected her words to make him back away and grow distant. "I'm still figuring things out myself."

"Let me know things as you figure them out, then. Bel, I think you're amazing. I'd be lying if I said I wasn't attracted to you, but the physical is only one aspect."

Zane pulled her in for another hug, and this time, she relaxed completely. The closeness of their bodies, his warmth, his breath on the top of her head, all of it was perfect. Despite everything, for that moment, she felt safe.

She smiled at him. "Are you still going to volunteer?"

"Yes. The sooner we solve this Ven problem, the sooner we can figure out how to get out of here. I was thinking about it, and I know a way off the planet, once this is over."

Bel arched her eyebrows. "How?"

"What if we could figure out how to fly their ship? I've been working on a translation program for the Ven language. Not the spoken stuff. I created a program that will run with a holo interface so we can read the Ven symbols in real time. It's not all of them, and I don't know if it will work…"

"Wait, the professor banned holo interfaces for the trip," Bel said.

Zane shrugged. "Oberon brought his own."

A light bulb went off for Bel. "Would your program work on the information stored in a Ven datacore?" The Ven datacore would give them all the information they needed about Ven rituals, their home world, and if they had any predators.

"It could be modified to read a core," he replied. "The hard part is getting it to work with a holo interface, but that wouldn't be necessary for translating a datacore. It should be easier."

Bel smiled. "So how did you put the program together?"

"It's incomplete," Zane admitted. "At first, it only had the language information that was in the public archives."

"That's not much," Bel said. She would know. She'd combed through every piece of data about the Vens after the attack on her home, looking for answers.

"You're right, but the language we do have skews toward the text we encounter most often. There's a higher percentage of ship language in the database. With what we have, you can't introduce yourself and order lunch, but we just might be able to identify ship systems and get them working."

"How can it be enough? There's hardly any Ven language available. I've looked."

"When I was using the Alliance access portal to find all those planet coordinates for Lithia, I got what info about Ven language I could. There's a lot they're keeping classified."

There was one thing Bel still didn't understand. "Why were you looking into the Vens?"

Zane blushed. "I knew how important it was to you. I thought if I could help…"

Bel smiled and squeezed his hand.

It was insane. Even as she did a happy dance on the inside, she feared that Oberon wouldn't allow it. Trying to steal, much less fly a Ven ship? She could imagine him calmly explaining the million reasons it would never work.

None of that mattered, though. There was a way to get off Kepos and prove her Ven hypothesis. All she needed was a Ven datacore.

"Why do you want the datacore?" Zane asked, as though reading her thoughts.

"I want to know the truth about the Vens. You know about my hypothesis. I think that some other creature hunted them, and I want to know everything about it so that we can finally stop the Vens."

"Don't you think the Alliance already has this information? They've taken Ven ships before."

"They're hiding things from us. Like all of the language data you got from their archives. Why hide that? There's something they're not telling us," Bel said.

Zane checked his manumed. "I need to meet Lithia and Dione at the shuttle, but I'll be back." He hesitated, like he was thinking about kissing her again, but thought better of it and gave her a short, solid hug. He turned to smile at her before he left.

As she watched him go, Bel felt happy but uncertain. She didn't like having something to lose, especially with the Vens around, but Kepos would not be a repeat of her old home. She wouldn't let that happen.

25. LITHIA

The flight from the mountain was a short one, though the landscapes below were so hilly, Lithia couldn't believe Cora had taken an ATV all the way back home. The Aratian settlement looked even brighter from above, and she imagined she could smell the spice and citrus of the open market. Lithia was looking for an open area to land when she realized there were no meandering people to avoid. The streets were empty. Dione, looking at one of the camera readouts, was the first to notice where all the Aratians were.

"What are they doing?" she asked.

Lithia pulled up the external camera feed and saw a crowd of people seated on blankets on the ground in front of a stage. On the stage were people, mostly girls, covered in garlands of flowers. Everything from the blankets, to the flowers, to the curtains at the back of the stage were blue, pink, and orange.

"What's going on? Some kind of talent show?" Lithia said.

Colm growled. He surprised her by replying, "It's the Matching, a barbaric festival that dehumanizes everyone involved. Of course, we'd come on the day of the Matching."

Lithia's dislike of Colm softened, just a little. His loose brown clothes were a stark contrast to their fitted blue and white StellAcademy uniforms. He had a handgun holstered at his hip and a rifle slung across his back. Lithia hated to admit it, but she was glad that he was well armed. She didn't trust him, but then again, she didn't trust the Aratians either.

"Can you land in that open space behind the stage?" he said.

"If we land that close, we'll probably blow the curtains down," Dione said.

"Good," Colm replied.

Lithia lowered them to the surface, and as expected, a few of the curtains fluttered to the ground, sending the girls on stage scrambling out of the way. *So much for a quiet entrance.*

Colm and Dione exited the craft first, followed by Zane and Evy. Lithia, stun rifle in hand, came last, but made her way to the front. She, Colm, and Zane had not raised their weapons, but they were ready. They stood, blocking the entrance to the back of the shuttle, until a few guards carrying batons showed up. Between Colm's large gun and Evy's presence, they looked nervous.

"Don't move," one of the guards commanded. "Put down your weapons."

No one put down their weapons.

"We're here to speak with Michael and Benjamin," Lithia said.

The guards exchanged looks, but none moved. They seemed unable to decide what to do about Evy. Just moments later, that decision was made for them.

Benjamin Bram hurried down the steps from the stage, looking relieved. "Evy," he said. In the moment, he looked like a father, rather than the First Geneticist.

"Father!" Evy rushed toward him, and he stooped to hug her.

He said nothing, but kissed the frizzy curls on top of her head. Amelia arrived shortly after, wrapping Evy in her own embrace.

Lithia stepped forward and lowered her stun rifle. Zane followed her lead, but Colm kept his weapon raised. Time to give this a try.

"Benjamin, we're here to talk. We don't want trouble," Lithia said.

"He looks ready for trouble." Benjamin nodded to Colm.

"Listen to them. Please," Evy said. "They are trustworthy."

"They kidnapped you," Amelia said, pulling Evy back to her, unwilling to let her child step out of reach.

Lithia couldn't blame her.

"We didn't kidnap her. She wanted to stay with us, and as soon as she asked to come home, we brought her," Lithia said.

"It's true," Evy said. She held up her bug container. "Their friend gave me a dragonfly. Look!"

Benjamin Bram looked at his daughter, half angry, half amazed. "We will speak about this later, Evy," he said. One nod to his wife, and she was leading their daughter away into the Temple. Evy didn't resist, but she did look at Lithia over her shoulder and smile.

"Thank you for returning my daughter. For this, I will let you leave unchallenged." He motioned to the guards, who took a step back.

Lithia turned to signal Dione, but she was already moving forward.

"We can't leave just yet. Where's Michael? We need to speak with him," she said.

"He took the cavalry to respond to the raid on the Hub," Benjamin said, "so you should leave before I change my mind."

"Did you see the ships that landed here a few nights ago?"

Benjamin frowned. "Yes."

"Those ships are full of an alien race called Venatorians, or Vens. You call them demons. They have already devastated the Field Temple. The Ficarans have relocated to the Mountain Base."

"That is not our problem," Benjamin said.

"The Vens won't stop after destroying the Ficaran settlement. They're coming here next," Dione said.

"The cavalry is already dealing with them as we speak," he said.

Dione turned back to exchange a look with Lithia.

"That won't be enough. Over two hundred Vens landed on this planet. Your cavalry alone won't be enough. You'll need Ficaran help." The First Geneticist opened his mouth to cut her off, but to Lithia's surprise, Dione kept going. "Benjamin, I know your people value genetic diversity. That is what this entire festival is about, right? Well, hundreds of Ficarans are dead. Erased from the gene pool, and the Vens are probably on their way as we speak. I doubt your people can absorb that kind of loss easily."

"I have faith in the Regnator and the cavalry's abilities," he said.

"Have you seen one of these *demons* with your own eyes?" It was Colm who spoke.

Benjamin frowned. "No."

"Then you have no idea what you're up against," Colm replied. "We have a Ven body at the base you can examine. Even with our weapons, we were overrun. With the Flyers, we barely escaped. I have no love for you and your disgusting rituals, but unless you meet with Victoria, all of our people will die, yours and mine."

"Meet with Victoria? Where is she?" He peered behind them into the shuttle.

"She's at the Mountain Base."

Benjamin's eyes widened in surprise. "You thought I would agree to go with you? You were probably at Victoria's side while our Hub was attacked and emptied. What happened to you is justice."

Colm bristled, and Lithia was about to step in when a woman with chin-length blond hair marched over. Lithia hadn't noticed her waiting nearby, but she recognized her from Cora's tour: Moira, the plant lady.

"Benjamin, you're going, and I'm coming with you," the woman said. Moira looked the group over and focused her gaze on Lithia.

"It's the little thief," she said. Moira apparently remembered her, too. Lithia didn't have a chance to deny the accusation because Moira kept talking, cutting Benjamin off.

"They've got one of these creatures, and I want to study it. They also have the anti-parasitics, and I'll need them back. I never had the chance to replicate the medicine, and some of our men are showing signs of infection. This can't wait."

"Then you can go. I'll grant you permission," Benjamin said.

"No, we both go. I talked to those boys who are sick and glowing green, and I'm worried these strangers are right. These... Venatorians are a more powerful enemy than we imagined."

Benjamin frowned at Moira, but Lithia saw respect there. He addressed Dione. "Leave a hostage here. An exchange. If I'm not back by nightfall, their life is forfeit," Benjamin said.

Colm stepped forward without hesitation. "I'm Victoria's brother and second-in-command. She will honor this deal." Apparently he had been planning this all along.

"Two of us are leaving, so two of you must stay," Benjamin said. Lithia scoffed, about to tell Benjamin off, but Zane spoke first.

"I will," he said.

Lithia's eyes widened. *Well, you picked a hell of a time to speak up.*

"Zane—" she began.

He brushed her off. "They need you at the talks. Plus, I might be of use here. I brought along some spare components, and I wanted to look at some of their broken equipment, just to see if I can help."

Dione handed Zane the bag of communicators. "These might help, too," she said.

"What are those?" Benjamin asked.

"Communicators. You can even stay in contact with your people while you're gone," Dione said.

Benjamin looked amazed, even though there were only two dozen communicators. The Ficarans had the rest. Benjamin tested one with a nearby guard. It worked perfectly.

"Where did you get these?" he asked.

"The Mountain Base where Jameson hid them from you," Lithia replied. "Come on, time to go."

Benjamin turned and spoke quietly to the guards, who nodded. Colm handed over his guns to Dione, and so did Zane. She looked uncomfortable under the weight of so many weapons.

"Be sure to show them the Field Temple on your way," Colm said. Lithia nodded.

As they returned to the Flyer, she had a good idea of why Colm wanted her to do that, but it didn't make it any easier. The

Field Temple was a fresh grave. She could still smell the blood on the stairs and see the lifeless faces of dead Ficarans when she closed her eyes. The black Ven crept into her thoughts, too, the one who seemed to be in charge of the Vens. He had almost killed her. What if he was still there? Could she escape another encounter with him?

Lithia tightened her grip on the controls to steady her hands and took them into the air.

26. CORA

Those wretched outsiders had to ruin her day. Nothing else would do. Now, instead of overseeing the Matching, her uncle was off talking to those liars. Cora took a few deep breaths and tried to calm herself. Even though the ceremony had been interrupted, she would still be matched with Will, and that was all that really mattered.

Her uncle had bade the ceremony go on without him. There were still several other girls before her, and she watched their faces as they got matched. They looked nervous. Unsettled. She couldn't blame them after what just happened. Lithia and the others had come just to create chaos on this special day.

Her uncle's assistant called the next name. "Claudia Lopez."

Cora recognized the girl to her right who had just been called. She stepped forward and clenched her jaw, as if bracing herself for impact. When her Match was announced, the girl reminded Cora of a tree in a storm. She inhaled sharply and swayed a little bit, but she did her best not to react. Cora could see her fingernails digging into the palms of her hands.

A man climbed onto the stage and took the girl's hands in his own so that they faced each other. When he turned, Cora examined the bald spot on the crown of his head. He had to be almost forty. He looked pale, and he spoke the words of the ceremony quietly, like he was afraid of them. Cora felt a knot tighten in her stomach.

The couple turned back toward the crowd and smiled before stepping off to one side. When she had been a part of the crowd, exchanges like that had looked so different. The whispered words that joined the couples in marriage had seemed romantic, and she had never looked too closely at the already-paired couples once they stepped out of the audience's gaze. Sometimes they cried, but her aunt had always told her it was just their nerves. Up close, Cora could tell that it was more than nerves.

Her uncle's aide spoke her name into the amplifier.

"Cora Bram, please step forward." The crowd cheered loudly for their next Regnator.

For the first time in this process, Cora felt afraid. It was finally happening, and all her faith in the Farmer was not enough to settle her anxiety. *Deep breaths. It's just nerves.*

"The Match for Cora Bram, which will best promote the health and longevity of our people, is… Jai Wilderson."

The knot in Cora's stomach disappeared and was replaced with nothing. A hollowness grew inside her, and the only thing she could feel was her heart pounding so hard that her fingers felt numb. Jai, a stranger, her Match, was walking across the stage, and his approach snapped her back to reality. He smiled widely. He had brown skin and dark, wavy hair. When he got close, she realized how tall he was. His brown eyes seemed kind. He couldn't be more than twenty, and she had to admit, he was extremely handsome.

But he was not Will. Will was still out there somewhere, in the crowd, watching. Jai took her hands, but he did not say the ritual words. They would not be married today onstage like the other couples had been. The crowd broke into thunderous applause. They approved of this Match, like they had all the others, but hers would yield the next generation of Aratian leadership.

She would hold onto the fact that they would not be married today. Her uncle, in his worry, had made a mistake. The aide had read the wrong name. No, those thoughts were wrong. They felt like the other things she had told herself that turned out later to be lies. They might not be married today, but they would be eventually.

Jai led her to the right side of the stage where the other pairs waited. In a low voice he spoke the first words she had heard from him.

"Cora, it is an honor to be your Match. I can see that you are uncertain, but all I ask is that you give me a chance. We have been paired for a reason."

Cora gave him a small smile that vanished as quickly as dew in the hot morning sun. She did not have the words right now. She looked out into the audience, examining every face in her search for Will, but there were too many people. She couldn't find him.

Will had known this would happen, even when she had been so certain that it was the Farmer's will for them to be together. This was the second time that her faith had been misplaced. She had believed that the Farmer chose her to help Lithia. Lithia had had a communicator, and she looked so much like her grandmother Miranda. Cora had believed her. That had gone poorly. Lithia told her that the Farmer was a liar. He was not a god. Now the Farmer had let her down again. Lithia might have been telling the truth about him after all.

Cora had believed that Will would be her Match. Why? Because she wanted it to be true. Her aunt had tried to warn her that morning, but she hadn't wanted to listen. Her aunt was probably enjoying this, watching her suffer up onstage. That thought was enough to put a fake smile on her face as she waited for the cheering to die down.

She looked around at the other girls. Some looked pleased with their strong, young husbands, while a few sniffed quietly to hold back tears. Did they have sweethearts, too? Or were they just unhappy with their Matches?

One girl, the second to be matched, stood next to a severe-looking man in his early thirties. He had a hand around the girl's waist, but she was leaning away from him. She tried to step away, but he closed his other hand over her wrist.

"That hurts," she whispered.

"If you don't move, I won't have to do this," he replied.

The sight sent chills down Cora's spine. How had she never seen this before? How could she have revered such a custom? Was this this the true face of Aratian honor and duty?

For the first time in her life, Cora questioned the wisdom of the Matching.

27. DIONE

Dione looked at the shuttle's camera feeds displaying the destroyed Ficaran settlement. She'd been there days ago, but now it was unrecognizable. The buildings were still standing, sure, but the town was marked.

She could see scorch marks and debris, and what could only be bodies. She even saw a bunch of green dots in the streets. Dead Vens.

Benjamin and Moira were silent. Benjamin got up and moved to the front of the Flyer. Dione was alarmed at first, but it became clear that he just wanted to see it with his own eyes.

The First Geneticist looked surprised, like he had expected the camera feeds to be a lie. Dione felt for the Ficarans. She had no idea what it must have been like, trying to escape from this place. She looked at Lithia, whose back was to her. What had happened to her and Brian as they tried to escape?

"There should be more Ven bodies," Lithia said. She took the Flyer for another pass over the town.

"I wish they were easier to kill, too, but—" Dione began.

"That's not what I mean. We killed more. I know we did."

Dione felt a shift in their movement. Lithia was taking them down.

"What's the meaning of this?" Benjamin said, taking up the communicator in his hand. Moira put her hand on his own, stopping him. She looked curious.

"Lithia, stop it. Take us to the Mountain Base," Dione said as calmly as she could.

"Just give me a minute," Lithia muttered. "I want to check something."

"Now's not the best time."

Benjamin looked angry, but Moira looked concerned.

Lithia set them down in the square. "Stay here. I'll be back in a minute. Di, give me your machete."

Now armed, Lithia headed off into the settlement. Dione was worried she would have to stall Benjamin, who looked eager to use his shiny, new communicator, but Lithia was back in just a few minutes. In fact, she was sprinting.

A Ven, moving more slowly than Dione would have expected, was in pursuit. Benjamin and Moira watched, agape.

Dione didn't wait to hop into the copilot seat. "Stay put," she said to the two passengers. Twenty seconds later, when Lithia arrived, everything was ready for take off.

"They aren't really dead, Di," Lithia said as she leapt aboard. "That one back there was in some sort of stasis, healing itself."

"That's... good to know," Dione said. She glanced back at Benjamin and Moira, who looked alarmed. Maybe this would help the talks?

Once back in the air, Lithia did not linger over the broken town. Soon the mountain was looming ahead of them. Lithia landed, and the professor was right outside the shuttle, waiting for them. He was wearing his own StellAcademy uniform so that he stood out among the Ficarans.

"Where's Zane?" he asked, furrowing his brow as he peered into the empty shuttle behind them.

"He volunteered to stay behind as a hostage with Colm," Dione said. "He wanted to see if he could fix any of their equipment with the spare parts he found here."

"Well, that was very nice of him, wasn't it?" Professor Oberon said, looking pointedly at the Aratian newcomers. A moment later, he was smiling again, welcoming them.

"This is Benjamin Bram," Dione said.

"I'm Elian Oberon of the *Calypso*," the professor said, motioning to his ship. "And you are?" He addressed the woman who had come with Benjamin.

"Moira," she said, giving him a terse smile and a nod. She and Benjamin stared at the *Calypso*.

Dione tried to imagine what they might think of the professor's ship. It was much larger than the Flyers, and it looked completely different. From their uniforms to his ship, Professor Oberon was trying to show them that he and his students were a third party. They were not on a side, no matter what Benjamin might think. Even so, Dione didn't think it was working.

"Victoria is in a conference room on one of the upper levels, if you'd like to get started," Professor Oberon said.

"Please. I'd like to get back as soon as possible," Benjamin said.

"I heard you have the body of one of these... Vens," Moira said. "I'd prefer to examine it, if you could point me in the right direction."

The professor gave Dione and Lithia a look. *Should we let her?*

Lithia nodded at him. "Moira is a scientist. She was working on replicating the anti-parasitics we used to cure Bel."

"Before you stole my sample, little thief. I'd like that back as well," Moira said, though she sounded more amused than angry.

"Bel can help you," Dione said. "She's already begun the dissection. She's the one we saved with the anti-parasitics," she added, in hopes it would help Moira excuse their crime.

Professor Oberon led them inside, past the armed guard at the entrance. Dione saw Benjamin shift uncomfortably. Inside was the confusion of ongoing triage and the treatment of minor injuries, though it was much more subdued than the night's chaos, from what she understood. Some were sleeping, but many had been sent down to the apartments in the lower levels.

Benjamin and Moira looked around the atrium, eyes wide, mouths closed. They seemed shocked. Even frightened.

Good. They should be. Maybe seeing so many wounded would make Benjamin approach these negotiations with the gravitas necessary to save this colony. From what Dione had seen so far, Benjamin was not a fighter. Hopefully that meant his ego would not prevent him from coming to an agreement.

"These are the minor injuries that still need monitoring. Down that hallway are the more serious injuries," the professor said.

While the professor showed the others around the atrium, Dione found Bel asleep in a chair at the entrance to what they had deemed the trauma ward. She reached out to wake her, but hesitated. Bel started awake on her own, like she could feel someone's eyes watching her. Dione wanted to tell her to get some rest, but now was not the time.

Bel arched her back and rotated her shoulders in a slow stretch. "Hey, you're back," she said. "Zane stayed behind, then?"

"You don't sound surprised," Dione said.

"No, he said he wanted to. Asked for help finding some supplies to take."

Dione crossed her arms. "Thanks for the heads-up," she said.

Bel rolled her eyes. "Like you could have done anything about it. He wants to help, and he has the skills. If you knew Zane a little better, you wouldn't be surprised either."

Dione backed down. The more she had gotten to know Zane, the more she had grown to respect him, both his talents and his desire to help others.

At that moment, the professor led the others over and made introductions. "Bel, this is Moira, an Aratian scientist. She would like to see the Ven body," the professor said.

"I want to understand what makes them tick, what their weaknesses are, and I am, of course, curious in general about what we have always called demons," Moira said.

Bel sized her up before responding. "I'll show you what records we have and then let you examine the body we brought back. It's in the lower levels. They're sealed to everyone right now, but I can take you there. Come on."

"You can also give her the anti-parasitics," Lithia said. "She's replicating them. Some Aratians are already infected with the parasite, and I imagine a few Ficarans are, as well. We'll need more than is left in that vial." Lithia nodded to Moira, whose shoulders relaxed just a little.

"This way," Bel said, leading their guest toward the lift.

"I met Moira when I was being held prisoner at the Vale Temple," Lithia said to the professor. "She seems like a good person, like she genuinely wants to help."

Benjamin scoffed. The professor nodded at Lithia, but didn't reply. Dione wished her friend wouldn't antagonize Benjamin, though she had good reason not to trust him. In another few minutes, they reached the conference room where Victoria stood, rather than sat, behind the table.

As soon as she saw Benjamin, she asked, "Where's Michael?"

There was no diplomacy in her voice, but also no artifice. She would not try to coax compliance with her words, though Dione didn't doubt she was still capable of manipulation.

"He took the cavalry to address threats to our supply Hubs, but you wouldn't know anything about that, would you?" Benjamin said.

"Of course, I would," she said. "I led the raids myself. Compliments on the dried polla. Well done to retain so much of the flavor." Benjamin bristled at this, but didn't rise to the bait. "But what keeps him away now? As you can see, we're no longer a threat."

"I won't underestimate what your people are capable of. Michael picked up the trail of the demons while he was out. He sent back the machi as runners after the first skirmish. He's still in pursuit."

Dione didn't like the sound of that. The Vens were the hunters, not the prey. Something was not right.

"How many?" Professor Oberon asked.

"Nearly forty on maximute, and another two dozen on machi."

"I mean, how many Vens?"

"A dozen," Benjamin said.

"Sounds like a large scouting party," the professor said.

Even the Vens wouldn't like those odds, but Dione didn't believe the Vens were just fleeing. Were they leading the defenders away to make the Aratians more vulnerable? Or were they leading them to something?

Victoria took back control of the conversation. "Let's have a seat and get to business." She sat and motioned for Benjamin to do the same. Professor Oberon took the seat opposite Victoria, the one which she had indicated for Benjamin. She looked annoyed, but the professor smiled.

"Elian? There's no need for you to stay," Victoria told him.

"I'd like to offer myself as a mediator. My years as department chair have unfortunately provided plenty of relevant experience. Though I have to say, these circumstances present a unique set of challenges." When Victoria opened her mouth to protest again, the professor held up a hand to cut her off. "Besides, one of my students is currently being held hostage on the condition of this man's safety. I won't be going anywhere."

Victoria nodded her reluctant approval.

"And these children?" Benjamin asked, gesturing to Dione and Lithia, who took the seats on the left, leaving the last one for Benjamin. Victoria had clearly wanted Benjamin directly opposite her, but having him to her side, closer, might make this meeting less confrontational.

"They have each spent time in your settlements. They are here to help me understand you both," the professor said.

"And how do I know you're not working with the Ficarans?" Benjamin asked.

"I obviously am. My students helped them evacuate and get set up in this base. But I want to work with you, too. You saw my ship outside. The *Calypso*. You must have noticed it's nothing like your Flyers. Whether you want to admit it or not, you know that I'm not from around here."

"But you can't expect me to believe you're a neutral party," Benjamin said.

The professor jabbed a finger into the table. "I have one goal, to protect my students. That means stopping the Vens, which is what we're here to discuss. Let's get started."

Victoria spoke first. "I asked them to fly you over the Field Temple on your way here because I wanted you to see that all of this is real."

"And get me killed in the process? The demons are still out there."

Victoria raised an eyebrow, and Lithia interjected. "I landed there for a few minutes. Some of the Vens are regenerating. I watched one come back to life with my own eyes."

Oberon shook his head, and Victoria's frown deepened. "So the rumors among the rescue teams are true," she said. "It doesn't change anything. Our home is gone. The Temple stands, but a third of us are lost. One third. I wanted you to meet me here so that you could see what we're up against. I do not show you the wounds of my people lightly, and I won't pretend that this meeting magically erases the hatred I have for you and your brother. Do not mistake this for something that it is not, but do not believe that the Ven threat can go unanswered. I put my anger at the Aratians before anything else, and I failed to protect my people. There are innocents among your ranks that I would not see harmed. Do not make my mistake."

Victoria meant every word, and Benjamin could tell. He sat there in silence for a moment, finding the words he wanted.

"I believe you. I believe that these demons are a great threat. Michael would agree, I'm sure, if he were here. But the question is, what do we do about it? Our people will not work together easily. But if you loaned us, or traded us, some of your weapons, we might—"

"Ficaran guns do not leave Ficaran hands. They are our only insurance against you."

"I thought that the demons were a threat to us all. Can't you help us defend ourselves, and by extension, Ficarans? You have the Flyers now. If there is to be peace between Aratians and Ficarans, there must be a balance of power. The Flyers have tipped that balance, you must agree."

"Our home was destroyed. We are at an even greater disadvantage than before! Ficaran guns do not leave Ficaran hands."

Dione could see this was spiraling fast, but Professor Oberon was there, ready to redirect them. "Victoria, what do you propose then, in terms of working together?"

"I had hoped their cavalry might be able to help, since I've heard how effective maximutes are against these Vens, but now I doubt that their cavalry is still alive. They have a fortified position, and we can reasonably expect the Vens to attack there next. It's the next opportunity to defeat the demons."

"But what are you offering, if not your weapons?" Benjamin said.

"I never said we wouldn't offer weapons, only that the guns stay in Ficaran hands."

"You're suggesting that I allow armed Ficaran soldiers inside the walls?" Benjamin laughed. "That's absurd."

"I'm suggesting an alliance," she said.

"More like a coup," Benjamin said.

"Benjamin, all we've ever wanted is our freedom."

"That's why you robbed our supply Hubs and spilled Aratian blood?"

"Michael is the one who starved the dog and taught it to bite. Before the embargo, we lived in relative peace."

Benjamin said nothing to this. "If you betray us, we will show no mercy. How many armed men?"

"Sixty armed men and women. We have many wounded."

"I hardly know whether to be glad or concerned to accept so few armed Ficarans to my settlement."

"Sixty soldiers, but there's another condition," Victoria said.

"A condition? Please, tell me what else besides access to the settlement you could possibly want."

"I want you to stop the Matching." Victoria did not smile as she stared him down. Dione felt Lithia tense next to her.

Benjamin laughed. "You must be joking! You know we'll never agree to that. Half the reason I came here is because we need to keep our losses low on both sides to preserve our genetic diversity."

Victoria wrinkled her nose in disgust. "The Matching is the worst kind of crime. Girls groomed for child bearing, boys and men forced into bonds they do not wish to honor. All for a madman's plan for Kepos."

"You may put no stock in the Farmer's vision, but all of the texts are quite clear about the dangers of a small population. One day, the Matching will no longer be necessary, but until that day comes, Aratians will perform their sacred duty in the Matching. It would be barbaric to let our people suffer from genetic diseases that we can prevent."

"Then give them a choice. Instead of having our smugglers handle those wishing to flee, let your people choose. There will be pressure from parents and society, but do not condemn those who are ill-suited to be sheep to your flock."

"You'll gladly take the wolves, I'm sure," Benjamin said. He was silent for some time, deep in thought. Dione thought it was a good sign until he spoke again.

"How much ammunition do you have left?" Benjamin asked.

"Enough," Victoria said, but even Dione could tell she had answered too quickly.

"The raids and the demon attacks must have significantly drained your supplies. Do you still have no way of making more?"

Dione sensed where he was going with this, and Victoria would not like it. The professor took a breath, like he was about to interject, but Victoria answered.

"Even if I send armed men to the Vale Temple, I will not leave my own defenseless. We will have bullets enough to defend ourselves if you're stupid enough to attack us after the Vens are defeated. Don't lose sight of the main threat."

"I think you'd be wise to heed your own advice," Benjamin said. "This whole negotiation has felt more like blackmail than an alliance."

"I'm not interested in how you feel. I want to know, can we come to an arrangement?"

Victoria leaned back in her chair and crossed her arms. Benjamin continued to sit in silence, making a show of thinking. His contemplation worried Dione. Each was still looking for weaknesses in the other to exploit. They kept trying to negotiate what things would be like *after* the Vens were taken care of. Both believed there would be an after.

Time was running short, and she was beginning to doubt if two people with such different worldviews could ever come to an agreement, even with a threat as compelling as the Vens. The Vens could be at the Vale Temple as early as that evening, and they needed to make plans, alliance or not.

28. BEL

Bel rolled her eyes. She didn't have time to babysit some Aratian. "This way to the *demon*."

"They're not demons, are they?" Moira said.

Bel looked at her. Was this a test? Was Moira looking for a reason to cause problems? "No, they're not."

"What are they?"

"Aliens. From a distant part of the galaxy."

"How do you know this?"

Bel was tired of the Ficaran and Aratian ignorance. She was going to call an alien an alien, and a liar a liar.

"The Farmer lied to all of you. He brought your people here, oppressed them, and made up a bunch of crap for you to believe in. Humans have our own corner of the galaxy out there, and this planet is on the edge of it."

Moira didn't look surprised. "How many worlds?"

"A lot," Bel said. Moira hadn't even blinked. "You're taking this well."

"The Farmer left a lot of gaps in his story. Many of us have little reason to want to believe it, and you'd be amazed how easy it is to just... stop."

"Are you saying that most Aratians don't believe in the story about the Farmer?"

"No, not most. But we exist. Most people keep quiet about it."

"So Michael doesn't find out."

"Yes, though he knows about my own doubts. I'm just lucky enough to be indispensable to him."

That was unexpected. If people like Brian and Moira among the colonists had doubts, and there were more just like them, there was hope for explaining the truth to them after all. The Ficarans had accepted it easily, but they were predisposed to disbelieve the Farmer's version of things. She imagined the Aratians would be a tougher audience.

As soon as Bel was on the lift with Moira, she produced a small vial from her pocket. "I never asked them to steal it, you know," she said, handing the anti-parasitics to Moira. "I told them not to come down to the planet's surface."

Moira looked puzzled. "But the infection would have killed you."

"I'm glad to be alive, trust me, but I would have done things differently."

Moira said nothing, but inspected and pocketed the vial.

They arrived at the small lab where Bel had locked up the juvenile Ven. She also had an adult Ven on ice that the Ficarans had retrieved at her request. She'd wanted to compare the two. She'd also been hoping that a fresh adult would be in better shape, but the Ficarans had brought her one dotted with bullet wounds. She checked that they had severed the neural membranes, too, just to be sure.

Bel pulled up the records of Ven physiology so Moira could review the basic anatomy.

"Fascinating," Moira said. "Are those all redundancies?" She was looking at the Ven organs. There were multiples of almost every vital organ. Even the brain was segmented in such a way that damage to one area was not lethal. Vens were filled with biological backup systems.

"They also have regenerative abilities, but we're not sure how they do it."

"Some gland that releases a stimulant?" Moira said.

"None that we've found. The Ven specimens examined also have some slight differences in the scope of their redundancies."

"So, the difference between having one extra heart versus two?" Moira asked.

"Basically. Some of them even have two separate circulatory systems, each with multiple hearts pumping their blood."

"Hmm… Could it be a result of rapid evolution? We see that here fairly often."

"How rapid?" Bel was curious now.

"We've seen a few of the pests and controllers go through cycles of it. It's my primary job, actually. Monitor the harvests, make sure that any problems that arise stay in check. A few years back, there was a blight of corn grylls that had me sweating."

"Grylls?"

Moira tilted her head and smiled. "It's a small insect, like a cricket. Normally, the gryll snakes would keep the population in check, but the grylls adapted to produce a pheromone very similar to that of another insect poisonous to the gryll snake."

"You're talking about allomones?"

"Yes!" Moira seemed genuinely excited. "When one organism uses a chemical signal that benefits itself but harms the receiver, it's called an allomone. So few people care to understand the difference."

Bel smiled, too, despite herself. Moira was actually pretty cool.

"The gryll snakes didn't eat the corn grylls, and didn't find an alternative food source. They started starving. Eventually, they started eating the grylls again, and taking the risk. Some ate the harmless grylls, others ate the poisonous insects. The ones who survived had a natural immunity to the poison, so the resulting offspring of the survivors had an overall higher chance of surviving an encounter with a poisonous insect."

That was fascinating. Moira was doing exactly the kind of thing she had always dreamed of, using her knowledge to help colonists on the edge of the Bubble. Blights on the Rim could wipe out entire colonies, but a competent scientist using a carefully calculated intervention could solve a problem like corn grylls. It had resolved on its own here, but not every colony was so lucky.

Bel had almost forgotten about the Vens and rapid evolution, which had started this whole tangent.

"As awesome as rapid evolution is, it doesn't usually appear in species that reproduce slowly. It takes multiple generations to see a change. It's led to the theory that Vens reproduce frequently, and in high numbers, since they accept such high casualty rates. Others just think that the Vens used to live in more isolated cohorts and the differences we see are a result of long-term adaptations to different environments."

"That sounds plausible," Moira agreed.

"We really don't know as much about these Vens as we'd like. We don't know why they attack primarily to kill."

"Is it to gather resources?" Moira asked.

"To an extent, but they want more than resources. They want to fight. They force fights and sow chaos with their bites, creating a risk to themselves. A bitten enemy is stronger and more aggressive, but they do it anyway. It doesn't seem to be done out of honor, trying to give their enemy a chance. They want to force their prey to fight back or create a distraction when they've got the disadvantage. People who are bitten will attack anyone."

"What do you mean?"

"When they bite you, they inject you with a chemical that causes you to overproduce adrenaline to dangerous levels. There are some other components that may cause hallucinations."

Moira's eyes widened in disbelief. "There has to be a reason the Vens attack with so little provocation. With a sentient species, I guess it could be anything really. Cultural motivations don't always make sense."

"Very true. If there is a reason, we don't know it yet," Bel said. She considered sharing her Ven hypothesis, that they were prey, but decided against it. She didn't see how it would help Moira and the Aratians survive.

Moira studied her for a long moment, which made Bel uncomfortable. She broke the silence. "Let's get to it." Despite the fact that Moira seemed like a decent human being, she wanted to get this over with and get Zane back. That thought stopped her in her tracks.

"What is it?" Moira asked.

"One of the people who stayed behind at the Vale Temple…" she began.

"The young man?" Moira took her silence as confirmation. "Your friend will be okay. With Michael gone, they won't hurt him. They won't risk Benjamin's life," Moira said. "Or mine."

Bel nodded. "Thanks." Of all the colonists she'd met so far, she thought she could trust Moira.

"Green or blue first?" she asked.

Moira gave her a puzzled look.

"We've got an adult, which is green, and the juvenile that attacked our ship, which is blue."

"Green. From what I've been told, the adults are the ones attacking the colony, and the demons from the stories are green."

Bel and Moira retrieved the green Ven from cold storage. After their talk, Bel had warmed up to Moira a bit more. She handed Moira a cover-up and mask before donning her own. This would be messy.

First Moira inspected the green plating, examining the intervals of fused and open plates. "Is there a pattern to which plates are fused?" she asked.

"Not really," Bel replied. "Usually one of the first two plate gaps is open—the best way to kill a Ven."

She ran back to the *Calypso* for a small saw and let Moira open the Ven up so she could see just how tough the plating was. This particular Ven was pockmarked with at least six bullets to the chest and one to the head.

It already smelled bad, but when Moira opened its chest cavity, the reek overpowered her. She staggered back and coughed.

"That's not decomp," she said once she recovered herself.

"No," Bel said, "they were born this way."

The chest cavity was full of fluid, so Bel helped Moira clear it out.

Even after suctioning the fluid, it was difficult to make much sense of the organs. Several had been damaged.

"So these pump blood," Moira said, pointing to the two hearts at opposite ends of the chest cavity.

"Yes, they work on two different circulatory systems so that if one is damaged, blood still makes it through the body. It's not exactly blood, but it performs the same function."

Moira leaned in to look more closely at the wounded heart. "What's this discoloration?"

"Scar tissue," Bel said. "Remember those regenerative properties I was talking about?"

Moira's eyes grew wide. "This scarring is from yesterday?" she said.

"Probably. That's why it's so hard to actually kill them. Even if they're down, they might not be dead. The body keeps making repairs as long as it can, and if the damage isn't too severe, they survive."

Moira continued examining the Ven's entrails. She sighed in frustration. "It's so hard to get a clear look at anything with all the bullet wounds. Weren't there any that didn't get shot a bunch of times?"

"I don't know. The Ficarans brought me the body when I asked. We did kill that blue one I mentioned when it attacked the *Calypso*. Even with the refrigeration, it's begun to decay. No bullet wounds, though."

"How'd you manage that?" Moira asked.

"We knocked it out with gas and severed its neural connections with a machete through two unfused plates in the back. Except it survived, nearly killed me, bit Zane, and took two people to kill it when it was already injured."

"So it's not a method we could try to replicate."

"I don't recommend it, no," Bel said. "Especially because it was just a juvenile."

Moira inspected the blue Ven. "This Ven has a different symbol painted on its face," she said. "The other had three parallel lines, but this…" Moira trailed off and looked up at Bel, who felt the spiral cut on her cheek burning.

Bel tensed and kept her eyes on the Ven, its spiral design drawing her gaze. She braced herself for the question.

"Can you hand me the saw?"

She looked up puzzled for a moment, but this time it was Moira who was looking down. Bel relaxed her shoulders and handed over the saw. Moira had figured it out and decided there was no need to ask.

Bel watched with interest as Moira went straight for the brain. The juvenile had not been shot, so the brain, aside from the neural connections, should be mostly intact.

"This is strange," Moira said. "I wanted to see how the brain was segmented, but look at this."

Bel looked where Moira was pointing. It was hard to see, but there was a small composite disc, the size of a coin.

"What is it?" Moira asked.

"I don't know," Bel said. Zane could figure it out, but she bet Oberon could, too. "We don't have any records on these, at least none that the public has access to." She quickly checked the classified data that Zane had sent her, but it yielded no results.

Though it was easy to miss in an exploratory dissection, she doubted the scans that Alliance pathologists took of dead Vens would have missed it. Why not include it in the public reports? What did this thing do?

Bel removed it and cleaned it with a cloth. "See if the big guy has one," she said, but Moira was already on it.

A few minutes later, Moira was cleaning off a second disc. Maybe whatever these were would give them an edge against the Vens, or at the very least, an insight.

"Thank you, Bel, for taking the time to teach me." Moira hesitated a moment, but smiled. "We have some exceptional ointments that kill infections in larger wounds, but they work wonders for smaller cuts. They heal so well you can't even see a scar most times."

Bel knew immediately what she was offering. The spiral cut on her face, still scabbed, would certainly scar. She would not pretend that this had never happened. When they did find a way home, her face would be on all the vids. A reminder.

"I'm grateful for the offer, but our scars make us stronger."

Moira bowed her head and sighed. "Some scars, yes."

29. ZANE

It had taken Zane a while to convince them to let him help. At first the guards ignored him, but when he showed them the spare parts he had brought, they had called over some other guy, presumably their boss. Then he went to find someone else, who brought along yet another young man, who finally looked like he knew what Zane was talking about. He didn't know whether it was bureaucracy that slowed them down, or if they didn't believe that their hostage wanted to help them for nothing in return.

"I knew the Ficarans were hoarding their tech supplies," the boss said.

"Actually, these supplies were in the Mountain Base. The Ficarans didn't have access to them until a few days ago."

The boss grumbled and prepared to leave with the supplies, but Zane locked eyes with him and said, "Let me help. If the Vens… the demons come here, you'll need as much of this stuff working as possible. Give me the unimportant stuff first, but let me help."

Colm laughed at him. "They're never gonna let you help, kid. You're a fool to offer. They'd rather roast in their own pot than let you take the kettle off the fire."

The boss frowned at that. The young man had a suggestion. "Maybe he could help fix some of the Ficaran lights. I see some bulbs in here. These supplies might be enough to restore some of the Artifacts. I've seen most of these supplies before, and I think we should use them if we can. Plus, without those Ficaran techs, we could use some help."

Zane wondered if he was talking about the same techs Lithia had freed when she took the shuttle to get Dione from the Field Temple.

"All right, take him to the graveyard," the boss said.

"The graveyard?" Zane said. He didn't like the sound of that.

"We've got a barn full of broken and dead Artifacts," the young man said. "I'm Diego, by the way."

"Zane."

The guards followed, bringing Colm along with them. Luckily, they saw him as the real threat and didn't bother Zane too much. Of course, Zane was also compliant and wasn't making rude jokes.

The graveyard was an enormous barn back near the wall. From the outside it was well kept, but once Diego slid open the double doors, Zane could see it was a complete mess. Somehow, based on everything he had heard, he wouldn't have expected this from the Aratians. The Ficarans, maybe. There were tables littered with gadgets, corners stuffed with boxes, and several farm vehicles parked haphazardly. Zane stopped in front of one monstrosity near the entrance. It was a giant tractor, and attached to the back was a device covered in fang-like blades.

"What is this?" he asked.

"Heavy tiller. They used to break up the soil and establish the farms on the steps." Diego gestured to the terraced hillside outside the walls. "It hasn't worked in over a decade. Here, help me with this."

Zane grabbed the other end of the floodlight Diego was carrying. They brought it out into the light where Zane's stuff was. Diego looked through what he had brought before selecting a replacement bulb. He held it up to Zane as if asking if he agreed, and Zane nodded.

"Here. Hold this steady while I remove the fasteners," Diego said. The light was designed to last a long time, but a good chunk of that time had already passed. Some of the tech that came from the bases was nearly a hundred years old. The newer stuff Jameson must have brought with him, but those things were aging, too, and with no new supply, they were breaking down. Zane wondered why Jameson hadn't brought a fabricator. They were expensive, sure, but he'd been able to afford a colonizer. It would have made sense to bring one along, especially since he would have known that he wouldn't be relying on trade for supplies.

Diego turned out not to be a talker, much like Zane. The two worked together in relative silence, repairing a few more floodlights before moving on to other small gadgets Diego brought out. Zane advised him to cannibalize some of them for parts in order to repair others, but Diego shook his head. "That's not something we do."

"Well, you should consider it, because a few of these things could work if you used other parts."

"The Farmer will provide. No need to destroy his Artifacts."

That explained a lot. A lot of this stuff could be usable. Hot plates, clocks, and Zane thought he even saw a holo-projector in the back. But they wouldn't sacrifice one piece of equipment to repair another.

"I think the Ficarans take broken Artifacts and use the parts."

"We're not Ficarans, are we?"

Zane thought he detected a hint of annoyance in Diego's voice. "Do you really think he would be mad?"

Diego shrugged.

Zane was actually enjoying this a lot. It was calming to work with something in his hands, find the problem, and repair it. Or, as the case often was, especially here, label it irreparable for the moment. Zane looked around for his next fix. The floodlights would help if the Vens attacked at night. The glowglobes he'd seen were beautiful, but just did not have the lumens to turn night into day. Looking around, he didn't see any weapons, but there could certainly be some in here, well hidden in the piles of crap. Somehow he doubted it. The Aratians would store broken guns somewhere off-limits to the general population.

His eyes settled back on the giant tiller. Yes, this was it. Right now, it had a safety bar blocking off its blades, but with the bar removed, the tiller could become a deadly, Ven-mowing machine.

"Diego, what's wrong with the tiller? Do you know?"

But Diego wasn't paying him any attention. His focus was on a young man close to Zane's age, who was talking to Colm's guards.

"Benjamin called. He wants me to ask these two a few questions. In private."

At first, they were reluctant, but the young man showed them something tucked into his waistband, and they nodded.

"Zane, we'll be back in a minute. Stay with Will," Diego said, sounding very annoyed. He motioned to the new guy, before following the guards off.

Will looked anxious, almost afraid, and he completely ignored Zane. He was focused on Colm. When Colm, who had been leaning against the barn, stood up, Will took a step back. Colm noticed and laughed.

"I don't bite," he said, "unless provoked. Why did you lie to those people? You told them Benjamin sent you."

"Why do you think I lied? We have the communicators, after all," Will said.

"Because you're bad at it. What do you want?" Colm said.

"I want to leave. I want to go with you to the Field Temple."

Colm stared at him a moment. "We were forced to leave the Temple when the Vens attacked. Our settlement is in ruins."

"Then let me help rebuild," Will said. "Please. There's nothing for me here."

"Another victim of the Matching, then?" Colm's voice was softer than usual. "Tell me."

"My girl, she was matched with someone else."

"Is she going to come with you?"

Zane realized he was not watching a hypothetical conversation. Colm was actually planning to get this guy out.

"I don't think that's an option."

"There's always an option for victims of the Matching. I am proof. Many Ficarans are proof."

"What made you leave?" Will asked.

Colm paused for a moment as if deliberating how much of his story to tell.

"I never wanted to be matched. I didn't want to marry. I was in love with a man who had not been matched, and when I got married, he couldn't stand it. He left. He tried to get me to come with him, but I was too afraid.

"At first, I tried to perform the duties of a husband, but after he left, I couldn't. Luckily, my wife was already pregnant, so I was left alone. But soon, she began complaining loudly to the others.

Shaming me. Everyone hated me, and I hated myself. Except for my sister and my daughter. Victoria and I talked about leaving, but she was afraid she wouldn't make it out. She was almost sixteen, so she destroyed the only thing of value in an Aratian woman so she wouldn't be kept. We left on the day of her Matching with a few others. I took my daughter. She cried and cried and cried for her mother, but I knew that one day she would thank me for freeing her. For giving her a choice."

Colm looked angry but resolved. Zane was willing to bet he had told that story before to Aratians with doubts. The Ficarans had needed numbers. At least, until their food shortage started.

"So your daughter doesn't have a mother?" Will said. There was judgment in his voice.

"No, she has two fathers. My story has a happy ending."

"Mine won't. My girl can't leave."

"Everyone feels like that. If she is truly as unhappy with her Match as you claim, she can leave, too."

"I don't think they would take the escape of Michael's daughter lightly." Will looked closely at Colm when he said this.

Cora. The guy was talking about Cora. Even Colm looked taken aback.

"That would be difficult, you're right. We don't have the resources to protect her. We don't even have the resources to protect ourselves at the moment."

"Even if you rebuild?"

Colm frowned. "Rebuilding will take time, resources, and manpower. The Vens hit us hard. We lost so many, and if you still wish to join us, we welcome you, but it will have to wait until the Vens are gone. We have learned a difficult lesson. I am only here as a hostage because the Vens are a bigger threat than any of us realized."

"Is it really that bad?" Will said.

Colm put a hand on Will's shoulder. "Here, they want you to feel safe. That is how they keep you sheep. They tell you stories of wolves, like me, to frighten you, and now that the true wolves are here, you do not believe that they will rip you to pieces. The Vens could kill us all. I've seen them, and in all my life, I've never been so afraid as when they were tearing down my world around me. Do you think I'd come back here—to this place I hate—for anything other than a deadly threat to everyone on Kepos? Do you think I'm here to save Aratian lives?"

Will said nothing.

"I'm here to save Ficarans, and that means working with the Aratians."

Will turned to Zane, as if noticing him for the first time. He wanted something. Reassurance? He looked so pale.

"It's true," Zane said, stepping away from the tiller. "The only way to stop the Vens is by working together. If your people really think that they can brush this threat off, then we'll all die."

"You're Zane, aren't you?" Will asked, cocking his head slightly. "Cora told me about you."

"Nothing good, I'm sure."

"You're friends with Lithia. Cora told me about where you claim to come from."

"Lithia told the truth. The Farmer was just a man. The Architect was just a woman. They were people, just like us."

"The Artifacts?" Will said, gesturing to the barn behind Zane.

"The components aren't magical. They just obey the laws of the universe. There's so much more out there than you can imagine."

Diego and the guards returned. Will gave Colm a meaningful look, nodded to Diego, and left.

The guards had apparently gone to get a snack, and offered Zane and Colm some crackers and dried fruit. The food tasted completely unfamiliar to Zane, but he ate it gratefully. He hadn't realized how hungry he was.

He got back to work. The sun was past its peak in the sky, but there was still a good chunk of daylight left. The days here were long. Zane took a break and wiped the sweat from his brow. He noticed Colm staring out across the town, deep in thought. His silence was deeper after their conversation with Will.

Zane couldn't imagine what it must be like for Colm to be back here, as a hostage no less. "Do you have any good memories from growing up here?" he asked.

"A few," Colm replied. "But they aren't the ones that stick out."

30. DIONE

"You don't have to solve all of your disputes today. You only have to figure out a way to work together for a few days," Professor Oberon said. It was the third time he had said it, by Dione's count. She was beginning to doubt that these two would be able to come to an agreement. Every time they got close, something pulled them off track.

Dione needed a break from the bickering, so the knock on the door came as a welcome interruption. Victoria and Benjamin stopped glaring at each other long enough to glare at the door.

Dione opened it, and Moira and Bel entered the room. Lithia pulled up a chair from the corner for Bel, who was holding something in her closed hand. Moira grabbed her own chair and moved it next Benjamin. She didn't wait for an invitation to speak.

"The demons, or rather Vens, are incredibly strong. Their plating is almost impenetrable. The cavalry's *pila* blades will not be effective. Any blows will glance off unless they are at the joints. Their organs are redundant, which explains why the Farmer and his men had such trouble defeating them. Even their brains are segmented to have redundancies. The threat is real, Benjamin. Michael would want you to act."

Benjamin seemed annoyed by the mention of his brother. "Michael wouldn't give up everything sacred to us for a few guns that won't do any good." Dione watched Benjamin check Victoria's reaction. He was trying to rile her, and the nasty frown she threw back told Dione it was working.

Bel, however, was staring at him. He seemed to notice and turned to her. She opened her closed fist to reveal a small white disc. Benjamin and Victoria looked unimpressed.

"Bel, what do you have there?" Professor Oberon said.

"I'm not sure. Moira found it attached to the juvenile's brain," she said, placing the disc in the professor's palm. "There was an identical device in the adult. We checked. If Zane were here, he could tell us."

"Lightweight. Small. I'll run it through some tests on the *Calypso* to find out what it is," the professor said.

"Do you think it will help us?" Dione asked.

"Until we figure out what it is, I've got no idea. Good work, Bel. And Moira," Professor Oberon said. He nodded to her. Dione thought Moira seemed like the most reasonable one of the three Kepos natives. Maybe her presence would moderate things.

"So if it's agreed that the Vens are a true threat, then what is the best way to defeat them?" Dione said.

Bel spoke up again. "Sam, can you use the Icon to kill any of the Vens?"

There was a long pause before Sam spoke. "The Icon is…" She trailed off.

"Sam?" Lithia said.

"I'm sorry, my attention is divided. I am walking one of the doctors through a surgery. The Icon can only hit targets above a certain altitude. It cannot be used for attacks on the ground."

Everyone around the table frowned. Dione worried about Sam. She was not used to doing so much. She was just beginning to realize the toll that caring for all these Ficarans was taking on her.

Benjamin looked worried as well, but for a different reason.

"Who is Sam? How could you forget to mention you have control over the Icon?" His eyes were wide as he leaned forward and looked around the room. Moira looked surprised, too, but relaxed back into her chair.

Professor Oberon sighed, but Dione knew he was going to tell the whole truth. "Samantha is the artificial intelligence, the AI, that controls this base and the Icon, the weapon which is installed here. They," he said, motioning to Dione and Lithia, "repaired it and used it to destroy one of the Ven ships that came here. Sam is currently coordinating the Ficaran refugees, which keeps her busy."

Moira arched her eyebrows. "Anything else?" Somehow Moira knew already.

"Sam was the Architect before joining herself to the AI here."

"And you didn't think to mention this?" Benjamin said. "Is that why you wanted me to come here, to be at her mercy?"

Victoria was losing her patience, Dione could see. "I've already explained my reasons for inviting you here."

"Enough, both of you," Moira said. "We are running out of time. If this AI hasn't killed us yet, I doubt she'll start now. Victoria, what do you need in return for the guns?"

"I would send armed men, not trade the guns themselves."

"Very well, what do you need, then?"

"I want the end of the Matching."

Moira laughed and turned to the professor. "I can see why the talks have stalled, Elian. Victoria, you know that the Matching is not something that Aratians can give up so easily. Tell us what you need, not what you want, because you need this alliance as much as we do."

"We need food, freedom, and a chance to rebuild."

"You have taken some of those things already, but I have a suggestion. We can negotiate a deal to include food and a temporary peace while you rebuild, but what if I could show you how to restore your farmland so that you can be independent once again?"

Benjamin interrupted. "No, Moira, you're giving them too much."

"Benjamin, she's offering to send her people to die for ours. Our offer must convey our gratitude without compromising our values. What do you say, Victoria?"

"I'm interested," Victoria said.

"Good, the process of phytoremediation takes many years, but in the end, your farmland will be usable again."

Dione gasped in excitement at the word phytoremediation. The professor also seemed impressed with Moira's ingenuity. Dione suspected that she had been working on this proposal for a long time, and was just now getting the chance to pitch it. It sounded like she didn't have permission to offer it, though.

"Years? That's hardly a fair deal."

"Perhaps not, but that's how nature works. Phytoremediation uses plants to remove the toxins from the earth. You will keep control of all the Flyers throughout the process, except for one, which you will give to us as a sign of good faith, along with the help of your armed men against the Vens."

Victoria thought about it for a long time. It didn't sound like a bad deal to Dione. In a few years, they wouldn't have to rely on the Aratians for food, but in the meantime, the Ficarans would no longer starve. They would also have time to rebuild.

"And you'll offer all of those Matched a choice, instead of imposing marriage on them," Victoria said.

Dione admired her dedication to this cause, but she doubted the Aratians would budge on such a central tenet of their culture.

Moira thought a moment. Benjamin took her silence as an invitation to speak, but she shook her head. *Amazing how he listens to her.*

"Victoria, we can't. Michael would never allow it, but consider this. Everyone already has a choice. They know that the Field Temple would welcome them if they left. They know there is an alternative. While I understand this is not the same thing, there are many Aratians who are dedicated to the Matching and what they owe to their people. That's the best we can offer."

Victoria pursed her lips. Dione could see the wheels turning in her mind. It was not enough. Nothing except complete compliance would be enough for her, but she saw that this was the only choice. Victoria had seen enough death at the hands of the Vens to agree to this proposal.

"Fine. We have a deal. Michael will honor it, as well?"

"Yes," Benjamin said. "You have my word."

Lithia's shoulders relaxed, and Dione let out an audible sigh, as if she'd been holding her breath. Bel, on the other hand, did not relax.

"Good. Now that you've agreed to work together, you need a plan. Moira has seen what you're up against. Do you have anything that might work against them?" Bel said.

Moira and Benjamin exchanged a knowing glance. If Dione noticed, she was sure Victoria had.

"What is it?" Bel asked.

"We have—" Moira began, but Benjamin interrupted.

"Moira, enough. You overstep your bounds."

"We need to incorporate anything of use in the defense of the Vale Temple," Professor Oberon said. Benjamin looked incredibly flustered, as if this whole negotiation had gotten away from him. Truthfully it had. Everyone, including Moira was staring at Benjamin.

"Tell them," she said. "It's our best weapon against these Vens."

Benjamin thought a moment before he spoke. "We have prepared some flaminaria vials."

This meant nothing to Dione, but Victoria slammed her palms on the table and stood up. "I knew it. I knew you were planning something. How many?"

"Enough to protect ourselves," Benjamin said, rising himself.

"With a preemptive strike," Victoria said. "You were planning an assault against us, weren't you?"

"You actually raided our supply Hub, and now you think *we* are the violent ones? You Ficarans are the biggest hypocrites!"

"We needed to steal food because you rejected our trade offers!" Victoria said. "We only used force when necessary. It's not even close to what you and Michael were planning to do with the flaminaria."

"Excuse me." Lithia interrupted before the dispute could gain any more steam. She directed her question toward Moira. "What's a flaminaria vial?"

"Flaminaria… I've heard that name before," Bel said. "In Sam's logs."

"It's a plant that, when dried and concentrated, becomes extremely volatile when mixed with water," Moira replied.

"It's an explosive?" Dione asked.

"Yes. It's localized, but extremely powerful. A small vial of the powder placed in a larger vial of water, if stepped on, could blow off an entire leg."

"Then we use it all. Take out as many Vens as we can with it. The fewer we have to face in close combat, the better off we are," Lithia said.

"How many vials do you have?" Victoria said.

Benjamin paused. "Almost a hundred."

Victoria scoffed.

"That could really make a dent in the Vens," Dione said.

"And what about the ones who make it to the walls?" Professor Oberon asked.

"They won't be able to get in," Benjamin replied.

"You hope that. The ones who make it inside the walls will answer to Ficaran bullets," Victoria said. "I'll prepare several squads of soldiers. If you've got a high vantage point, I'll coordinate from there."

Dione should have felt optimistic, or at least relieved, but she couldn't, not after that conversation. An agreement born of fear would be short-lived. She had doubts about whether this alliance could last days, let alone the years it would take for Moira to hold up her end of the bargain. With all of the tense situations that could rise up instantly in a battle, things could go very, very wrong.

31. CORA

Cora's world, so bright and organized just a few days ago, was completely in shambles. She had thought the Farmer was going to return. She had thought that the Matching would join her to Will, while her father watched with pride.

Instead, her father was still gone, she had not seen or spoken to Will since the Matching, and now the evening meals for the Matched couples had been postponed on her uncle's orders. Uncle Benjamin had returned and called an assembly to share the news.

"The demons have destroyed the Field Temple," he said. There was tepid clapping from some until Benjamin cut them off. "And they are coming here next."

"Can you be sure?" A grim voice rose from the front of the crowd, and a man stepped forward. "Can an enemy of the Ficarans truly be our enemy as well? Perhaps we can negotiate with them."

Cora recognized the man. His brown hair was slicked back against his scalp, accentuating his crooked nose. She tried to recall his name, but her uncle saved her the trouble.

"Elijah, I've seen the destruction myself, and these creatures are brutal beyond anything I could have imagined."

Elijah. The name was familiar. He had wanted to speak to her father about the demons before the cavalry left, but her father hadn't had the time.

Murmurs swept through the crowd, but Benjamin hushed them and continued. "We have formed an alliance with the surviving Ficarans."

Elijah pushed back at once. "That can't be wise. They were attacking us just yesterday!" Shouts of agreement rose up in the crowd.

"The Ficarans suffered heavy casualties. The demons forced them to flee their homes. Under normal circumstances, I agree it would be foolish to trust the Ficarans, but Moira examined the body of one of the demons, and the Farmer's accounts have not been exaggerated. It's unorthodox, but I promise that the demons are the real threat."

"I'd trust the demons before I trusted a Ficaran," muttered Elijah, loud enough for those around him to hear, but he settled back into the crowd.

Cora felt sick. The demons were coming, and there was a new alliance between the Field and Vale Temples. She didn't know which was worse.

***

Hours later, Ficarans with guns were stationed in the streets. Certain areas were still off-limits to them, of course, but they were being quartered in the public buildings by the market.

What made it worse was that Cora had no idea what to think. Before she met Lithia, her world was safe and logical. Now, she had questions. She had been able to ignore Lithia before, but now that Jai was her match, she didn't know what to do. Beliefs that had been crystal clear before were now out of focus. She couldn't see straight. She didn't know where to look, even.

No, that wasn't entirely true. She knew that there was only one way to be with Will, but she didn't think she could do it. There was no way she could leave her father, her home, and her responsibility. *Duty.* It was an Aratian virtue, and she was the future Regnator.

The Ficarans landed their Flyers in the open area where the stage had been just hours earlier. Cora had been watching them from a distance, their loose shorts and dull, sleeveless shirts out of place inside Aratian walls. Then, she saw someone else whose fitted pants and tight white tank top looked even more alien. *Lithia.*

Cora needed to talk to her. Lithia had the answers. Cora might not trust her, but she would listen this time. Doubt, she had begun to realize, was a powerful thing.

Cora caught her newly-discovered cousin on her way back to one of the Flyers. "Lithia, I need to talk to you."

The girl looked surprised to see her. "Last time I saw you, you shot me."

"I'm sorry."

"And tried to steal the meds that would save my friend."

"My people needed them, too."

"Now Moira has them back. There you go."

"I need you to tell me more about where you came from."

Lithia stopped walking and faced Cora. "You didn't want to listen before, and you don't want to listen now."

"I do, please," Cora said. This was not going well.

"Why? What changed? Finally believe us about the Vens now that they're knocking on your door?"

"The Matching. It's all wrong."

Lithia paused a moment and gave her a searching look.

"Of course, it's all wrong," she said. Cora shifted, uncomfortable under her gaze. "That's it, isn't it? You got matched with someone you don't like, and now you want out. How convenient that it only becomes a problem when it affects you."

"That's not fair," Cora said, blinking hard.

Lithia's expression softened. "I don't have time for this right now. We've got to set these flaminaria mines before we lose the daylight. The Vens are regrouping, based on Sam's satellite images, and we need to get these set up around the perimeter before they arrive."

Lithia's manumed came to life, and Cora recognized Dione's voice. "Come on, we're waiting on you."

Lithia brushed by Cora and hesitated. "Find me later. We'll talk." She jogged to one of the Flyers, which were beginning to take off, each filled with a mix of Aratians and Ficarans.

Left alone, Cora retreated to the overlook she liked to visit with Will. She reached the top, too out of breath to cry, only to find Will had had the same idea.

"Cora," he said, "I'm sorry I didn't come find you."

"Will, what are we going to do?" Cora said.

"There's nothing we can do. The Ficaran town was destroyed, and there's no way they could protect you. There's nowhere in the world we could be together." Will took her hand in his. "Do you think the visitors are telling the truth?" he asked. "That there are other worlds?"

"I don't know what to believe," Cora replied softly.

"That would change everything. It would make the Matching unnecessary, if there are other humans who can prevent population drift…"

Cora was beginning to understand the danger of believing what she wanted to believe, and Will's line of thinking felt like another trap. The problem was, Lithia's story made sense. She'd seen the *Calypso*. It was like nothing on Kepos. They had their own communicators. She had thought it was a sign from the Farmer, but now she just couldn't believe that.

"It would mean everything we've ever known was a lie," Cora said. "But where did they come from? They're not demons in disguise. We always thought the Farmer would come back, but he never has. And now, after the Matching, I just…"

"Don't want to believe anymore," Will finished her thought. "With all that's happening, I didn't want to say it, but more and more things aren't adding up. So what do we do?"

"I don't know yet. Lithia just told me that the demons are getting ready to come here. She calls them Vens and says that they're aliens," Cora said. It felt strange to repeat the things that Lithia had told her, now that she might believe them. It felt wrong. But looking down at the Aratians rushing around, everything had to be real. "I think we should help prepare the settlement. We might know about a few weaknesses in the walls that others don't."

"I bet Evy could help with that," Will said, laughing. "Your aunt still doesn't know how she escapes half the time when the sentries are told specifically to watch for her."

Cora matched his smile and looked into his eyes. She may never have another moment alone with Will. Once the demons were defeated and things returned to normal, she would have to marry Jai.

As if reading her thoughts, Will wrapped his arms around her in a long, warm embrace. When he let go, Cora refused. Instead, she stepped back just to look into his eyes once more.

It happened so fast she hardly had time to think, but Will leaned down and kissed her, his lips lingering on hers. Their first kiss. Cora couldn't bear for it to be their last.

***

When they found her, Evy was sprawled on the floor of her room, cheeks wet and red. She wiped her eyes when she saw Cora and Will enter. Evy rushed to give Cora a hug. She hadn't seen Evy since she came back in the middle of the Matching ceremony, and this explained it.

"Did Aunt Amelia lock you in here?" Cora asked. Evy sniffed and nodded. Her aunt wasn't going to let Evy escape again. As annoying as Evy was sometimes, like when she refused to come home with Cora, she hadn't meant to worry Amelia. Locking Evy up was the surest way to get her to run again. Cora had more than enough experience with her stubbornness.

"Well, you're free now. We want you to help us with something," Cora said.

"Like what?" Evy said, sniffing again. Cora could see she was calming down.

"The Vens are on their way here, so you really can't go running off, but we want you to help us block off any exits you use to leave the town."

Evy looked skeptical. "How do I know you won't tell my mom where they are?"

It was a fair question. It was something she would do. "I promise I won't."

"What if you get really mad at me?"

"Even if I get mad. Here." Cora kissed her palm and held it out to Evy. "Kiss on it?"

Evy studied her outstretched hand for a moment before kissing her own palm and wrapping Cora's hand in her own. "All right, come on."

Evy led them outside to a portion of the fence protected by a number of trees and bushes. This stretch of wall had a sentry tower, but it was rather far away, and the summer growth hid them well. Evy was examining the wall, looking for something when Will touched her shoulder and put a finger to his lips. She could hear it, too. Someone was coming. Cora beckoned to Evy, who joined her in hiding behind some shrubs. Maybe someone else had had the same idea, to look for weaknesses in the defenses. Still, she had promised not to give away Evy's secrets, and she wasn't inclined to explain what they were doing out there.

Cora didn't recognize the strangers' voices, even when they got closer. She couldn't tell how many there were in all, but she only heard two distinct voices.

"Do you see the mark?" a man asked. Cora thought she recognized the voice, but she couldn't place it.

"Yes, I've found it. You're sure they are using the flaminaria?" the woman asked.

"I've seen the empty storeroom myself, and the Ficarans are already here. We can't let this happen. It might be enough to stop the Vens, and we can't risk it," the man said. "They are our only hope of discovering the truth the Farmer kept from us."

"And the others have already left?" the woman said.

"Yes, or they will soon. We'll reconvene before we find our targets."

What in the world were they talking about? Cora peered through the bushes to see who was speaking, but the branches and leaves were too thick. All she could see were dark green cloaks. It was odd that they were wearing travel cloaks in the summer season.

One by one they passed through the wall. Cora could tell because their footsteps grew more distant. It sounded like five or six of them had passed through the wall.

"Who were those people?" Will said once they were out of earshot.

"I have no idea. What were they talking about?" Cora said.

"I don't know, but I've seen them once before," Evy said. "The green cloaks. I was out catching bugs. I hid, and they didn't see me. I thought they'd take me home if they found me."

When the coast was clear, they examined the wall again, and this time Evy found what she was looking for. Someone had removed a portion of the stone wall and replaced it with a wooden door disguised to look just like the wall. Carved into one of the stones was a symbol, a triangle with a spiral inside it. Cora thought she had seen it before, but couldn't remember where.

"This must be the symbol they were talking about, but what does it mean?" she said.

"I don't know. I've seen it before on my trips to the farms, carved onto trees in the woods, but I assumed it was something the Ficaran smugglers used to communicate. There's all kinds of graffiti in the forest," Will said.

Cora frowned. Were those Aratians in the green cloaks working for the Ficaran smugglers? If so, what were they up to?

"So how do we block this entrance?" she said.

"I brought along sealant. It's water tight and extremely strong. I thought we might have to patch an Evy-sized hole, not seal a door, but this should still work," Will said.

"What about the people who left?" Evy said. "They'll be stuck out there."

"They knew the risks. Uncle Benjamin warned everyone to stay inside the walls. They'll still be able to come through the main gate, anyway," Cora said.

Half an hour later, the secret door was sealed, and they were on their way back to the center of town. She offered to lock Evy back in her room before Amelia noticed, but Evy declined by running off into the market, which was packed with people buying up over a week's worth of supplies. Shopkeepers were packing up their wares, preparing to leave the shells of their businesses behind. They were taking Benjamin's warning to heart, which Cora thought was a good thing. They would be prepared. The Aratians had a plan.

After saying goodbye to Will, Cora ate dinner alone in her room that evening. She didn't want to feel her father's absence at the dinner table or suffer her aunt's wrath. They hadn't received any more news from the cavalry or her father, but she knew he was okay. The Ficaran Flyers had circled around looking for them, but hadn't seen anything. Cora looked out her window. The sun was low, still an hour from setting, and its golden warmth gilded the empty market, the walls, and the treetops beyond. He would send them word when he had news, and no sooner. Perhaps in the morning, he would already be home.

With that hope in her heart, Cora went to bed early.

32. DIONE

In the Flyer, Dione watched the video feed from the external cameras. Everything was green and alive, and it was hard to believe that the Vens were on their way.

It was a very short ride, but it was the safest way to transport the supplies. From what she could gather, it had taken a long time for the Aratians to harvest and refine the flaminaria plant into a concentrate that would explode when it came into contact with water. Dione wanted to know what kind of plant it was and how they isolated the compounds they needed, but the Aratians hadn't taken kindly to her questions, so she stopped asking.

After they landed, Dione grabbed her box of supplies and followed Lithia and the others to the area where they would be working. The Aratians knew the area very well, and they were designating specific avenues leading to and from the settlement that would be free from mines.

They had been briefed very specifically on how to assemble each explosive. First Dione checked the seal on the plant compound. She checked the glass vial for any cracks and added a small dab of Bolma resin at the top in case the seal was imperfect. Once the resin was dry, she would hand the glass vial to the next person, who would carefully place it in a second cylinder full of water before sealing it. The cylinders were made of some kind of flexible, biodegradable plastic. If stepped on, the cylinder wouldn't break, but the glass vial would, causing the flaminaria compound to come into contact with the water. They would react, then *boom*. Explosion.

Dione refused to let her mind wander while she worked. It was too important to check every single seal and to make sure that the water would not make premature contact with the compound. Brian and Bel had gone with a different group, but she imagined they were just as tense as she was. Lithia, on the other hand, looked distracted. She paused for half a minute, lost in thought, until Dione cleared her throat. Lithia snapped back to the task at hand.

"Lithia, if you need to take a break, you can go back to the shuttle. You had a long night."

"I'm fine, Di," Lithia replied, speeding up her work.

Two Aratian men were setting up the charges, and everyone else kept behind a certain line. Before they even began, they put up coded warnings for the cavalry that the area was booby-trapped. The Flyer had been parked at a distance so they wouldn't set off the charges when they left. Things were going smoothly, until Lithia fumbled one of the glass vials and it hit the ground with a clink. Lithia flinched, and everyone stood completely still and silent. The birds chirped on and the bugs hummed away, but no human breathed. The undergrowth was covered in evening dew, which could be finding its way through a crack in the vial as they waited.

"Don't move." The project manager, an older man, carefully picked up and examined the vial. "It's a crack," he said after inspecting it a moment, "but it didn't go all the way through. I'll put it in a dry, empty cylinder and pack it in the sawdust, just to be safe."

The group heaved a collective sigh and got back to work. The manager approached Lithia.

"Not you. Take a walk," he said, pointing back in the direction of the shuttle. Dione saw the rapid rise and fall of Lithia's chest. Something had been bothering Lithia ever since the Ficaran settlement fell, and whether or not she wanted to talk, she needed a break. She knew her best friend well enough to recognize that.

"I'll go with her," Dione said to the man in charge.

He nodded, frowning at them, as if he hadn't wanted them there in the first place.

Once they were out of earshot, Lithia began to cry.

"Talk to me, Lithia," Dione put a hand on her friend's shoulder. "Something's been bothering you."

"I can't take it anymore, Di. This place is a death trap. I almost killed everyone back there. If that vial had broken..." Lithia tried to hold in another sob. She closed her eyes hard, forcing more tears down her cheek. Lithia never cried. She had to hate every minute of this.

"But it didn't break. It's not your fault."

"Isn't it? I'm the one who brought us to this planet."

"You made the best decision you could with what you knew. And we know now that the Vens would have found this place sooner or later. This way, we can at least help."

"We might actually die here. I didn't believe it when we first arrived, but now it's all I can think about. I can't stop seeing his face, Di."

"What are you talking about? Did something happen at the Field Temple?" Dione asked.

Lithia stopped trying to hold in her sobs. She stopped walking and collapsed against the nearest tree, clutching her stomach.

"Roy. H-he's dead be-because of me."

Dione still wasn't sure what she was talking about, but she didn't ask. She wrapped her arms around Lithia and hugged her while she cried. Eventually Lithia hugged her back. After a few more minutes, the worst of it was over. Lithia took a few deep breaths before launching into the story.

"At the Field Temple, we had to fly out in Nate, even though he was a complete mess, because Victoria had sent away all the Flyers. There was this kid, Roy, who came at the last minute, but we couldn't take any more weight. The Vens were right behind him, and I left him. I was flying. We crashed in the lake anyway. We could have taken him, Di." More silent tears streamed down Lithia's cheeks.

"You can't blame yourself for that. How many people did you save?" Dione asked.

"I don't know," she whispered.

"Would the others have gotten out without you? Do you think any of them could have flown that shuttle in the shape it was in?"

Lithia shook her head. "No, I barely got us out of there."

"And you went out with Brian afterward, didn't you, to look for survivors? How many did you help save then?"

"I don't know."

"I bet it was a lot."

"Di, I keep seeing his face. The look of betrayal in his eyes when I left. I can't live with that memory."

Dione suddenly remembered the river stone she had in her pocket.

"This," she said to Lithia, "is good luck. When my grandma died, my uncle took me to the Red River and found me a white river stone." Dione put the rock in Lithia's palm. She repeated the words her uncle had said to her. "Feel how smooth the edges are? This rock used to be sharp. It used to hurt to squeeze in your hand, but not anymore. The flow of the river is like the flow of time. It smooths the rough edges of your pain."

"And if I want to be rough around the edges?" She handed the stone back to Dione.

Dione sighed. So stubborn.

"Then take the rest of the day. Hate yourself if you need to, but tonight, in the darkness, let the light back in. I'm so sorry you have to go through this, but you're not alone. I'm not going to tell you to forget him. I know you can't do that. But when you remember his face, remember all the other faces of the people in that shuttle that you saved. We can't save everyone. It's just not possible. We have to focus on the good we can do, and let our failures inform our decisions moving forward, not cripple us. *You* are the hero, Lithia. You always have been." Dione forced the stone into Lithia's hand. "I won't let you forget it."

Lithia stared her straight in the eyes, but Dione didn't break eye contact. Lithia needed to know that she had meant every word.

"Thanks, Di. This is why you're my best friend. I think I'm going to hang out in the shuttle, though. We're almost done, and I'm pretty useless right now." Lithia shivered and held out a hand to show that she was still shaking.

"Take this," Dione said, handing Lithia her jacket. "I'm going to head back. Shouldn't be long now." It was already getting darker. The sun was on the verge of setting, and they needed to be back before dark. There was still no sign that the Vens were approaching.

Just as they were finishing up, she got a message from Bel. Dione's group was the only one still out. They quickly packed up their empty crates and returned to the Flyer. Lithia was ready to take them to the settlement and within minutes they were up in the air.

In the failing light, Dione saw something bright flash in the distance, followed by a boom. Then more flashes and booms.

Something was detonating the charges. Were the Vens already here?

"Lithia, fly toward the explosions, but keep us high," Dione said.

"Already on it."

Immediately, chatter erupted over the communicators. Victoria cut in, her voice sharp with authority. "Amanda, what's going on out there?"

"We're heading to investigate now. It looks like some of the mines went off."

"Keep me informed, and cut the comms chatter." They were still getting the hang of the communicators, and they hadn't all set up separate channels yet, so everything had come over the main channel.

"Everyone, check the external cameras. Keep an eye out for Vens and see where they're headed next," Dione said. They needed as much information as possible.

"I don't see anything. It's getting too dark," one woman said.

She was right. It was nearly too dark to see. Before they could reach the site of the explosions, the next set of charges went off just up ahead to their right. In the light from the explosions, she saw dark green figures darting through the trees.

"It's the Vens," Amanda said. "I'll inform Victoria to get ready."

They were green, but they were far too small to be Vens. They didn't move like Vens either.

"Those aren't Vens," Dione said. "They're people dressed in green robes. And they're heading to the next site where we just set our charges. They're detonating the mines prematurely."

"That doesn't make any sense," Amanda said.

Dione's thoughts flickered to the shrine they had found near the distress beacon. Could the Ficarans be behind this?

"You're just playing innocent! I'll bet this was a ruse to destroy our flaminaria so you all can take over the Vale Temple," the project manager snapped.

"I just watched my friends and family flee their homes or die. Don't you dare try to blame this on us," Amanda said, clenching her fist by her side.

There were two Ficarans and four Aratians on board, and they were beginning to separate and face each other. This was about to get bad.

"Stop it," Dione said. "Let's get back and figure this out. Tell Victoria we're on our way. She and Benjamin need to meet us when we land, and we'll figure this out."

Right as she finished speaking, another set of charges went off, this time behind them.

"So we're just going to let them set off the charges?" Amanda said.

"Do you have a way of stopping them?" Lithia said. "I'm not taking this Flyer anywhere near the explosions. That's suicide."

"Whoever those people are, they're clearly not on our side, whether they're Aratian or Ficaran. We need to regroup," Dione said.

Amanda reported back to Victoria, asking her to meet them when they landed. Victoria agreed, though it was clear she did not like to be kept waiting.

Dione's manumed buzzed with a new message from Bel: *What's going on?*

Dione replied: *Not sure. Meet us when we land.*

Less than ten minutes later, they landed back inside the Aratian walls. By the time the shuttle door opened, a small crowd had gathered. Many Aratians and Ficarans were armed, and Dione feared that mistrust, fueled by the tension, would end this alliance before it could even begin.

33. DIONE

Dione could barely hear her own thoughts over the chaos and confusion. There were Ficaran floodlights and Aratian glowglobes illuminating everything in an eerie mix of light. The glowglobes left too much to the shadows while the Ficaran lights were too bright and exposed every angry wrinkle on the faces of the crowd. There was shouting. Everyone wanted explanations. The Aratians and Ficarans on board the shuttle were pulled out by their comrades. A space was beginning to form down the middle, dividing the two sides. Ficaran guards with weapons stepped back inside the shuttle, reaffirming their claim.

A strong hand grabbed her and pulled her off to the side, out of the fray.

"Professor Oberon," she said, voice heavy with relief. He must have come over with one of the last groups of Ficaran soldiers. Bel and Zane were all there, too. Lithia followed close behind them.

"Your arm," Dione said to the professor. It was no longer in a sling.

"The Aratians shared their healing tea as part of the agreement, and many of the injured are recovering with its help, myself included. Are you all right?" he asked.

He looked at her, then at Lithia. His brow was furrowed, and he had bags under his eyes, unnaturally darkened by the strange illumination.

"Someone sabotaged the flaminaria," Dione began.

Before she could continue, Brian appeared at her side. "What's happening? Are the Vens here?" He looked pale, and Dione couldn't tell if it was fear or floodlights.

"I don't know, it was getting dark—"

Before she could continue, a horn blew. She recognized that horn. To her, it was the sound of Aratian trackers. Now it was a call for order.

It worked. The crowds settled a bit, and turned to the source of the sound.

Benjamin stood on top of an empty crate. "We are going to get to the bottom of this. This was no accident. Crew of this Flyer," he said, gesturing to their shuttle, "step forward."

Victoria strode up to him and said something in a soft voice. Even as Dione approached, she couldn't make out the words. Benjamin replied in a voice meant to be heard. "No, we'll conduct the interviews in the open, unless you have something to hide." Dione could guess what Victoria had said.

"Very well," Victoria said, pursing her lips. She turned to one of the Ficarans. "Amanda, tell us what you saw."

"We saw people running through the trees, away from the explosions. At first we thought they were Vens," she said.

"Why are you sure they were people, not Vens?" Victoria asked.

"They didn't move like Vens."

"Then why did you think they were Vens in the first place?"

"Because they were dressed in green," Amanda said. "It was getting dark, and I wasn't sure. It didn't make sense for people to be setting off the charges."

"No, it doesn't," Benjamin said. He turned to the Aratian project manager. "Do you agree with her account?"

"Yes, they weren't demons. Which means they must have been Ficarans. They must have figured it was the best way to weaken us. They convinced us to use our flaminaria so they could destroy it." The manager glared at Amanda, who looked ready to punch him in the face.

"We are *helping* you! You have no idea the destruction these Vens are capable of." Amanda's voice broke at the end.

Dione stepped forward. A horrible fear crept down from her mind into the pit of her stomach.

"When we were in the forest trying to stop the Ven distress beacon, we found a small shrine near the site. A few rocks piled up, some flowers, and a symbol, like a triangle." She paused. She didn't want to tell Benjamin this next part. It would probably make things worse, but she had information that everyone needed to hear. "The shrine had an inscription on one of the stones: *The Farmer lies. Do the demons tell the truth?*"

"A shrine? You're suggesting these people worship the Vens?" Victoria said. Her expression betrayed the pain she felt.

"If they don't believe the Farmer, then they must be Ficarans," the manager said, still glaring at Amanda and Victoria with distrust.

Benjamin crossed his arms, and Dione held her breath. The Aratians were reaching the same conclusion she and Zane had earlier. Maybe she shouldn't have said anything, but if there were people on the inside working against them, they needed to know. There had to be a way to salvage the alliance.

She prepared to speak, if only to stall Benjamin, but a new voice broke into the inquiry: "They were Aratians."

Everyone turned to look at the accuser, and a few, Dione included, gasped when Cora stepped forward. "Dione, that triangle symbol you found, did it have a spiral in it?" she asked.

"Yes, it did," Dione said with a frown. "How did you know?"

"We found the same symbol on a secret exit out of the town."

"I've seen it, too," Brian added. "In the woods, carved into rocks and trees. I figured it was a symbol your trackers used."

"It's not," Cora said. "I was securing one of the unofficial and lesser known entrances to the settlement when several of our own Aratians left, even though they knew no one was supposed to leave."

"How do you know they were Aratians?" her uncle asked.

"They mentioned that the Ficarans were here. They had a strange conversation that didn't make sense at the time, but now it's clear. They were worried that the flaminaria might work. They were worried that the demons might be harmed. No"—she shook her head—"the Vens. It's time we called them by their name."

It took a few moments for Dione to realize that she was staring with her mouth open. Cora was openly opposing her uncle and accusing her own people of treason. What on earth had happened?

"Cora, that doesn't make any sense. Why would Aratians choose to help these Vens? Do you have any proof?" Benjamin said.

"Will was with me," she replied, motioning to a cute, blond guy in the crowd. He moved forward and stood next to her.

"I saw them, too," he said, "sneaking out through a secret exit."

"Why would they do this? What possible motive could they have?" Benjamin said.

"That question didn't stop you from accusing us, even after everything we've lost," Victoria said. "You thought we wanted to weaken you, even though we've sworn to work as allies against this common threat. Now your people have broken that promise. Why?"

That was the real question, Dione thought. Why would a human want to protect a Ven? A Ven would not want help and wouldn't offer anything in return. But not everyone knew that.

She interjected once more. "I don't think the people who helped are part of the alliance. They're not true Aratians, at least, and it sounds like they don't really understand who or what the Vens are. They see them as a way to get answers that the Farmer wouldn't give."

"Which is a stupid plan," Lithia added.

"All the more reason to think the Ficarans are behind it," muttered the manager.

"I'm telling you, they were Aratians," Will said. "I don't like it any more than you do, but the evidence is there."

Benjamin lowered his head and raised his hand. "Enough," he boomed. "We'll look into these claims. In the meantime, there's work to be done, and rest to be had. We will need to be vigilant tomorrow."

Someone called out from the crowd. "What are we going to do without the flaminaria?"

"Fight," Victoria said, "and win."

The Ficarans cheered at that. Even some of the Aratians joined in, but Dione shivered as a chill went through her body.

Without the flaminaria mines to thin out the Vens, what chance did Kepos have? What chance did she and her friends have of surviving? Now on top of the Vens, they would have to worry about the Green Cloaks.

Dione approached Benjamin. She had to talk to him about the inscription.

"About the rock we found at the shrine." He turned towards her as she spoke. "It was carved with a message. It said, 'The Farmer lies. Do the Vens tell the truth?'"

Benjamin's frown deepened. "You mentioned this already. What's your point?"

"Some of your people may believe that the Vens are the only way they can learn the truth. So they're doing everything in their power to help them. They're tired of being lied to."

"We don't lie to our people," Benjamin spoke sharply.

"Maybe not intentionally, but they'll find out the truth soon enough. If these Ven worshipers beat you to it, your people will never trust you again. Doubt can be powerful. They must be asking questions with everything that's going on."

As Dione walked away, Benjamin looked shaken, but skeptical about what he had learned about the Vens. The Vens were a terrible enemy, but they weren't shy about it. These Green Cloaks on the other hand? They could be anywhere. They could be everywhere. And they were desperate enough for answers that they would sacrifice their own people.

***

"I have more bad news," Oberon said, once they were away from the crowds. It was just the five of them, the original crew of the *Calypso*. "We figured out what these discs are for." He held up one of the white composite discs that Bel and Moira had fished out of the Ven.

"Why, what are they?" Lithia asked.

"They are short-range communicators and memory recording devices. A record of all that a Ven sees, hears, and experiences is stored on this device."

"How is that possible?" Dione said. She had never heard of technology like that.

"I'm not entirely sure, but I imagine it's somehow linked to their already-confusing physiology. They may not store memories in the same way we do."

Dione closed her eyes. She didn't want to ask her next question, because she thought she knew the answer. "Why record their memories?"

Professor Oberon frowned. "I'm not sure how detailed the memories are, but we know they link up to the ships. When a Ven dies, its memories get sent to its ship. From there, we think it gets transmitted to nearby Ven ships, or all the way to a Citadel ship."

"A Citadel ship?" Lithia asked.

"Only one or two exist, but they house tens of thousands of Vens. All of the smaller ships we encounter have launched from one of these Citadels."

Dione's hands were shaking. "How do you know the recordings aren't sent out automatically?" she asked.

"We don't, but Sam has been monitoring their ships for transmissions. She's picked up a lot of short-range communications, but she hasn't detected any sent off-world. We know that several Vens have already been killed, and they haven't sent those memories back yet. They might just use the memories as a teaching tool," the professor said.

"It explains why they're so willing to sacrifice themselves. Maybe if they die heroically, they are honored somehow," Dione said.

"Or maybe they believe they'll be reincarnated as a bigger, more powerful Ven," Bel said.

"You don't think they use clones?" Zane said.

"I don't know. But once we get their datacore, we'll know a lot more," Bel said.

"What do you mean?" Dione said. Bel and the professor exchanged a look. They had already talked this over, it seemed.

"We can't take the chance that they'll come find Kepos if the memories get sent," Professor Oberon said. "We have to shut down Ven communications permanently, and as soon as possible. The Vens haven't sent a distress signal yet, probably because they think they can win and that there's no need to share the glory. But if we do defeat them all, their memories will get loaded into a transmission and sent back to the Citadel ship. Or the closest Ven ship. It's not efficient. It could take years for the signal to be found, but we haven't exactly been lucky in that regard."

Dione felt the despair that she had been keeping at bay threaten to overwhelm her. "What about a dampening field? Does Sam have enough power yet?"

"Even with the Ficarans jumpstarting more of her energy cells, it will be days, at least, before she can initiate another field," Oberon said.

"There's more," Zane said. "Remember how I said that you'd go crazy if you downloaded your consciousness into a computer? Well, Sam's been working over time. She's been splitting her attention a lot, which is really taxing on her... mind. She's starting to forget things. I don't know if she'll still be able to initiate a field in a few days even if she has the power."

"Why doesn't she just shut down? It sounds like she's dying," Lithia said.

"I don't think she wants to," Professor Oberon said. "She feels responsible for these people, and she'll help as long as she can."

"You're right," Sam said over Zane's manumed. "It is becoming increasingly difficult to focus, but I don't think the situation is quite as dire as Zane makes it out to be. I think in a week I will be able to initiate a dampening field, but we don't know if that's soon enough."

"Then what do we do?" Dione said. Her heart was racing, and adrenaline was driving off the exhaustion that had come with the end of a long day. She needed to know they had a plan.

"I've already told Benjamin and Victoria, but they don't want to send anyone. They won't admit it, but they're afraid," Professor Oberon said.

Dione saw where this was going. "You want to go to the ships ourselves."

"Yes, we need to disable their power and their transmissions array," he said. "There's also a chance we could get one flying."

A way home. That's what the professor was talking about.

"Is that even possible?" Lithia asked. "Flying a Ven ship? *Jumping* a Ven ship?"

"I don't know," Bel said, "but unless Kepos is hiding an interstellar vessel, a Ven ship is our only way out of here."

Lithia was unconvinced. "And how are we supposed to fly a completely alien ship? It's not like we have a user manual, and if we did, we couldn't read it anyway."

Bel beamed at them. "Zane wrote a translation program."

"I'm sending it to your manumeds now," he said. "Oberon, you already have it, and it will work with your holo interface."

Lithia's jaw dropped, though Dione wasn't sure if it was because of Zane's program or the fact that the professor had brought a holo interface for himself.

"Who's going?" Despite the glimmer of hope that she'd make it home again, Dione shuddered at the thought of returning to a Ven ship.

"I am," the professor said, "and so is Bel."

"I'm going to download their datacore once we disable the communications." Dione barely had time to wonder what Bel wanted with a Ven datacore before Lithia volunteered.

"I'll go," she said.

"No, they need you here," the professor said. "You're the best shot of us all, and if the Vens breach the walls, your stun rifle will save a lot of lives if they start biting people."

Lithia opened her mouth to protest, but stopped. "All right," she said with some resignation.

Dione wondered if her desire to atone for Roy kept her from arguing. The professor looked a little surprised that he wouldn't have to press the issue.

"I'd like to stay as well," Zane said. "I'm close to getting some of their larger machinery running. Might come in handy."

"Dione," the professor said, "you've been on one of the ships before."

It was a not a statement, but a request. "I'll do it."

He looked at them each in turn. "I'm sorry that you've all been put in this situation. It's something that no one should have to go through, and I hate to put your lives in danger. But we have no choice. Locking you all up in the Mountain Base might keep you safe for a while, but it would only be a matter of time before the Vens found their way there. This is our best chance. I have to trust you. You are the most capable students I've ever taught and, as I can now see, the bravest."

Dione could see Professor Oberon's eyes watering. He was afraid, not just for himself, but for all of them. She was afraid, too, but the professor was right. This was their best chance.

Melanie approached them. "Things have cooled down a bit," she said. "The Aratians are serving dinner for everyone, if you're interested."

She didn't need to offer twice. Some food, then rest, sounded like the perfect end to what had been a very long day.

"I'll catch up," Lithia said, falling behind.

Dione reached the front of the Temple where a bunch of tables lit by glowglobes had been assembled. Despite the earlier tensions, and a general division between Aratians and Ficarans, some groups did seem to be mingling, even laughing. It seemed a simple meal could bring people together.

Dione shivered in the cool night breeze. She had left her jacket on the shuttle. Despite her hunger, she knew that she'd enjoy her meal much more if she were warm, so she headed back to the Flyer.

As she approached, she could see that two figures were talking, dark silhouettes backlit by a floodlight. She couldn't make out who they were, but they looked like they wanted privacy. She decided to walk around the other way, when she heard the girl laugh.

Lithia. What was she doing? Who was she—? *Brian.* Her heart sank into her stomach. This would explain why he had been acting so weird around her lately. Dione stopped in her tracks, and that's when they noticed her.

"Di, I thought you were getting food," Lithia said, like nothing was the matter.

"Forgot my jacket."

"Grab it. We'll wait for you."

"Let me come with you. Lithia, we'll catch you at dinner," Brian said.

Lithia nodded and left her alone with Brian.

"Hey, I wanted to talk to you," he said. He put a warm hand on her back, and it gave her butterflies. She couldn't control those involuntary reactions, but that didn't mean she was helpless around him. Dione quickened her pace and felt the cold settle back in where his hand had been. She shivered.

"How's Canto doing?" she said. She would take control of the conversation.

"He's a lot better. Still at the mountain, though. I figured he could use the rest."

"That's good." Dione was at the shuttle. There was no guard now, but she assumed that Victoria had figured out how to lock the controls herself. She went inside to grab her jacket, and when she turned, Brian was standing in the doorway, almost blocking her exit.

He didn't back away when she approached, and she grew aware of how tall he was. She tried not to look him in the face, but he put a hand on her shoulder. She looked up at him and tried to ignore how his wavy hair had fallen to cover one of his warm, brown eyes. Her heart pounded in her chest when he leaned down to kiss her gently on the lips. She let him, but when he tried to pull her into an embrace, she got a hold of herself and stepped back.

"What's wrong?" he asked.

"Look, I don't know what's going on between you and Lithia, but—"

"She told you?" he said.

"Told me what?" Dione's chest constricted. She knew what was coming.

He looked confused but explained anyway. "The night the Vens first attacked, we kissed. Technically, she kissed me. There was alcohol involved, and..." He trailed off. "But that was it. We decided it wouldn't happen again. It meant nothing."

"Well, it didn't look like you were talking about nothing." Dione brushed past him. She was sick of feeling this way. Lithia always got the guy, and that was fine. Normally the guy didn't kiss Dione first, though.

"That? We... we were talking about..." He trailed off again.

She shook her head. "I don't want to hear it. We're not together, and you can make out with whoever you like. I never told Lithia about the kiss in the smuggler's den, anyway, and I've gathered that you just tend to go around kissing girls. That's what Melanie said, right?" She was getting angry.

"That's true," he said defensively, "or at least it used to be. But you're different. Even before Lithia, I realized that. I was drunk, and I honestly thought I was going to die."

"And you just couldn't bear to die without kissing someone first. Is that what this is? End of the world, take two, and this time I'm the most convenient girl?"

Brian took one of her hands in his. "That's not it. You always find some clever solution to your problems, and I think I'd forgotten that. Here we've been so focused on fighting that we've lost sight of other possibilities. Dione, you're special."

He was right about that last part, but she didn't need him to realize it. She pulled her hand away. "I'm not interested in competing with other girls for your attention. Or any guy's attention. I am enough, and if you need to tell me that I'm *special*, then you're probably trying to convince yourself, not me."

Dione had no idea where that came from, but she filed it away for later. She zipped up her jacket and walked back toward the cheerful glow and laughter of the dinner, refusing to shed a single tear or look back.

I am enough. I have always been enough.

34. DIONE

A good night's sleep was like washing clothes. All the stains of yesterday were a little faded, and things looked brighter. Dione woke up in the Ficaran quarters between Lithia and Bel. Cora had offered them the floor of her room, another surprising gesture of good will, but they had decided to stay in the town in case the Vens arrived in the middle of the night.

The Aratians were preparing more *pila* blades, wrapping their ends in a rubbery material to form makeshift hilts. The "blades" came from something called *pila* trees, which looked a lot like large pinecones with very sharp points growing out of the ground. They were flat, like her machete, rather than round, and while they were not as tough as metal, they were strong and abundant and slightly flexible. The cavalry used them, from what she could gather.

Dione spent the day fortifying the settlement, and by late afternoon, she was more than ready to get her mission over with. She waited in one of the shuttles for the professor, but Colm arrived first. Ever since she had seen his reaction to the Matching, she hated him a little bit less. There was a story there, and she could tell it was painful.

"Are you coming with us?" Dione actually wouldn't mind his company on this mission. She didn't know what to expect, and having some muscle along was probably a good thing.

"No, I'm just dropping you off," he replied. "It's not too late to abandon this fool's errand." He gave her a concerned frown.

He was right to be skeptical. How in the world were the three of them going to pull this off?

As if in answer to her unasked question, the professor and Bel came on board. Professor Oberon said, "Sam's latest images show that the Vens are on the move, and they've only left a handful guarding the ships. Now's the time to go. They probably don't expect anyone to attack their ships in the middle of a battle, and they can't fly them away, or Sam will shoot them down with the Icon."

By Dione's count, that left plenty of Vens to attack the Aratian settlement. A strange weapon at the professor's waist caught her eye.

"What's that?" she asked.

"Flare gun. Figured it was better than nothing."

Like Dione, Bel was wielding a machete.

"So should we head out, then?" Dione asked.

"We're waiting on one more. Brian said he wanted to come along."

Dione's heart pounded in her chest. This was the last thing she needed right now. "If he'd meant it, he'd be here already. We should go."

The professor raised an eyebrow at her. She wished she wasn't completely transparent. "I... thought you might appreciate his help. I'm sorry," Professor Oberon said.

Before she could object further, Brian entered the shuttle, carrying a *pila* blade and a pistol. Dione quickly buckled into the copilot seat so she wouldn't have to make small talk with him. He seemed cheerful after last night—all the proof she needed that he didn't really care about her.

She decided to move on to a different topic, only to realize she was now running through the layout of the Ven ship in her mind. She had memorized the layouts of the two ships, based on the scant information available. The Invader class layout, though, was an extrapolation based on the study of other ships. Apparently one had never been captured, or at least the records hadn't been made public.

Colm dropped them off a short walk from the ships so that the Vens wouldn't be expecting them. Still, the Vens had landed their two surviving ships in the open fields. She and the others would be exposed the moment they left the cover of the forest. She hoped the professor had a good distraction planned.

"All right, Dione, I want you to take the Marauder," he said. "You've been on it before. You'll be heading to the energy hub, pulling the power, and making sure you've taken out back up power to the transmissions array."

"Bel, you coming with me?" Dione asked.

"No, I'm going with the professor. I want to download the datacore from the Invader."

"Can't you just download the Marauder's datacore?"

"No," Bel said, "its datacore is much more limited. I want to see if we can find evidence to support my Ven hypothesis."

Once again, Dione tried to imagine what a creature that hunted Vens would look like. She shuddered. "No offense, but I hope you're wrong about it."

She looked over Bel's shoulder to Brian, who gave her a hopeful grin. Dione rolled her eyes. *Guess there's no escaping him now.*

They arrived near the tree line and crouched behind a copse of trees. There was a group of Vens patrolling directly in front of the ships. A few of them looked like they were sparring.

"I thought you said a handful. There must be a dozen," Dione said.

"Baker's dozen," Bel corrected. Dione had missed one hanging back closer to the ships.

"That's what Sam said. It's possible she missed some," the professor whispered.

"We need a diversion," Brian said, running his hand through his loose hair, pulling it back into a bun. "Looks like you won't have to put up with me after all." He looked right at Dione before jogging off down the forest line.

"Brian," she whispered, but she didn't dare shout. He was going to die. He didn't even have Canto! Was this her fault? Was he trying to impress her or make amends? She might not want to kiss him anymore, but she didn't want him to die.

Heart-pounding minutes passed while she watched the hulking, green monsters. She wouldn't be able to see Brian, but she would be able to tell from their reaction when he reappeared from the woods.

One of the Vens' heads snapped up, and he growled. The others joined in his growling. She still didn't see Brian on the open plain, but maybe they had spotted him in the woods. Before he was ready. *Please don't let him die.*

The Vens formed up and armed themselves with their clubs. A few even put on strange-looking helmets. They were black and gleamed in the late morning sun with long, cape-like attachments fitted to the back. Their thick straps fastened in the front, creating a giant X, a useless bull's-eye on the Vens' impenetrable chests.

"What is that? It's like a breastplate, except..." Dione began.

"It's a back plate. Vens know where their natural armor is weakest," Bel said. Dione realized that with the armor, it would be nearly impossible to shove a blade between the typically vulnerable back plates to sever the neural connections like she had done before.

The Vens rushed off to the right, in the same direction Brian had gone. A dozen Vens. Dione could barely breathe. They would kill him in a heartbeat once they found him. Was there something she could do? Create a distraction, perhaps, that wouldn't give them away? Her mind raced, and she was so engrossed in her planning that she jumped when Brian reappeared between her and Bel.

"What are you doing?" Dione yelped. She turned to see if the Vens had followed Brian back. They were still charging in the opposite direction. "What are *they* doing? I thought they were chasing you."

"You're not going to believe it," Brian began, but before he could finish, her eyes told her the story.

Sprinting across the field was a group of twenty maximutes, maybe more, each with a rider. This must be the Aratian cavalry. At their front was a dark-haired man whom she assumed was Michael.

They were chasing a few Vens across the field, determined in their pursuit, and she dared to hope. She had seen what maximutes were capable of, and she thought the cavalry could take care of these Vens. If the cavalry was surprised to find more enemies here, she couldn't tell in the darkness. The maximutes pressed on, and the dozen Vens who had been blocking the way to the ships rushed to meet the approaching force.

"Come on, this is our opportunity," Professor Oberon said. Without further discussion, he led Bel to the Invader, while Brian and Dione dashed to the Marauder.

***

She felt cold. She was about to go back onto the Venatorian ship that had attacked them a few days ago, but this time, she was prepared. Dione led the way through the vessel's twists and turns. The layout was beginning to make sense to her since she'd actually had the opportunity to study it.

Dione stopped when they emerged in a large, circular room. The energy hub. It was the heart of the vessel, pumping power through every ship system. She felt exposed under its high ceiling and overwhelmed by all of the monitors and control panels.

"First, we disrupt power to the transmissions array," she said, standing in front of a panel with a lot of alien symbols on it. The professor had the only holo interface, and therefore, the only working translator. Dione had studied the few symbols that were public record by now, and Zane's translation program had provided her with specific sequences that she would need. Actually using the program was tedious, though, because she had to input each individual symbol. Hence all the time spent the time memorizing what sequences she could.

Figuring out what everything did was still a nightmare. She scoured the console for the right sequences, but it was like trying to complete a word search of hieroglyphs. There was no pattern recognition that helped the words jump out at her.

Brian was staring over her shoulder at the panel. It was annoying. He didn't have to be so close.

"What's that one?" he asked, pointing to a cluster of symbols.

She recognized them. "How did you find them? That's part of what we'll need to shut down the power. Can you read that? When did you learn Venatorian?"

"I didn't read it," he replied. "I was looking for patterns."

"But the Vens are completely alien. We don't think the same. There shouldn't be any patterns to pick up on."

"Some things transcend language," he argued.

Dione put her hands on her hips. "Our differences go far beyond language. They have a completely different way of thinking, of looking at the universe."

"Maybe they're not as different as you think. One plus one is always two, right?"

She didn't have time for this argument. "Whatever. Let's just do this." Now that she had the first sequence, she found the others easily. If anything about the Vens made sense, this would shut down power to the primary transmissions array and force any backups online.

Warning lights flashed on the panel. "It worked!" Dione said. "It looks like there's a secondary array and... there it is! The auxiliary power."

Dione smiled. This was going better than she thought. She'd be out of here, away from Brian, and back with the professor in no time.

Brian frowned at the panel. He looked around the energy hub, glancing in every direction.

"Did you hear something? A Ven?" Dione whispered.

Brian shook his head. "Here." He pointed at one of the power readouts. "What's this?"

"I don't know."

"Figure it out. It's changed. Something else happened when you shut down the power. This is it."

Of course she had to be the one to actually figure it out. It took Dione a minute to decipher enough symbols to get an idea of what was happening.

She stopped cold. There wasn't much time. She checked the map in her manumed once to find her target, then sprinted out of the room. She could hear Brian's feet pounding the floor behind her.

"What are you doing?" he shouted.

Dione didn't bother to turn around. She just shouted back and hoped he could hear her.

"We tripped a failsafe. The secondary array is preparing to send a transmission. We can't let the message send. It will lead more Vens straight to Kepos!"

Brian must have heard because he blew by her in a burst of speed.

"Left!" she shouted after him.

He disappeared around the corner. They were almost there.

"Through that door," she said, just before he passed it.

Panting, she entered the room. She pressed against the stitch in her side and advanced to help Brian who had barely broken a sweat.

The secondary array was in the corner.

"Argh! What does it say?" Brian pounded the console in frustration.

His world was at stake. Not his dreams, ambitions, or even his family. His entire world. If the colonists survived the current Ven attack, another assault would be too much. The Vens would know about the Icon.

Dione inspected the panel. She couldn't read the symbols fast enough. This wasn't about doubting herself. She knew her limitations. Based on her other translations, she'd need more than ten minutes, and they had less than one by now.

"I can't," she panted. "Not in time."

He looked at her with such disappointment in his eyes that she broke his gaze. She looked down and caught sight of the pistol holstered at his hip.

"Brian, your gun!"

It had worked on the beacon in the woods. Maybe it would work now.

He drew the weapon and pointed it at the array controls, giving Dione just enough time to cover her ears.

He fired three successive shots, which clustered near the center of the panel. It went dark.

"Sam, are you detecting any signals from the Ven Marauder?"

There was a pause. Brian fired another shot before she had time to react.

"Stop it!" she said, flinching at the noise. Her ears were ringing. She wondered if he could even hear her, because her own voice sounded distant.

"Sam," she tried again, shouting into her manumed. "Is the Ven Marauder transmitting?"

After a few moments, Sam replied. Her voice was muffled as if she was trying to talk to Dione underwater. "No, and the short-range communications have stopped as well."

Dione smiled and gave Brian a thumbs-up. He looked relieved and rubbed one of his ears.

The moment of triumph was short-lived. If this had happened to them, would the same thing happen to the professor when he disabled the array on the Invader?

She called the professor and hoped she wasn't shouting too loudly.

"Don't disable the primary array. Over here it triggered the secondary array to start up automatically. It almost got a signal out."

"Understood." Professor Oberon's voice, a little less murky than Sam's, rang out over her manumed. "Dione, I need you over here if you're finished."

"On our way. What's wrong?"

"There's a Ven still on board, and I can't reach Bel."

35. LITHIA

The growling had started just before sunset. The Vens had arrived. Lithia could feel the vibrations on her skin, and when the growls crescendoed in volume and pitch, a shiver swept through her whole body despite the warmth of the night.

The moon was half full, and lights kept the darkness at bay with a patchwork quilt of illumination. The bright floodlights were aimed at the gate, and the town was lit by variously colored glowglobes. Most were softer yellows and pinks, though a few were blue. The green ones, however, gave Lithia the creeps. They reminded her of the infection that had nearly killed Bel.

Everyone who could fight was assembled by the gate, with the exception of the patrols walking the perimeter, watching for breaches. Luckily, the settlement was backed into an unscalable cliff, providing safety from that direction. Lithia couldn't help feeling like they were backed up against a wall.

The fighters were divided into teams of four, and there wasn't much mixing between Ficarans and Aratians. Despite death humming outside the walls, there was still mistrust and fear within.

Melanie found her staring hard at the ground.

"Want to partner up? No one should be alone," she said.

"Sure," Lithia answered. Zane was still tinkering away in the barn, and most of the others kept their distance from her. A few of the Ficarans had nodded to her, like they remembered her help at the Field Temple, but hadn't asked her to join them. Lithia had never been picked last for any kind of team, and this feeling of isolation was almost as off-putting as the growling.

That's when Lithia noticed that the growling had stopped. *It won't be long now.*

"Lithia, wait!" A voice piped up in the silence.

Lithia sighed. Cora approached them, followed closely by the blond guy from earlier.

"Hi, Cora. This is Melanie." Lithia turned to the blond guy. "And you're Will, right?" He nodded, and she turned back to Cora. "I didn't think they'd let you out for the fight."

"This is my place," Cora said, taking a deep breath. "With my people. It's what my father would do if he were here."

"Do you have any combat training?" Lithia asked. She felt ridiculous asking, because her own combat training amounted to a few trips to the shooting range and a lot of VR simulations.

"I have basic training with *pila* blades," she said. Lithia could tell she was nervous.

Another guy with brown skin and intense dark eyes ran up behind Cora.

"Cora, you shouldn't be out here," he said. He gave Will a disapproving glance.

"And you are?" Lithia said. She might not think Cora should be out here either, but she wasn't about to put up with the "girls are delicate flowers" crap, which is where it seemed like this was heading. Cora looked annoyed to see him.

"My name is Jai. I'm Cora's intended Match."

Lithia glanced from Jai to Will, then to Cora. She cracked a smile, which seemed to vex him.

"If you're her *intended* Match, then it sounds like you don't own her yet. So let her be," Lithia said. "Sure, I think it's stupid she's out here, but everyone deserves the chance to be stupid, especially for a good cause." Cora's presence might give the Aratians confidence, at the very least.

"Own her? What are you talking about about?" Jai said.

Lithia put a finger to her lips. "Listen."

Screams in the distance. One of the patrols.

"You don't think they've crossed the walls already?" Will said.

"I won't underestimate them. Come on," she said to Melanie. Everyone followed.

A couple of teams were already on their way, but most stayed by the gates. Lithia was willing to bet that this was another distraction, just like the Vens had done at the Field Temple, but it was worth checking out.

Once they reached the edge of the buildings, there were no more glowglobes except those on the wall. Lithia couldn't be sure, but she thought that a few were missing, because of their uneven distribution. She wished the Vens hadn't picked this side. It was lightly wooded, which obscured any moving figures, while the other side of the settlement was open. Melanie had a headlamp, but other than that, they had only moonlight, which failed to penetrate the summer foliage.

"This is where the people in green cloaks left from," Will said.

"How?" Lithia asked. "Is there a breach in the wall?"

"No, we sealed it earlier, after they left," he replied.

"What were you two doing out here?" Jai said looking from Cora to Will.

This was getting awkward. "Jai, friend." Lithia patted his shoulder. "Now's not the time or the place."

"We were with Evy looking for weak spots in the wall," Cora said, all the same.

Lithia smiled at the mention of Evy, who was safe inside the Temple with her aunt.

They had just entered the wooded area, and Lithia could see nothing. She tripped over a root and nearly knocked over Melanie before regaining her balance on a nearby tree.

"Ow, what the—" Melanie said, turning back to look at the obstacle, casting the beam of her headlamp on the ground. She squeaked in surprise and recoiled with the rest of them.

A body, Aratian by the look of the clothes. Lithia wished Melanie would look away. Her light illuminated the dead man's fear-widened eyes and the blood still trickling from an open throat. It was clearly the work of Vens. Cora managed not scream, but Lithia could hear her sniffing, trying to hold in her tears.

"They're here. Come on," Lithia said. "Back to the others."

"No," Will said. "We need to check the gate."

Melanie notified Victoria of the body on her comm device, but warned her it could be a diversion. "Another team is on its way," she said.

Will forged ahead and pulled a miniature glowglobe from his pocket, examining the wall. "Here," he said, pointing to a symbol, a triangle with a spiral, carved into the wall. Next to it was a hidden gate, still ajar. "We sealed this. These are tool marks! Someone must have come here after us and reopened it."

"From the inside?" Jai asked. "Why would someone do that?"

"Vens aren't the first evil that people have worshiped," Lithia said. "And they won't be the last. It doesn't matter right now. We need to find those Vens. I don't hear gunfire, so it doesn't sound like they've gone to our main force."

"Then what are they doing?" Will asked. "Why aren't more coming in through this breach?"

As much as she didn't want to, Lithia thought back to the attack at the Field Temple and quickly found her answer. "Sowing chaos. They're going to find victims to bite and create confusion before sending the rest in."

"But if they're not heading for our soldiers…" Jai began, but stopped as he realized the answer to his question.

"The town. We need to go now," Lithia said. As they ran back through the trees, Lithia got Victoria on her manumed. "Victoria, there's at least one pack of Vens inside the walls. Do you see anything in the town?"

There was a long pause, and just before Lithia tried her again, she heard the sharp crack of Victoria's sniper rifle before she answered. "Two of them just entered the market. I just shot a third in the chest, and that slowed him down. They've got on some kind of helmets, though, that extend down their backs. If you can lead them out in the open, I'll be able to get a better shot. This new armor makes head shots nearly impossible, so you'll still have to take them down while they're injured."

At least three Vens, loose in the town, looking for victims. Most people were secured in the Temple, but if these people were anything like the folks back home, some would have stayed in their houses, unwilling or unable to leave, even in the face of a disaster. These were the Vens' first targets.

Lithia's team exited the woods just in time to meet the two other teams, one Aratian, one Ficaran, who were coming to investigate. As they passed, Will tossed one of the Aratians a bottle.

"Use that to seal up the gate before any more Vens can enter," he said.

"Gate?" the Aratian replied.

Jai gave them directions to find the secret gate, and the Aratians hurried into the wooded area.

In minutes, Lithia and the others reached the market. Empty stalls cast eerie shadows, and she expected the Vens to pop out from behind the counters at any moment. She heard another crack of gunfire.

"They're moving toward the houses," Victoria said, "but I got a second shot in. One has slowed down near the west market entrance. If you move now, you can get to it."

"Why doesn't she just finish him off?" Cora asked.

"They're conserving ammo," Lithia said. Victoria tried to play down how much ammo they had already used, but she knew that the Ficarans had been given strict orders. The armor complicated things. Head shots had been the most effective way to slow Vens down, but now their chests were the next vital zone.

Cora rushed for the west entrance, and the others followed. It wasn't long before they caught up to the injured Ven.

Aside from Lithia and her stun rifle, Melanie was the only one with a gun, a mere pistol. All of them had *pila* swords.

Now that Lithia could see it for herself, the new armor presented a major challenge. It covered the plate gap on their backs and made it more difficult to kill them. That was the point of armor, though. Still, there were other plate gaps they could take advantage of.

"The back is covered, but try for the gaps at its leg joints." If they could bring the Ven down, they might be able to bypass the armor. The trick was avoiding those sharp Ven claws.

Five on one were good odds, especially when the one was oozing from its chest wounds. Two high-caliber bullets to the chest, and it was still swinging. Unbelievable. Will moved in for an attack, but the Ven swung and connected, just barely, leaving a shallow, bleeding scratch on his arm. In that moment, Jai and Lithia lunged for both of its legs. Jai's strike was true and deep. The Ven bent to one knee and bellowed in pain. Lithia's blow missed, and she dodged a claw swipe.

Cora surprised her by coming in next and aiming for one of the straps that kept the armor in place, slicing through the material.

Great idea. "If you can't get the legs, aim for the armor straps!" Lithia called, playing off of Cora's move. "All we need is an entry point." She and Jai made another attack, but the Ven was ready for them, and they had to pull back. Melanie stood with her gun trained on it, ready to fire if the tide began to turn but reluctant to waste even a single bullet on an already disadvantaged opponent.

Will and Cora moved forward, and this time Will sliced through a strap on the other side. The Ven moved back to his feet, but stumbled on his injured leg. In that moment, Lithia burst forward and shoved her *pila* sword up its back plate. The effect was immediate. The green monster fell forward, face on the ground, dead.

As they caught their breath, Lithia assessed that the kill was relatively easy for one reason. This Ven did not have backup. Its companions were looking for victims to send into a frenzy. When the rest of the Vens arrived, they would not wait on the sidelines while a team of humans slowly wounded and killed one of their own. They had to find the others before they found any victims.

Lithia's head pounded with adrenaline, but before she could calm down, Victoria was back on her manumed. "The other two are headed toward the Residential Quarter. They're among the houses now. I can't get a shot."

Victoria and the other two snipers had set up on the tallest building in town after the Temple, the Beacon. It was mostly ceremonial, but at times in the past, it had served as a guide back home for lost Aratians. According to Evy, it also attracted lost machi. The Beacon was not lit tonight.

"Let's go," Lithia said. "If we can lure them into the open area in front of the temple, Victoria will have a shot."

"They won't follow us. They're not looking for a fight," Will said.

"Then we make them," Melanie said, brandishing her gun.

Cora was already running in the direction of the Vens with no hesitation, and they all followed. Lithia snorted. *I thought I was supposed to be the reckless one.*

She could see them at the end of a long, narrow street. The houses here were very close together. The two Vens moved together gracefully. They seemed to be looking for any stragglers. Lithia heard a baby's wail, and at the same time, the Vens rushed off in that direction.

"Hurry," she said. They had to move. No one else was coming to help that family.

The Vens were already inside the home when Lithia got there. A man and a boy, presumably his son, had already been bitten, and were turning on the women in their family. Lithia needed to get a shot with her stun rifle now, but the Vens blocked the doorway. The Vens turned to face them. They seemed energized. Excited, even. They didn't engage, though, and rushed on to the next occupied house.

The man and boy were punching the woman who was crying and using her body to shield her daughters and the baby. A few quick shots from Lithia's stun rifle, and they were down. The woman was still sobbing.

"Cora and Will, can you take them up to the temple? Tell them to monitor the boy closely. They can't stay here, and we need to stop the other Vens," Lithia said.

Cora had tears in her eyes, but she nodded. They were unlike any tears that Lithia had seen Cora shed before. She was crying for someone else. Jai, however, glared at her, not thrilled that Cora would be leaving with Will.

"I should go with them," he said.

"Melanie and I need your help," Lithia replied.

More screams. The Vens had found someone else, and there was no time to argue. "Come on!" Lithia rushed off into the night, moving as quickly as the narrow streets would allow. The Vens would barely fit through them.

The next house held a young couple. Both had been bitten. Lithia stunned the woman, but the man had already disappeared out of her line of sight, running toward the gate where all the lights and fighters were. He would either attack everyone or be killed. Probably both.

"I've got him," Jai said, climbing up a rain barrel onto the flat roof. The houses where close enough together that he could jump from one to the next.

Lithia called Benjamin who was leading the force at the gate. "Jai's chasing one of the Ven-bitten your way. Don't shoot him."

Another shot rang out in the night. Victoria was back on the line. "They're moving toward the Temple. Only got it in the arm. There's a group of people headed that way, but the Vens are holding position. I don't know what's stopping them."

The group of people had to be Cora and Will with the family. Had this been the Vens' plan all along, to find a way to get into the Temple? She could believe it, especially after Dione told her about the blue Ven, how he had waited until she input the code to get to the engine room on the *Calypso*.

Lithia was getting tired. All this running and adrenaline were wearing her out quickly. How did proper soldiers do it, fight continuously for hours at a time? Now it was just her and Melanie. Finally the Temple doors came into view.

Lithia could see, up ahead, that the Vens had reached Cora and Will just before they reached the Temple. The goal had been to keep the fighting away from the Aratian stronghold for as long as possible. They handed off the man and boy to the women and directed them toward the Temple. Cora and Will raised their *pila* blades, ready to fight.

The two Vens loomed, dark green monsters undaunted by children with sticks. One's arm was oozing, though Lithia smelled it rather than saw it. Her nose wrinkled in disgust, and she tightened her grip on her own *pila* blade.

Melanie aimed her gun and fired twice, once in the chest, once in the leg. The injured Ven whirled, and both lunged at her in unison. Melanie barely dodged out of the way, and they lunged again. This time, one managed to scratch her leg. She cried out in pain.

Lithia ran forward as a distraction, but they were set on Melanie. Her next dodge cost her. She lost her grip on the gun, which now lay on the ground. Lithia saw terror in Melanie's eyes. She couldn't keep this up much longer.

"Come on!" Lithia shouted to Will and Cora, and they charged in. Lithia aimed for the already weak leg, and the other two aimed for the armor straps. All of them failed to hit their targets, but their united attack accomplished one thing. One of the Vens turned to face them, leaving the injured Ven to Melanie. *That's the best we can do right now, Melanie.*

Lithia tried to pass the Ven to get to her friend, but the Ven blocked her every time. It wanted to keep her isolated. Lithia kept trying, waiting until Will and Cora attacked before trying to rush past, but it intercepted her with a swipe of its claws. It was doing this on purpose. She tried watched its torso for telegraphed movements, just like she would in a hylaball game, but even knowing where it was going only allowed her to react more quickly in her own dodges, not her breaks. She thought she saw flashlights in the distance, but didn't dare look more closely.

Lithia heard a cry from Melanie and looked over. She was on the ground, scrambling backward. There was no time. Lithia saw Melanie's gun and broke for it. She felt the sting of claws on her back, but she had known that was coming. She grabbed the gun and fired into the Ven's lower torso, stopping it for just a moment so Melanie could get back on her feet and out of the way.

That was all she needed. What Lithia had assumed were flashlights were actually headlights. A sickening crunch followed by a more sickening smell signaled the end of Melanie's attacker. It was Zane and a young Aratian man, driving a large tractor.

"I didn't even hear you!" Lithia said.

"Battery-powered," Zane replied.

They all focused their attention on the last Ven. Zane pinned it to the ground with the tractor while the others sliced through its armor. Melanie did the honors and shoved a blade into its brain.

For a moment, Lithia felt hopeful. They had stopped the advance scouts from getting to the Temple. Then someone called over all their communication devices. "They're pouring through a breach in the wall."

The Aratian patrol had failed to seal the wall. They were probably all dead.

"There are still some Vens outside the gate, but I'm sending most of our men to hold them off from the Temple," Benjamin said.

Lithia thought he sounded afraid, and she couldn't fault him. *This is it.*

36. ZANE

After saving Lithia and the others, Zane had left the tractor to Diego and hurried back to the barn. He wanted to try out the monstrous tiller he'd spent the day repairing. He thought he could probably mow several Vens down with it.

He rushed there while Lithia and the others moved back to join the main force that was coming up to meet the invading horde.

The tiller had a safety bar to prevent anyone from getting caught under the blades, but since that was the whole point of his plan, he had removed it. He thought it would make a good weapon.

He was certain he'd left the safety bar leaning against the toolbox built into the seatback, but it now lay across the seat. He was probably imagining it, but he felt his stomach do a nervous flip.

He started her up and headed out into the chaos. The tiller was loud compared to the battery-powered tractor Diego was driving around. He heard a strange banging sound and worried that something had gone wrong with his repairs.

No matter how many times you test something, it always seems to get performance anxiety. He decided he would just roll with it. If she broke, well, hopefully at that point he would have killed a few Vens.

He heard the banging again, and realized that it was coming from the toolbox, which doubled as the back rest for the seats.

At that moment, his heart filled with fear. He knew what was inside that box even before he opened it to reveal Evy.

"Evy, you're supposed to be in the Temple!" he said.

"I'm coming with you. I want to help," she said.

"Do you have any idea how dangerous this is? I'm taking you back," he said.

But it was too late. The Vens were beginning to fill the area. Floodlights were being moved from the gate to illuminate the battleground they had chosen. Soon, there would be too many people to use the tiller to mow down Vens. He thought about closing Evy back up in the toolbox, but if something happened to him, he didn't want her to be trapped there.

"If anything happens to me, hide in the toolbox." Evy nodded in compliance.

Zane felt more glee than he probably should have in such a situation. Vens were pouring from the trees, their dark green bodies like shadows moving toward the men and women taking a stand against them.

"Get down," he told the girl. He powered the machine forward, catching a Ven underneath it. It made a sickening crunch that Zane found strangely satisfying. He had no sympathy for these monsters in his heart. If he could press a button and remove every last Ven from the galaxy, he would. For now, he would settle for running a few over.

As powerful as the machine was, the Vens were much faster. After the initial few failed to get out of the way, they caught on. They directed their attacks toward him, and by extension, Evy. The Aratians and Ficarans caught on quickly and did their best to keep the Vens off him, wounding them so that he could back over them with the tiller blades spinning. Soon Diego arrived on his smaller tractor, which was much more maneuverable. For a while he was driving circles around Zane, sending Vens hurtling back through the air, but he was lower to the ground. On his third pass, his luck ran out. A Ven rammed into the side of his tractor and knocked it over, pinning his leg underneath.

"Help Diego!" Zane shouted to the teams on the ground. "He's pinned!"

No one heard him in the chaos, but no one would have gotten to him in time anyway. Zane watched in horror, helpless, as another Ven lifted his club and brought it down with impossible force. Zane barely knew him, and even in the midst of all the death around him, Diego's death sent a chill through his whole body.

This was no place for Evy. He needed to get her out of here. The area was becoming too chaotic anyway. Soon he wouldn't be able to maneuver around the humans, putting them in danger of getting crushed or torn to pieces.

"Look out!" Evy said.

Before Zane realized what was happening, a clawed hand, wet with blood, dragged him out of the tractor and threw him on the ground. A Ven loomed over him, ready to finish him off, but something stole its attention away from Zane. An Aratian melee team appeared, making cuts, trying to force it to the ground. It turned and smashed one of its attackers in the head with its club. With a sharp crack of breaking bones, the Aratian went down.

The Ven was not alone. Its pack arrived, trailed by another Aratian team and a Ficaran team who were following their marks. In the time it took for them to reach Zane near the tiller, another Aratian and Ficaran were dead at Ven hands. Humans might outnumber them three to one, but the Vens were built for murder and survival.

The heavy safety bar thumped to the ground next to him. *Thanks, Evy,* he thought. He grabbed it with two hands, just in time to deflect a blow from a Ven club, but he wasn't strong enough. It knocked the bar back into him. The bar struck painfully across his chest. He was dazed, but grateful. If it had been the club unchecked, he'd be dead.

Zane got to his feet and prepared to join the others against this pack. His earlier glee having now vanished, he felt sick with fear. He had never intended to be in the thick of the battle. His talents did not lie in the physical brute force required to kill a Ven, but a quick glance at his companions told him that he was not alone. Most of these people did not have the necessary skills or training to fight, but they didn't have a choice. He was just like them. There was no escape. His fate was tied to that of these colonists, and they were dying, one after another all around him, crumpling like paper under Venatorian clubs.

The communicator of a dead man crackled to life at Zane's feet. "They're at the gates, trying to break through!" His heart sank. There were even more Vens out there.

Zane tightened his grip on the heavy bar and watched the Ven for patterns in its attacks as he dodged. Patterns he could handle.

37. LITHIA

Lithia looked into the fray and felt almost hopeless. Even in teams of four, the colonists struggled to take down one Ven. Some just weren't fast enough, and eventually they missed a dodge or fumbled an attack. One mistake, one misstep, and that was it. She tried to block out the intermittent screams of the dying.

One group, however, appeared to be taking Vens down systematically, coming to the aid of their pinned-down comrades. What was this group doing differently?

Six people. Four Aratians, two Ficarans. The Ficarans were not afraid to use their weapons, but Lithia watched carefully when they fired. Whenever one of their Aratian teammates was in trouble, they fired another round into the Ven plating, aiming for the legs. This distracted and injured the Ven long enough for the Aratian to recover, and even allowed an attack from another Aratian.

"Victoria, Benjamin," Lithia said into her manumed, "call a retreat to the gate and regroup. You need to put people into mixed teams of Aratians and Ficarans. Whenever a Ven is about to land a blow, the Ficaran fires. That is the only way to win this.

It's not enough for the Ficarans to fire a few bullets into the Vens and hope they are badly injured. They have to shoot at just the right moments and keep the Vens off-balance."

"I agree," Victoria said.

"The other group of Vens has nearly knocked down the gate," Benjamin said.

"Then we'd better join you soon. You can reorganize your people, and then give the order to retreat to your position."

"Are you sure—" he began, but Lithia didn't hear the rest of what he said. A small figure, much too small to be out here on the edge of the battle, was approaching.

"Evy? What are you doing out here?" Lithia said. Her chest tightened as she pulled the girl close.

"Lithia, please help," Evy said.

The line was still open to Benjamin. "Evy is there with you?! You have to get her to the Temple!"

Lithia bit her lip as she scanned the scene. "I would if I could, but there's no way. I can't promise that there are no Vens prowling the houses near the Temple."

"Zane needs help," Evy said.

That caught Lithia's attention. "Five minutes, Benjamin. Hope the gate holds, and get your people ready to cover us." She cut off the call.

"Where is he?"

"By the tiller."

"Evy, go hide in the market. Somewhere no one can find you, and don't come out until I get you. Run," Lithia said. Evy gave her one last look, eyes wide, full of uncertainty. Bravery and stupidity walked hand in hand, but Lithia refused to let anything happen to Evy.

Lithia was not the only one to find Zane. Melanie and another Ficaran were already there, laying down cover for the Aratian bladesmen. Zane was wielding a metal bar, which was not particularly useful for killing Vens.

It looked like they had already killed two Vens and were working on the other one.

"Zane, Benjamin is about to call a retreat so we can regroup," Lithia said. The Ven was occupied by the Aratians at the moment.

"Evy's here. She stowed away on the tiller."

"I know. I sent her to hide in the market. We'll go through and get her on our way back to the gate."

Melanie shot the Ven in the leg again, and it went down, leaving it vulnerable to *pila* blades. The Ven was catching on, though. As the Aratian stepped in to slice at its armor straps, it slashed the man across the stomach. He dropped his blade and fell down. Lithia moved in to strike back immediately. Another shot from Melanie elicited a cry of pain from the Ven before Lithia silenced it.

Zane was already with the man on the ground, whose shaking hands clutched his own stomach. Lithia was afraid of what she might see if he moved them. He struggled to keep his eyes open. The other Aratians who had been helping made a protective semicircle around them. The tiller prevented an attack from behind.

"How bad is it?" one of them asked, glancing back.

Zane shook his head. "There's nothing we can do for him." The Aratian woman cursed. Moments later, his eyes closed and his whole body, including his shaking, bloody hands, relaxed.

Lithia didn't say anything. There was nothing to say. She looked around at the carnage. Everything stank of metal, sweat, and rancid Ven. There were a lot of Ven bodies, but even more humans. Parents, siblings, children. How many more would die?

Before the despair took over, Benjamin came over the comms and called the retreat. Victoria followed up with her own order, just to be sure.

Most people stayed in groups and fought their way to a better position to fall back, but some just ran. The Vens quickly caught on to what they were doing and began a new tactic. As people fled, Vens grabbed at them and bit them, spiking their adrenaline and compelling them to fight. Berserkers.

A few of the bitten turned on their own, making the retreat more panicked than it already was. Some chased Aratians into the market, and set Lithia into immediate motion.

"Evy."

Zane followed her into the market, but Melanie and the others in their group kept moving toward the gate. She hoped someone would warn Benjamin about the Ven-bitten Berserkers.

Lithia wove in and out of the stalls, calling Evy's name, but she only seemed to attract the Berserkers, whom she stunned. Finally, Evy came crawling out of a cabinet several rows down.

"Look out!" Zane said, but it was too late. In the distraction of finding Evy, she didn't notice the Berserker until it burst from behind one of the draped sheets between stalls. It knocked her down and pinned her rifle to her body. Evy screamed. The Berserker, an enraged woman, clawed at her face, scratching her neck with her fingernails. Zane tried to pull her off, but she elbowed him in the face. The break gave Lithia just enough freedom to roll out from underneath the woman.

Zane grabbed the woman's braid, yanking her back, giving Lithia the time she needed to raise her weapon and fire. Zane caught her and laid her gently on the ground. There was no time to move her or any other Berserkers they'd stunned here in the market.

"Take Evy to the gate," Lithia said.

"Where are you going?" Zane said.

"I'm the only one with a stun rifle," she said, climbing up on top of a counter. She reached, grabbed the roof of the stall, and swung a leg up. She pulled herself on top of the market stall and looked at the chaos, men and women trailed by Vens. Above the colored fabric covering the market's walkways, she had a clear view. It was hard to be sure which ones had been bitten, but a Berserker's gait was uneven. Some of them were running off into the town itself. She stunned as many as she could, jumping from rooftop to rooftop until she reached the edge of the market.

The Vens paused at a distance from the people who had retreated to the gate. They, too, seemed to be regrouping, but there was something more. They were waiting for something.

Lithia hopped down and jogged toward the gate area, which was well lit by Ficaran floodlights. She could see the men and women who had just retreated and regrouped applying bandages and reloading their weapons behind a wall of militiamen led by Benjamin.

In that moment, the gate finally gave way, and a horde of fresh, growling Vens poured inside the walls. The other group of Vens who had been holding back at a distance poured in from the opposite side, flanking the humans. The exhausted soldiers scrambled into formation, and Lithia put on a burst of speed.

Somewhere in the chaos were Evy and Zane, and she had to find them.

38. DIONE

Dione left the darkness of the Ven ship, only to emerge into the darkness of the night. The moon loomed large in the sky, even though it was half full. She had never been on a planet with only one moon before. Home had two, and Barusia would have had five.

After her eyes adjusted, she blinked a few more times, just to make sure what she was seeing was real.

Michael's forces still engaged the Vens who had been guarding the ships. She saw a few bodies from both sides on the ground, but behind them, another force was emerging. From the tree line, from the same direction as Michael had come, another band of Vens was preparing to attack.

Michael hadn't been pursuing a few remaining Vens. They had herded him here. The other group of Vens moved into position to flank his men. Their shouts indicated they saw the incoming threat and prepared to fight on two fronts, but Dione was not close enough to see the fear she knew must be on their faces.

She hesitated, then took a few steps toward the battle that raged in the distance. There had to be something she could do.

Brian grabbed her by the hand, gently pulling her back toward the larger ship. "We need to complete our mission," he said. "Michael's men can handle themselves."

She hoped so. If Michael lost, more Vens would come for them. She and Brian ducked into the Invader. They had to be quick.

Wary of the professor's warning about a Ven on board, Dione led the way in silence. She only checked her manumed once for directions as she made her way through the ship to the professor. He was on the main bridge. Alone.

Professor Oberon looked up when they entered, hand twitching to the flare gun at his hip.

"Where's Bel?" she asked.

"She's downloading the datacore onto her manumed. She's got something to prove," Professor Oberon said. He sounded annoyed. Or stressed.

"Why do you think there's a Ven on board?" Brian asked.

"Bel sent me a message that she saw one," the professor said. "I told her to come back, but she wouldn't."

"What if it got her?" Dione said.

"I don't think that's the reason she's not responding. She was dead set on getting that datacore."

"Then we need to find that Ven," Dione said.

"Yes, but there's something else," the professor said. "I've looked into shutting off the power to the primary array, but there are too many backups. If it triggers an automatic signal like it did for you on the Marauder, it will be impossible to shut them all down in time on a ship this size."

"Then how can we help?" Dione asked.

"We need to fly the ship to Sam. She can destroy it."

Dione's head snapped up to meet the professor's eyes. "While we're on board?"

"No, we'll get it into position, then take the escape pods. We'll be at a safe distance when Sam blows it up."

Dione looked around the bridge. So many symbols. Zane's plan was to eventually figure out how to fly a Ven ship, but not in the limited time she and the professor had. Once the Vens were defeated, they could take the necessary time to decode the controls. "How are you going to fly this thing?"

"We don't have to fly it properly. We just have to get it off the ground and high enough in the air for Sam to blast it."

Sam interrupted, speaking over the professor's manumed. "I've sent you the altitude requirements."

"Here's my concern," Professor Oberon began. "That's navigation up there." He pointed to the console. "In order to initialize the engines and lift off, you have to put your hand in *that*."

Dione looked more closely and discovered the problem. "It's designed for Ven physiology. Even my small fingers won't go far enough into those openings."

"They were meant for the tips of Ven claws. We need to find that Ven Bel saw and bring back its right hand."

Dione wrinkled her nose, but she was surprised to find that it was more in anticipation of how bad a severed Ven hand would smell, rather than discomfort with dismembering one.

"Where do we start?" Brian asked. "This ship is huge."

"I have a feeling it will find us," Professor Oberon said.

They made a fair bit of noise as they made their way to the energy hub, hoping to increase their chances. Considering the size of the ship, Dione was surprised by how quickly they crossed its path. As soon as she saw the Ven, she realized why it had stayed behind.

The Ven looked like it had survived an explosion of some kind. Its face was blackened on one side, and some of its plating was cracked or completely missing. Dione wondered just how much a Ven's regenerative capabilities could repair. She glanced at its right side. The claws there looked intact. And sharp.

Even injured, the Ven growled fiercely, but it moved to retreat.

"It's backing up," Brian said.

"It's running away," the professor said. "I've never heard of a Ven running away from a battle before."

"It may be leading us into a trap," Dione said, recalling the Ven who tried to use Bel as bait back on the *Calypso*. "Be careful."

The three followed at a distance, unsure of what was happening. The Ven stopped at a console for a moment. Brian rushed forward, seizing the opportunity, but before Dione could follow, a door closed in front of her, cutting her off.

"Brian!" Dione shouted. To the professor, she said, "It must have been trying to separate us."

"Vens don't run without a reason," the professor said. "That room is the location of a backup communications terminal."

"Brian is trapped in there," Dione said, trying to temper the panic in her voice. "I don't think he's worried about shutting down the system at the moment."

"You misunderstand. I think I've figured it out," Professor Oberon said. "Those recorder discs. Not only do they transmit memories, they are also used for short-range communication. This Ven's recorder is damaged. You saw its face. It needs to tell its comrades that there are intruders on the ship."

"It's going to kill Brian," she said.

"Not if he keeps it busy for a few minutes. I'm going to try to open the door."

Dione waited impatiently for about fifteen seconds before she heard a single gunshot. How many times had Brian fired at the secondary array console back on the Marauder? Four times? Five? He was probably out of ammo, and she'd had enough of waiting.

"I've got another idea," she said. "Keep working on the door."

Dione found the nearest access to the vents. They were even colder than she remembered, but they were the fastest way into that room. In another minute, she'd made her way to the vents in the room. She could see Brian and the Ven, but didn't waste time trying to figure out who was winning. With a few kicks, she broke through the vent register and fell to the floor.

She landed on her feet, then tumbled, banging up her knee. It hurt, but she'd live. She unsheathed the machete and charged.

She was reckless. The Ven swatted her back with its clawed hand, drawing blood. Another gunshot echoed in the enclosed space, leaving her ears ringing again. Brian was on the ground, but had pushed himself up against a wall. He tried to fire again, but the gun clicked in vain. The Ven continued to advance. It knew an easy target when it saw one.

At that moment, the doors opened and Professor Oberon entered. Dione watched him size up the situation in an instant, draw the flare gun, and fire at the Ven's weakened plating.

The Ven's wail of pain was almost as bad as the gunshots. Dione looked away for just a moment before coming to her senses. She took the machete and jammed it between the Ven's plates. The wailing stopped.

The professor was helping Brian to his feet.

"I'm fine," Brian insisted. "Just a bit dazed."

"We'll check you out later," the professor replied. "Dione, get the arm. We can't be sure if he got a message out. We need to move fast."

Dione hacked away at the joint until she was holding her oozing prize, a Venatorian hand, complete with claws.

They hustled back to the bridge, where the professor held up the holo display. In the time it took Dione to blink, the Ven symbols had turned into words. At least, some of them. There were a lot of Ven symbols that would not translate.

Brian stared at the holo display, amazed. Apparently, they didn't have holos here, at least among the Ficarans. His awe shifted to confusion. "You're sure we can get off the ship?"

"In the escape pods," Professor Oberon said. "I need Dione here to help me, but someone has to check on the pods, make sure they're here and intact."

"That leaves me, then," he said. "I'll need directions."

"Dione, do you mind?" Oberon asked, nodding to her manumed. She could tell he was uncertain about what was going on with her and Brian, but he knew something was up.

"Here, it's fine," she said. The communicator he had was not as sophisticated as her manumed and didn't have the Ven ship layouts loaded. She programmed her manumed to give him directions. "The pods should be here or here," she said, pointing to the display.

"Thanks," he said. He looked into her eyes and took a breath like he was going to say something, but she turned away before he had the chance. She didn't have time for this right now. She heard his steps fade away.

Professor Oberon gave her a questioning look, but she ignored it. They had a Ven ship to get off the ground, and that needed all of her focus.

The professor took his time scanning each panel, and Dione looked over his shoulder, trying to fill in the blanks.

"So, what do you think? That one's navigation," he said, "but I don't know which of those two stations over there controls the power flow." Dione had wondered the same thing. There were too many of what she assumed were abbreviations on these panels. Once or twice it was actually easier to look at the incomplete Ven symbol to see if it matched one she had studied.

"Trial and error?" she asked. She was annoyed to fall back on that process yet again under such serious circumstances.

"I guess so," he said.

The professor pressed some buttons on the first station, and nothing happened. When he gave the second a try, the claw interface lit up. Breathing through her mouth, she inserted the Ven hand, which initiated the display. Professor Oberon looked over her shoulder.

"Let's give it a try," he said, using the holo interface to help him start the ship. Everything shook as they lifted off the ground, but they'd done it. They were in the air, rising higher each minute.

"Brian, did you find the escape pods?" the professor asked over his manumed.

"Yes, they were at the first location, just like you said, but I don't know how to get them working."

"We'll be there soon," the professor said, ending the call. "I'll get us up to altitude, while you grab Bel on the way. Here." He offered her the manumed.

"Keep it. I memorized the layout. I can find my way to Bel. You think you can set an autopilot?"

"No, that's why I'm sending you ahead. At least take the holo interface with the translator. That way you can figure out the escape pods by the time I get there." The professor would keep them moving up in the air without any significant forward motion while she figured out the escape pods.

"See you soon," she said, rushing down the corridor toward the energy hub. That's where Bel was, downloading all of the data she could. As terrifying as all this was, the prospect of finding out more about the Vens was exciting. Dione couldn't help but think what they could do with all that tactical, biological, and cultural information, whether or not Bel was right that the Vens were prey.

Bel was still downloading the datacore when she arrived.

"Bel, come on. We've got to go. We're in the air and we need to get to the escape pods," Dione said. "Sam's going to destroy this ship with the Icon."

"Not yet. This is taking forever because of my stupid manumed. I bet your fancy next-gen model is a lot faster. You could download the rest in no time."

"Brian's got my manumed. How much have you gotten?"

"Almost sixty percent," she replied.

"You'll have to hope you got what you needed, because we're out of time," Dione said.

"I'm not leaving, Dione," Bel said, raising her voice. "The answers are here, I know it. Why they kill everything they come across, why they won't negotiate a real peace. I'm not leaving without answers. Leave without me if you have to."

"What are you doing? Let's go," Dione said, putting a hand on her shoulder.

Bel shrugged her off. "Don't touch me." Her brown eyes glared up at Dione.

Dione took a step back and put up her hands.

"Okay, fine." What was she supposed to do? She couldn't call the professor for back up, and even though Dione was a few centimeters taller and probably weighed more, Bel was strong. More than that, she was fierce. Dione wasn't a fighter. She was a thinker. What had Zane told her? *Don't try to brute-force your way through things.*

"Bel, Professor Oberon is expecting us to be at the pods, ready to go. Once he leaves the controls, we're going to start falling back to the ground and Sam will either have to destroy the ship with us on board or risk a transmission from it. I know which one she'll choose."

"Then I'll tell Oberon to stay at the controls until I'm ready," she said.

"Listen to yourself. This information is not our priority. You're willing to risk the lives of these colonists for data."

"This data could save lives," Bel said. "On the Rim, no one looks out for them. If I don't do this, no one will."

"If you do this, we might all die. I don't know if you've been paying attention, but Sam is getting a little worn out. She will happily blow this ship out of the sky with us on board because she has an obligation to the people here on Kepos. You've got to hope what you need has already been downloaded, because we have to get out of here."

Bel's manumed buzzed. She ignored it. A call would slow the download.

"That's the professor, isn't it?" Dione asked. "He's probably wondering where we are. Please, Bel, come with me. If we leave you to die on this ship, then the people on the Rim get nothing from you."

Bel turned around, but Dione had already seen the tears in her eyes. She was getting through to her. "I have to go. I have the holo interface for the translator. I was supposed to bring it to Brian. Come with me."

Bel didn't respond. Dione turned to leave. Bel would follow. She had to follow. She wasn't an idiot. She knew that getting sixty percent of the datacore was huge.

Dione made it to the end of the second corridor, and still Bel wasn't following. She began to doubt herself, hesitating at the next intersection. She should go back and drag Bel out of there. If brute force was the only thing left, then—

Footsteps. She turned to see Bel racing down the corridor.

"It's a left," she said, running past Dione, who followed, keeping pace with her.

Soon they reached the professor and Brian, who returned her manumed.

"Where have you been?"

"The download wasn't finished," Bel said.

The professor frowned at her. "There's not much time. Sam says we've only got minutes until we're out of her range," Professor Oberon said, holding out his hand to Dione. She gave him the holo interface, and moments later they were deciphering the directions. Luckily, the emergency directions were designed to be crystal clear. Once they got a few symbols translated, it became apparent what to do.

"Two to a pod," the professor said, herding Bel into the pod in front of him, following her in like she might run off.

This, of course, left Dione to share the next pod down with Brian. She closed the hatch, strapped in, and Brian entered the release sequence. They were falling, faster than she thought they should be, but she trusted the fully-automated pod to land. It was probably a good thing that their descent started at such high velocity, because less than a minute later, an explosion thundered in the sky above them.

They had done their part, leaving Sam to do hers. Kepos was safe from more Ven ships for now. At least, whatever was left of the colony.

39. LITHIA

Lithia couldn't find Zane or Evy in the fray, so she joined up with a nearby team that looked like it could use some help. The Ficarans and Aratians were working in mixed groups now. Maybe Lithia's hope was making her delusional, but she thought she saw a difference. When the Vens charged forward, the Ficarans fired and the Aratians moved in. Someone had given the order to go for the legs. The Vens were pressing in from both sides, but they were falling more quickly and staying down. The battle wasn't over yet, and Lithia allowed herself the tiniest hope that they might prevail.

This strategy worked for a while, but the Vens soon caught on and began swarming areas, overwhelming the Aratian bladesmen, offering the Ficarans too many targets to hit.

In the chaos, she was separated from her momentary allies, but Zane found her.

"Where's Evy?" Lithia shouted over the din of battle.

"I sent her to hide in the houses," he replied. "Can't be more dangerous than it is here."

Lithia sighed in relief. Evy might survive the night, whatever the morning brought.

The Vens were pushing in, and Aratians and Ficarans alike were losing men and closing ranks. Then, a new cry bounced among the soldiers.

"Out of ammo."

"Me, too."

"That's the last of what we brought."

Despite their careful use of ammunition, whatever the Ficarans had in the guns was it. There may have been loaded weapons on the ground or more ammo on dead Ficarans, but they were surrounded with no way to get to it.

The Vens had whittled away at their numbers, but so had the colonists. There were maybe a hundred Vens left and nearly twice as many humans still standing. Those sounded like decent odds when Lithia said it to herself, but standing was a loose term. They were wounded and exhausted, and couldn't maintain the level of exertion needed to fight off the Vens for much longer.

The Vens showed no such weakness, vicious in spite of their wounds. For the first time since the battle began, Lithia truly believed she was going to die. Before, it had been only a fear as others died around her, but now, with death closing in on all sides, she could see no other future.

She readied her *pila* blade and planned her attack on the nearest Ven. As she approached, a bright flash in the distance caught her eye. A loud boom reverberated through the sky. Even if the flaminaria mines hadn't been prematurely triggered, they wouldn't have made that kind of sound.

"What was that?" she said out loud.

"Lithia, look," Zane said. Every last Ven was staggering. Several Aratians took immediate advantage. Five Vens fell simultaneously. This was it. Their last chance. Already the Vens seemed to be recovering.

Two more Vens fell, and Lithia, just like the fighters around her, felt reinvigorated by their progress. For the first time since the battle began, the colonists reclaimed ground. The Vens pulled back a little and began growling.

This was not like the ominous growling before a battle that struck fear into their prey. This was different. Discordant. It came in shorter bursts, with varying pitch and tones.

Lithia wasn't sure what was going on, but she pressed forward, bringing a Ven to its knees so another pair could cut off its armor and slide the *pila* blade into its brain.

The Vens were in chaos. Before they had been methodical and bloodthirsty; now, they were utterly disorganized. Their attacks grew more conservative, and they began to cluster together. They did not react as quickly.

This was it. This was their chance to defeat the Vens.

No sooner had hope swelled in her heart than she saw him. The black Ven. He emitted a shrill growl that sent shivers down her spine. Its effect was immediate. The Vens were regrouping. The black Ven was imposing order on their chaos.

If the Vens reorganized, the colonists didn't have a chance. Already Lithia could see her companions' burst of energy waning in the face of renewed organization.

She got on her manumed and called Victoria and Benjamin. "The black one. In the middle. Take him down."

"I don't have a shot," Victoria said. "He's surrounded and at the edge of my range."

"Then get in range," Lithia said. "He was calling the shots at the Field Temple. He's the only thing keeping them together." They had to see that.

"We can barely fend off the Vens coming at us," Benjamin said.

It was true. Any ground the colonists had regained in the confusion had been lost. The Vens were closing in. Soon the colonists would be backed up against the town's wall with no escape.

"Help me out, Zane. What do we do?"

"There are two bullets in this gun I found," he replied, holding up a high-caliber handgun. "But my aim sucks." He handed the weapon to Lithia.

"This Ven is bigger than all the others," she said. "It's going to take more than two bullets."

"*Pila* blade?"

"I'm not fast enough. Plus, he's in the middle of the rest of them. How do we even get to him?"

"Get Victoria to clear a path," Melanie suggested, appearing next to Lithia. "I'll come with you."

"The three of us can't take that thing alone. You saw him, back in the square in front of the Field Temple. He's faster and more powerful than the other Vens," Lithia said.

"Once the path is clear, we rush him. As many of us as possible."

"That's suicide," Zane said.

"The alternative is the same result," Melanie replied.

A few minutes later, everyone was in position. Everyone not actively engaged in holding off the Vens, at least, which was a smaller number than Lithia liked. Benjamin was a part of their group, *pila* blade in hand. For all his failings, he at least had the integrity to stand beside his people. Lithia respected that.

Victoria and her crew were no longer in the tower but had taken up position on the closest roofs. Their vantage point was not good, but it was the best they could do.

Victoria's voice came through Melanie's communicator. "This is going to consume the rest of our ammo. You can't afford to fail."

"We understand," Melanie replied.

Shots began to ring out in quick succession, and nearly every bang was met with an angry growl. The group of colonists pushed forward into the crowd of Vens as the injured monsters momentarily stumbled.

The crowd of colonists thinned as they were pulled into combat with the Vens around them. Then the gunshots stopped.

Victoria called. "That's all we can do. You're close."

"We're not going to make it," Zane said.

Lithia looked around. Even though they were close, he was right. The black Ven was still too protected. There weren't enough colonists left in their group, and behind them the gap they had hurried through had closed again. They were surrounded.

"There's only one way we can go," Lithia said. She raised the gun Zane had given her, took careful aim, and fired at the pale green spot on his chest that she had noticed at the Field Temple. Maybe it was weaker than the rest of his plating.

Lithia's shot hit the edge of the discolored patch, and the black Ven howled, focusing his slitted eyes on her. *Perfect.*

If she couldn't get to him, she would force him to come to her. And her allies. She was not alone. She had help, but that meant she had something to lose. Zane. Melanie. Those were her stakes. The strangers around her were fighting for home and family.

The Ven growled, but didn't seem to be bothered by his wound. He made his way toward them. Lithia took stock of her surroundings. The firm ground was littered with metal bars and broken boards. Some small building had once stood here, though she didn't know what. By now, most of the colonists, including Benjamin, had broken away from her group, but there were still a few left.

An Aratian man charged forward, aiming for the black Ven's armor straps, but the man was reckless. The Ven knocked him down in seconds with a swift swing of his club. The rest of them, including Lithia, took a step back.

"No one goes it alone," Melanie said. Their small group took turns making attacks. First one armor strap went, then the other, though it cost a Ficaran her life. The Ven cast off the useless armor, exposing the plating on his head and back.

Lithia hoped she was right, and that this Ven was the one keeping the others together. Melanie made a feint while she and Zane charged. Using the *pila* blade, she aimed for the first plate gap. She hit her mark, but the blade went nowhere. The Ven whirled, whipping the blade from her hands before she scrambled away.

"The first plate is fused!" she shouted over the noise.

Lithia was panting. Her heart thrummed in her ears with the effort of her exertion. They were so close. A few more attempts, and someone would take him down. They had to.

The Ven killed another Aratian in the charge. She didn't need to look around her to see that the progress the colonists had made was rapidly vanishing. They were exhausted. Slow. Doomed. They had to end this now.

She grabbed an abandoned *pila* blade from the ground to replace the one she'd lost and charged again with Zane and Melanie. Zane's blade found its target, the gap between the second and third plate, but it didn't go anywhere.

"Second plate's fused, too," he groaned.

"Move!" Lithia shouted, but it was too late. Zane was too slow and took a club to his arm. Lithia heard the crack over his scream as he fell to the ground. The Ven was about to make his finishing strike when Lithia pulled the gun and shot the monster straight in the back of the head. He flinched, but didn't stumble.

Both plates fused? That hadn't happened before.

"Do we try the third plate?" Melanie asked.

"I don't think the *pila* blades have enough reach to sever the neural connections from that entry point."

"Then what do we do?" Melanie's eyes were wide.

"Watch out," Lithia said, pushing Melanie to the left as she dodged right. Lithia rolled on the ground, losing her *pila* blade again. She couldn't even hold on to her only working weapon. She scoured the ground for a gun with even one bullet left in it, but there was nothing. Only the rubble from a destroyed floodlight. Her fingers wrapped around a thin but sturdy metal pole. There was nothing else.

She heard another gunshot and looked up. Melanie. Her last bullet. Lithia could see the exit wound oozing. It was a small hole, black on black and hard to see, but it was her only entry point. *Wait.* No, it wasn't. She had shot him in the back of the head. That was the closest she would get to his neural connections. A bullet to the head couldn't stop him, but maybe a metal bar could.

She needed a plan.

"Victoria, if you have even one more shot, I need it. The black Ven's plates are all fused. I've got a plan, but I need him distracted."

"Tell me," she replied.

"I'm going to jam this metal bar into its brain through a bullet hole, but it's a small target. Can you stagger him?"

"Yes, but you've got only one chance. This is my last round."

"Understood," Lithia replied.

"Get ready," Victoria said.

Lithia focused on the black mass in front of her. He seemed to sense that she was up to something and began to turn...

Crack.

He stumbled. In that moment Lithia leapt forward and thrust the metal bar at her target. It struck the edge of the hole, and with a slight movement, Lithia plunged it into the hole and levered down with all her might. The Ven howled then collapsed as she levered the bar in the other direction.

Melanie grabbed another piece of debris, a shorter metal pole, and drove it into another hole on the Ven's back. He wasn't moving, but a few nearby Vens growled and moved toward them. They needed to get out of there, but Zane was still on the ground.

Lithia got into a protective position over Zane and another Aratian who was barely alive, and Melanie and the few remaining colonists of their group joined her. Before they got within striking distance, the approaching Vens broke off. The chaotic growling from earlier resumed. She watched the Vens get separated and dissolve into disarray around her. It was gradual, but they began to fall. They failed to work together in groups as she had seen them do earlier.

The colonists pulled energy from somewhere, scraping the bottom of the barrel, and began to take down the Vens, one at a time, until the Vens pulled back. In a short time, fewer than twenty Vens remained, grouped together and marked by discordant growls. They fled into the woods. Lithia couldn't believe it. She must be delirious from her exertion. Victory was theirs.

Zane moaned on the ground and wiped his mouth with his good hand. The pain was enough to make him vomit.

"Let me find you some help," Lithia said.

"It's just my arm. I can make it to the Temple on my own. Get him help," Zane said, nodding to the Aratian coughing next to him.

Melanie was already on it, waving down some weary soldiers.

"All right, but be careful," Lithia said. There was still so much to do.

A few of the more vigilant colonists replaced the gate, propping it in place, as if it would offer some protection. Many fell down from exhaustion, but others cried out, suddenly gripped by the pain of wounds and grief. An Aratian woman cradled an Aratian man, a husband or brother or friend, and wailed into the night. A translucent cloud dulled the moon, and a shadow passed over them in the darkness.

Loss surrounded her. A pyrrhic victory, however painful, was still better than defeat, but that was easy for her to say. This wasn't her home. She could never feel their grief.

Word had gotten back to the temple, and those too old or young to fight rushed out to help. More sobs and cries and wails echoed around the settlement. Victoria's people were gathering the Ficaran dead and their guns.

Lithia had stunned more than a dozen people, but they were scattered among the dead. She came across an old woman weeping over a young woman, except the young woman had a bite mark. She was still warm to the touch, and Lithia bet the old woman had not checked for a pulse.

"She's alive," Lithia said. "Just unconscious, see?" She put the old woman's hand on the young woman's chest so she could feel the heart beat. With a sob of relief, the woman hugged Lithia.

"She'll come around in a few hours. Tell others to look for the bite marks." Lithia pointed to the oval of small puncture wounds. "Those with bite marks might still be alive."

Benjamin found her next. "Where's Evy? Where is my daughter?"

"She's hiding somewhere in the town." Benjamin hurried off, but Lithia didn't pay attention to what direction he went. There was too much else going on around her.

"Will they come back?" said a cold voice behind her. It was Victoria. Her expression was grave, and the tension of battle had not quite left her shoulders. Her eyes were bloodshot, and her forehead creased with worry.

"I don't know." Lithia wanted to collapse, fall asleep, and forget this mess. She was physically exhausted, but there was so much left to do. "Tell everyone to take the *pila* blades and make sure all the Vens are really dead. Mark them after, so we can be sure. We can't have any coming back to life like at the Field Temple." Victoria nodded. Had she really just taken an order from Lithia?

Lithia looked out across the battlefield, dotted with bodies, crackling with the shouts of Aratians identifying the survivors and waving down care.

She noticed that the Aratians were helping everyone, Ficarans included. She searched among the dead, looking for those who had been stunned. She found more dead than alive, but she kept moving until she physically collapsed.

***

She didn't realize she'd fallen asleep until her manumed buzzed. It was Dione: *Ven ship destroyed. Status?*

Lithia looked around. *Alive. Zane too. Battle over. It's bad here.*

That was an understatement. She willed herself back to her feet and kept moving. Everywhere she turned, people were weeping. They were carrying bodies to the square or to the Temple. In the darkness, Lithia saw a familiar face.

Cora.

She was draped over a body on the ground, shaking with rhythmic sobs. *Don't let it be Evy.* Lithia picked up her pace. *Please, not Evy.* She approached and recognized the body. The blond hair gave him away. Will did not look like he was sleeping. His eyes were open and unfocused. His face looked untouched, but Cora covered his body.

Lithia put a gentle hand on Cora's shoulder, but she gave no sign of recognition. After a few moments, Lithia pulled her away from the body. Lithia gasped.

The girl was covered in blood. "Cora!" Lithia said. "Are you hurt?"

Cora shook her head. She couldn't speak. Lithia looked down at the body and saw the gruesome wound that had undoubtedly killed him. It looked like Will had taken a Venatorian club straight to the chest. It matched up to the bloodstain on Cora's clothes.

Jai found them moments later. Lithia held out a hand to stop him before he could say anything.

"It's Will's blood," Lithia said softly.

Jai looked down at the body and back at Cora. She had burst into fresh sobs. Jai nodded to her. He understood. He waved over a few others, then approached Cora.

"We'll take him to the square," he said.

Cora wailed and covered her face, but nodded all the same.

"I'll take Cora to get cleaned up after," he said. He looked as exhausted as she felt, but she was glad he was taking over here.

Lithia couldn't take much more of this emotional labor. She sent another message to Dione: *Come back ASAP.*

40. DIONE

Lithia's messages did little to set Dione at ease. The Vens had lost, but Lithia's tone made that revelation joyless. Behind the tree line, the forest was black to her eyes. She hoped that no more Vens were working their way through the trees. In the moonlight, she could see that the cavalry was prevailing. The maximutes were powerful weapons against the Vens, something the Vens clearly hadn't planned for. Still, her heart broke for the massive creatures that lay in motionless heaps on the battlefield. Many of the maximutes had died protecting their masters, and she imagined many others were wounded.

She only saw two Vens left, and the remaining maximutes and riders were engaging them. One of the Vens fell, and Dione's heart pounded with hope. They just might make it through this.

"What's that?" Brian asked, squinting across the plain.

Dione had been so focused on the battle, she hadn't noticed the single figure emerge from the forest. A woman. In the pale moonlight, her cloak seemed dark gray, but Dione knew without a doubt that it was deep green.

"Ven worshipers," she said, but Brian had figured it out at the same time and was rushing toward them. They were so much farther from the battle than the Green Cloak that they were barely within shouting range when she reached them. The Aratian in charge dismounted to meet the cavalry.

"That's Michael. He must think she's a runner with a message," Brian said.

"What does she want?" Dione said.

The answer was immediate. The Green Cloak pulled something from her robes and plunged it into Michael's throat.

"No!" Dione screamed, stopping for just a moment before rushing ahead. She was panting. Michael fell to his knees first before falling completely. One rider closed in and killed the woman while another dismounted and tended to Michael. Even from a distance, Dione saw the shake of his head. Michael was dead.

The remaining cavalry, suddenly alert, noticed Dione and Brian running toward them and raised their *pila* blades when they got close. Two mounted men came to stop them.

Bel and the professor had landed after them and were still a bit behind. They were probably just as confused as the men.

Dione held up her hands. "Wait! The Green Cloak," Dione nodded to the dead woman, "is a Ven worshiper. She's been helping the… demons." These men had been away for a few days, and probably hadn't heard the whole aliens-not-demons story.

The Aratians lowered their weapons just a little, but still looked skeptical. "Michael sent back a small contingent of the cavalry when we heard explosions last night," one said. "What happened?"

He must have meant the flaminaria mines. The cavalry had missed a lot.

"Here," Brian said, handing over his communicator to the tall one, presumably the new commander. "Call Benjamin." Brian showed him how to use the device, and the man seemed shocked to hear Benjamin's voice. Once he confirmed that it was Benjamin, he took the device to make the call privately. Afterward, the riders seemed to relax and put their blades away, so Benjamin had to have vouched for them. By this time, Bel and the professor had reached them.

"A lot has happened while we've been away," the commander said, returning the communicator to Brian. "He says that the Ficarans will send Flyers for us. When we left, we were trying to defend against the Ficaran attacks."

"The Vens—you call them demons—posed a threat to everyone on Kepos. You should also know that they destroyed the Ficaran settlement," Professor Oberon said.

"I won't lose much sleep over that," the commander said. Brian tensed next to her, but he said nothing.

"Just remember that they came to your aid when it counted," Dione said.

＊

Dione fell asleep on the Flyer. It wasn't a long ride, but that short nap gave her the energy she needed to confront the devastation she witnessed once they arrived. She had noticed that bad news always seemed slightly less awful after a good night's sleep, but a short nap could do nothing to mitigate the collective grief of the Aratians and Ficarans.

The sun hadn't yet risen, but the gentle blue before dawn cast a ghostly filter over the settlement.

Even though the battle was over, people were still running about and shouting. And crying. One woman moaned above the rest, giving Dione goose bumps. She looked to her left at Bel, who was nearly paralyzed. She had seen this before. Dione reached out and squeezed Bel's hand.

"I hate the Vens so much, Dione. I would kill every last one if I could."

"I know. Let's find Lithia and Zane."

Professor Oberon followed close behind, somber. Brian saw a pocket of Ficarans and joined them to see what he could do.

Suddenly, Bel let go of Dione's hand and rushed forward. Zane. His arm was in sling, but he wrapped Bel in an embrace, his good hand pressing the back of her head against his chest. He kissed her forehead, then just held her. Bel was crying into his shoulder. She deserved a piece of happiness and comfort after everything. Dione smiled and nodded at Zane. He nodded back, and Dione turned away. She would give them privacy.

"Lithia!" Professor Oberon said.

Lithia hurried toward them and hugged Dione.

"Are you okay?" Dione asked.

"I'm alive."

"What about Melanie and Cora?"

"Cora's physically okay. Melanie has some cuts and bruises. Evy's fine, too."

Dione gave her a puzzled look. "Wasn't she in the Temple?"

"Evy made her way onto the battlefield. We sent her to hide, and we finally found her after the battle."

"Holy crap" was all Dione could think to say.

"I still can't believe we survived," Lithia said. "They had us surrounded, but then their ship exploded and they lost it."

"Why did they retreat?" Bel asked. It was a good question. Retreat was not a very Ven thing to do.

"After the ship blew up, they were dazed. We took advantage of that, and they didn't really recover. The remnants ran off."

Professor Oberon broke in before Dione could even reach the conclusion she was heading for. "The implants also work as short-range communication. Just as the *Calypso* manages our manumed channels, their ship must serve a similar function. When Sam destroyed it, their communications were cut off. The Vens must heavily rely on that communication in battle."

"But why flee?" Bel wasn't going to let it go.

"I don't know, but we can figure it out later," Professor Oberon said.

Dione looked around at the devastation. "Do you know where Cora is?" she asked.

"No, Jai took her to get cleaned up."

"Jai?" Dione said.

"He's the guy she got matched with. Why?" Lithia asked. Dione could detect the worry in Lithia's voice.

"The Green Cloaks, well, one of them, killed Michael." Dione explained how it had happened. How she had been too far away to do anything. How Michael had no idea what to expect.

"I... I'll try and find her," Lithia said. "Someone needs to break the news gently."

Dione didn't like the tremor in her friend's voice. "You should get some rest."

"No," Lithia said. "I need to tell her. She deserves to hear what happened before some rumor reaches her first." With that, she headed toward the Temple. Dione considered following, but she got the feeling Lithia just wanted to be left alone for a while.

Dione didn't know what else to do. She saw some weary Aratians struggling to move a body. She rushed in to help, and the professor, Zane, and Bel followed. They took the stretcher, Zane using his good arm, and followed the Aratians to the square.

The square, a day ago filled with people to witness the Matching, was filled again, this time with the dead. Seeing the bodies laid out was nothing like hearing a number of casualties. It was a grave visual of Ven destruction.

In that moment, Dione felt a kind of hatred well up inside her unlike anything she had felt before. It was the kind of hatred that stopped her from thinking clearly. It was the kind of hatred that needed no justification. It was the kind of hatred that Bel must have felt every single day since her family was killed. Bel was right. There was nothing about Vens that was worth preserving. Every single Ven needed to die.

41. CORA

Cora had dreamed about her father. Not the body that the cavalry had returned to her for burial, but the man he had been when alive. Sometimes, as a girl, she had imagined him made of stone, carved and animated by the Farmer himself. It seemed like something a god might do, but she knew it wasn't really the truth. As hard and unyielding as he often was, she loved him.

The flowers from the Matching had been brought out, even though they were wilting. There was no time to pick enough fresh flowers for all these bodies, and Cora thought it was fitting, anyway. Dying flowers for dead bodies.

She was not the only one walking the rows in the morning haze. She stopped at the center of the first row and stared at her father. She knelt and reached out her hand to his. He was cold to the touch, and it sent shivers down her spine.

"Goodbye." She had already said everything to his ghost in her dream. She hoped she could still believe in ghosts, even if everything else she had believed in was a lie. She draped the bridal garland that she had worn during the Matching across him and onto the body next to his. Silent tears blurred her vision.

Will. The future she had envisioned for herself was truly gone now. Even when she had not been matched with him, she had never given up. She hadn't wanted him to, but he had leapt between her and a Ven club, his *pila* blade not sturdy enough to stop the club's momentum. One strike to the chest was all it had taken. Someone had cleaned away the blood and covered the wound, but she knew it was there.

She felt hollow. She had lost two pieces of herself yesterday, but she was not alone among the Aratians. Others had lost just as much. Or more.

She looked back across the rows of dead. In the back lay bodies too mangled to leave uncovered, so she had asked her aunt to find an appropriate cloth, one that could mask the blood. The Ficarans had taken their own, though there were fewer. Her heart ached for their sacrifice. Somehow yesterday's hatred just didn't mean as much today.

Every name had been recorded. Four hundred and fifty-one. So far. Some of the wounded were not expected to recover. She had plans for a memorial. She tried to imagine it: the names carved into polished stone, a statue keeping watch, but it all blurred into nothing. Before any of that, they would burn their dead. So many lives lost, all because of the Green Cloaks. They had sabotaged the flaminaria. They had let the Vens into the town.

The hole inside her was filling up with anger, and truthfully, it was the best she had felt all morning. It warmed her. She felt stronger. She no longer felt lost. She had a purpose. She would hunt down every last traitorous Green Cloak.

The edges around the viewing area were growing crowded. It was almost time. A small platform had been set up next to three unlit pyres. There were far too many bodies to be burned on the pyres themselves, so instead the cremations would take place in the crematorium inside the Temple. The pyres would stay lit to honor the dead. Cora stepped up on the dais and removed the amplifier from her pocket.

Her uncle figured it out almost immediately.

"Cora!" He rushed toward her, but Lithia, who had become an unexpected ally, stopped him. He had thought he was going to be the one to give this speech, but it was one only she could give. Whatever Lithia said to him worked, because he backed off. She would be allowed to speak.

When Cora looked out on the gathered crowd, her voice caught in her throat. They were broken, heads bowed and shoulders sagging. She would be the one to lift them back up. That was what her father would have done.

"Every person who lies before us today is an Aratian hero," she began. "Remember their faces. Remember their names. Keep their lives in your hearts the next time you walk through the forest, cook dinner, or tell a story to your child. Death may take our minds to the beyond, but survival takes our hearts." Cora took a deep breath. "Those of you who fought in the battle may look down on your companions and wonder, why them? When I look on my father's body, I wish I could switch places with him. Trade my life for his, and let him stand here and find the right words. The words that will comfort you and give you faith."

Faith. Cora stumbled over the word. She was not ready to talk about that today, about how the Farmer was a liar. But she would, and soon.

"Today, we will mourn our dead. Everyone is welcome to take up watch at the pyres and bear witness to the transition of the dead. Spare a thought for the Ficarans who stood and fell alongside us. I once believed that the Ficarans were our enemies, but between the surviving demons and the Green Cloaks, it is now more important than ever to strengthen our alliance. We can have no peace while our true enemies are free."

Cora nodded, and bundles of sweet-burning wood were carried to the pyres. She stepped off the platform to join her uncle in lighting the pyres. Benjamin looked tired, but he wasn't crying like she was.

"He loved you, child," he said. "And he was proud of you."

Her tears flowed more freely now, as her guilt overtook her. He had died before she had gotten a chance to explain herself. He would never understand. Or maybe, in a way, he had. What would she do with the truth she now possessed? The knowledge that the Farmer was a fraud, and that everything they believed in was a lie? Would she keep to tradition for the sake of stability? There were things she would need to figure out in the coming days.

She pulled a small wooden ring from her pocket and examined its design one last time. A growling maximute. A symbol of the cavalry. She had bought it as a gift for her father in the market when she was ten, and he'd worn it until it no longer fit on any of his fingers. She tossed the token of her father on the pyre, then put her hand on the torch handle her uncle was holding. They lowered it together, igniting the kindling, setting the pyre ablaze. The pyres on either side caught fire, too, and the crowd began to sing.

Her people didn't believe in an afterlife, so much as a renewal. The ash from the cremations would be collected and used as fertilizer. Plants would grow and sustain new life. The sentiment was beautiful, but the reality was not.

Cora felt overwhelmed. She didn't even want to be Regnator. She just wanted to make sure that justice was served for her father's death. She had one goal now: to find and execute every last Green Cloak still lurking among them.

Cora saw Lithia approach. "Are you okay?" Lithia said, her eyebrows lowered in concern.

"I'm fine."

"I'm heading back to the Mountain Base, but you can call me if you need anything. Even if…" Lithia hesitated. "Even if it's just to talk."

Cora cocked her head to one side, studying Lithia. She still didn't know what to make of her cousin. *Cousin*. She still wasn't used to it.

"Thanks," Cora said. Lithia nodded and left.

Cora turned back to the pyre. Her father was dead. The man she loved was dead. What little faith she had left seemed to burn away in the flames.

42. LITHIA

When Lithia got Dione's message, she sighed in relief. Dione had found her stun rifle and would bring it back with her. Lithia had lost it somewhere in the aftermath of the battle, and Dione was the only one left at the Vale Temple. Unless she counted Brian, that is. Everyone else had returned to the Mountain Base.

Lithia paused in the hallway to compose a response when she heard a familiar voice coming from the closest room.

"Brian will be on his way back soon with a load of provisions," Colm was saying. "Benjamin is honoring our trade agreement, but I've heard some rumors about challenges to his leadership. Are you still going to give Brian a Flyer?"

"Brian's Flyer is at the bottom of the lake. With everything that's happened, I can't let him take one," Victoria said.

"He's done a lot the past few days. Maybe you could give him a break?" Colm said.

Lithia wanted to peek around the corner again just to make sure it was actually Colm speaking, but she recognized his deep bass. Somewhere in that broad chest of his, the man did have a heart.

"Everyone has done a lot, Colm. I don't understand why people think that they should be rewarded for defending the colony. It's his colony. It's his duty to protect it, just like the rest of us. Why should he be rewarded for meeting expectations?"

"If all he's done is meet expectations, then I agree with you."

"No, you don't, but that doesn't matter. I'm not giving the boy a Flyer, at least not any time soon."

Lithia was furious. Brian had risked everything to help them, even when they didn't want his help, and this woman couldn't lend him a shuttle for a few days? She was about to barge in and give Victoria a piece of her mind when she saw her half-completed reply to Dione. She and Brian weren't back. They were still at the Aratian settlement. She had an idea.

Lithia slipped away, out of earshot of any Ficarans, and called Dione.

"Di, have you left yet?"

"Not yet," she replied. "Why?"

"Victoria isn't going to give Brian a shuttle to go find his dad. You need to tell him."

Dione scoffed. "What? Why? What's her problem?"

"Too many to count. He deserves to know."

"You're right, but… man, this is going to be awkward."

"What do you mean?"

"We're not really talking. He told me about the kiss, and I don't blame you or anything, because you didn't know he kissed me when you were being held prisoner by the Aratians."

Well, that explained a lot. Suddenly Melanie's interruption made sense. And Brian's weirdness the next day. How had she missed that?

"Why didn't you tell me?" Lithia was pretty sure that even her drunk, the-world-is-ending self would not have made out with him if she had known.

"There were other more pressing matters, like Bel's impending death."

She has a point. "Well, tell him anyway. It's not really his fault. You know how I am. I'm sorry, Di. We need to work on our I-wanna-jump-this-guy communication so this doesn't happen again."

"Crap. Here he comes," Dione said in a hurry. "I'll update you later." She signed off.

43. DIONE

Despite the serious look on Brian's face, he was handsome as ever. His long, dark hair was back in a bun, and his brown eyes looked almost golden in the sunlight. There were just a few shuttles left, still being packed with food. The dead had been carried back to the Mountain Base for burial. Or cremation. She could see the smoke from the Aratian funeral pyre. Now they were loading up the supplies the Aratians had given them as part of Benjamin's deal with Victoria.

Brian kept his distance. When she waved him over, he looked confused. "What's wrong?" he said. *Because something had to be wrong for her to talk to him.*

"Lithia just overheard Colm and Victoria talking about you. They're not going to give you a Flyer."

"No, Victoria wouldn't—" He broke off, frowning. "That's what she wants to see me about. She told me to report to her when I got back."

"I'm sorry, Brian. I know how much it means to you to find your father."

Despite the bad news, he smiled. "Why do you think Lithia told you?"

"So you wouldn't be blindsided by Victoria?"

He shook his head mischievously. "She knows that there are still Flyers here. We can take one."

"I don't think that's what she had in mind." As soon as Dione said it, though, she disagreed with herself. Of course, that's what Lithia had meant. Brian raised his eyebrows at her, and she conceded. "Okay, you're right." She sighed. "Need a diversion?"

"I need your help. You said you would go with me, and I know that was before..." He began, but thought better of it. "Please, Dione. I can't do this alone, and you're the only one here who's not afraid to piss off Victoria."

Convenient that I'm here, then. "Maybe Melanie could—"

"There's no time. She's at the Mountain. Once we take the Flyer, we'll have to go straight to the southern island."

He put a hand on her shoulder and looked into her eyes, a technique he had used on girls dozens of times, no doubt. Rather than staring back, as he must have expected, Dione looked at the hand on her shoulder that was sending warmth through her body. *Dammit, biology.* He pulled it back like he had been burned.

When she did glance up, he looked desperate, and Dione saw the pain there that only an absent father could bring. She thought for a moment about her own mother. She'd died when Dione was young, and Dione had felt her absence every day for years. It was probably why she and her uncle were so close.

Brian's dad had left because he didn't believe the stories of gods and monsters. He went on a mission of discovery and had probably gotten stranded. He might be dead, but Brian deserved to know for sure. Wasn't that what she was all about, seeking answers, no matter if they weren't the ones she wanted?

Dione looked over at the two remaining shuttles. One was nearly packed and prepared for takeoff. She had to decide.

"I'll help you, Brian," she said. His furrowed brow was replaced with a grin of relief. "That last one there only has a few crates on board."

"No time to remove them," he said.

She shrugged. "We'll need supplies anyway."

They exchanged a look. Her heart was racing. She was surprised to find herself excited to steal another shuttle. With Brian.

They strolled up to the shuttle just as a Ficaran was arriving with a crate.

"Here, let me get that," Brian said. The Ficaran was panting with exertion and nodded his thanks to Brian before leaving, presumably to get another. There was one Ficaran on board, but the others were off at a distance, apparently more worried about treachery from the Aratians in the settlement than their own people.

"Just put it over—"

The man never got to finish his sentence because Dione stunned him. She wasn't used to the weight of the rifle, but it was easy enough to use at close range. No one was close enough to notice, so Brian picked him up and ran out of the shuttle, calling for help.

"He just passed out," she heard Brian saying. Within seconds, a group of Ficarans and a few Aratians were crowded around the man. None of them noticed Dione strap into the pilot's seat, nor did they realize that Brian had withdrawn from those attending the man.

No one noticed, that is, until the back ramp was already closed, and there was nothing they could do. The two were in the air in no time.

"I can't believe we just did that!" Dione said. She felt a thrill, as well as a pang of guilt as she wondered what the professor would think. He'd understand.

Less than ten minutes later, Victoria called Brian's communicator. He ignored it. After the third call, it stopped buzzing.

They passed over the open plains and the coast until the windswept sea rolled out under them like rough, blue scales. Dione sighed and stretched in her seat as if she finally had enough room to breathe. After all the struggles she'd witnessed on the mainland, she wondered what the southern island would be like. Her sense of discovery, of searching out answers, was waking up.

THANK YOU

Thank you for reading! If you have a minute, I'd appreciate it if you could leave a review on Amazon or Goodreads. Every review helps me get the word out about my books!

If you want to receive updates about my books, like new releases and deals, sign up for my mailing list at **subscribe.ericarue.com**. I send out emails when I have news.

If you want to read about some of the real-life inspiration for the biology in this book, check out the blog post "About the Science: The Ven Hypothesis" at **ericarue.com**.

ACKNOWLEDGMENTS

Without the support of my husband **Jacob** and my mom **Jane,** I couldn't pursue this dream. Their encouragement means the world to me. As always, a huge thank you goes to my beta readers: **Maggie Burnside, TR Dillon, Jane Eickhoff, Adrianna Foster, Donna Royston, Bradford Karl Slocum,** and **Martin Wilsey.** I'd also like to thank **Tannhauser Press** for taking on the series. I'm grateful to my writing group, The Hourlings, whose feedback has been indispensable. Thank you for being my sounding board for ideas, especially the previously unmentioned members **John Dwight, Evan Friedman, Liz Hayes, Jeffrey C. Jacobs,** and **David Keener**, who are regulars at our meetings along with TR, Donna, and Marty. Thanks also to **Ryan Loomis** for helping me wrap my head around the physics of Delta P. I'd also like thank **Jessica Hatch** of Hatch Editorial Services for her wonderful suggestions and her sharp eye for typos.

Most importantly, thank you, dear reader, for your support. I hope you're enjoying reading about this adventure as much as I enjoy writing it!

ABOUT THE AUTHOR

Erica Rue is a reader and writer of science fiction and fantasy, especially YA. Her abandoned biology major and handful of astronomy classes have prepared her well for writing sci-fi. She enjoys learning new words and promptly forgetting them so that she can rediscover them. When she's not writing, she forgets to water her garden, completes every side quest she triggers, and boosts her dog's self-esteem.